"THERE'S SOMETHING WRONG, DOCTOR . . ."

Pulaski turned to see Badnajian's bulk fill the doorway.

"No one's answering my security checks," he finished.

"I know," she told him. "I had some trouble, too. But I've managed to contact the ship. Now . . ."

She was completely unprepared for what happened next. First, a web of slender green filaments came out of nowhere. Then it closed down around Badnajian. Finally, man and web just vanished.

All in the space of a heartbeat, maybe less.

Pulaski felt light-headed. She clutched at a bulkhead for support.

"Doctor Pulaski?" It was Riker's voice, coming over the communicator, strident with alarm. "Doctor, what's going on over there?"

Look for STAR TREK Fiction from Pocket Books

Star Trek: The Original Series

Star Trek: The Next Generation

#9

STAR TREK®
THE NEXT GENERATION ™

A CALL TO DARKNESS

MICHAEL JAN FRIEDMAN

POCKET BOOKS

New York   London   Toronto   Sydney   Tokyo   Singapore

An *Original* Publication of POCKET BOOKS

POCKET BOOKS, a division of Simon & Schuster Inc.
1230 Avenue of the Americas, New York, NY 10020

STAR TREK is a Registered Trademark of
Paramount Pictures.

This book is published by Pocket Books, a division of
Simon & Schuster Inc., under exclusive license from
Paramount Pictures.

ISBN: 0-671-74141-1

First Pocket Books printing November 1989

10 9 8 7 6 5 4 3

POCKET and colophon are registered trademarks of
Simon & Schuster Inc.

Printed in the U.S.A.

For Amy, Craig and Matthew—
the next generation

Acknowledgments

Some people like to read acknowledgments. Some don't. In this case, you have little choice. If you decide to skip to the story, this book will self-destruct right in your hands. No fooling.

Okay, so it didn't. But I had you going for a second there, right?

In any case, I do owe some thanks for this one. I'd be remiss (not to mention deceased) if I didn't mention my wife Joan up top. She stoically played Supermom, taking care of our son Brett, our domestic affairs and our general well-being—not to mention holding down a pretty demanding job of her own—while yours truly tried to meet an impossible deadline. (For me, anything under a year is impossible.) Thanks, babe.

Dr. Seth Asser of the University of California at San Diego and Dr. Keith Ditkowsky of Long Island Jewish Hospital in New York spent long hours trying to explain the intricacies of immunology and neurology to me ("No, Mike. Bacteria is plural. Bacterium is singular. And we're running up quite a phone bill here . . ."). I hope they're pleased with the results.

I'd also like to thank Dave Stern, that most perceptive of editors ("Sure I'd like you to do a Next Generation book. I'm just not sure this is it . . ."); Kevin Ryan, the world's most indefatigable publishing associate; the other *Star Trek* novelists and Bob Greenberger at D.C. Comics, who have made a non-Trekkie newcomer feel welcome in their midst; and the folks at Paramount, who guard the integrity of the *Star Trek* mythos with such single-minded dedication.

Acknowledgments

Others deserving of a grateful nod: my parents, Gloria and Wynn, for taking the kind of interest they do; all my friends who carry my books in their stores or turn them face-front in other people's stores or otherwise make a nuisance of themselves promoting me; my mom-in-law Lorraine, for taking up some of the slack while Supermom's at work; Lori and Lee, Carol and What's-his-name, Cliff and Lois, Patti and Marc and all the kids; Rick Hautala, for timely support; Kathy Malley and Brian Thomsen, who had the good sense to publish my first four books, *The Hammer and the Horn, The Seekers and the Sword, The Fortress and the Fire* and *The Glove of Maiden's Hair* (whaddaya mean, plug?); and the New York Yankees, who make everything else in life seem so much less frustrating by comparison.

Chapter One

Captain's Log, Stardate 42908.6:

Our efforts to find the research ship *Gregor Mendel* have led us to the Trilik'kon Mahk'ti system, well outside the boundaries of Federation space. I do not believe it is an overdramatization to call Trilik'kon Mahk'ti our last hope.

We have been searching this sector for weeks, painstakingly inspecting every system, every planet—without so much as a hint of success. Even our communications beacons have been unproductive, their broadcasts met with silence.

Yet there is only so much margin for error in the calculations of our ship's computer. And the research vessel's last communication, a subspace distress signal, was determined to have originated in this vicinity.

Nor could the *Mendel* have gotten very much farther—at least, not under her own power. The same sudden and unusually treacherous Murasaki disturbance that threw her off course also effectively crippled her propulsion systems—or so we were given to understand.

1

It seems more and more likely that the *Mendel* has fallen victim to one of the myriad dangers awaiting a crippled ship in space. Or that the damage to the ship's systems was more profound than first reported—profound enough to result in a devastating explosion.

Nonetheless, we carry on.

CAPTAIN JEAN-LUC PICARD sat back in his command chair, the words from the log entry he'd made almost an hour ago still echoing ominously in his ears.

Log entries are so neat, so concise. And for good reason. Starfleet deals in facts, not sentiments.

But there were times when the facts alone were insufficient. When a man's emotions cried out to be heard as well.

Out of the corner of his eye, Picard noticed Counselor Troi gazing at him. He turned to regard her.

Troi was a Betazoid, an empath; she could feel the turbulence that was going on inside him. But she would not bring it up for discussion—not here, on the bridge. She knew better than that.

Still, something passed between them as their eyes met. A warmth—no, more. An assurance that whatever he was going through, he was not going through it alone. It calmed him somewhat, gave him a little more perspective.

Picard inclined his head almost imperceptibly—a token of his gratitude that only she would notice or understand.

Troi smiled and looked away again, went back to her scrutiny of the main viewscreen. In her own way, she too was searching for the *Gregor Mendel*—or rather, for its crew. Her talents were not nearly as far-reaching as the *Enterprise*'s long-range scanner/sensor systems, but that did not stop her from trying.

Picard looked around the bridge. He wondered if anyone else had noticed his increasing agitation. If so, they gave no sign of it.

First Officer Riker was hovering over the conn station, discussing some navigational issue with the officer in charge.

Though Riker probably knew the captain better than anyone else—with the exception of Troi, of course—there were too many others who needed his help and guidance for him to have thought much about Picard lately.

Data, positioned at the Ops console, was intent on the information scrolling across his monitor—nor was he likely to have perceived any change in Picard anyway. Regrettably, the android had certain limitations when it came to nuances of human nature.

Worf was actually quite discerning at times—particularly in recognizing the less gentle emotions. But the Klingon was entrenched now among the science-section people on the afterbridge, too busy to notice much of anything that didn't have to do with thorium ion concentrations. Impulse engines routinely shed such particles—and Worf was gambling that the *Mendel* had had enough engine function to leave a trail of them.

Picard's musings were interrupted as his first officer crossed the bridge. Graceful for a man his size, he folded himself into his customary seat at the captain's right hand.

"It appears that you were right," said Riker.

"About what, Number One?"

"About our precautions. There's nothing left of the Klah'kimmbri. Plenty of debris that might once have been ships, free stations and satellites—but no evidence that the Klah'kimmbri themselves are still around."

With a little tilt of his head, he indicated the main viewscreen—where Trilik'kon Mahk'ti's outermost world was a slowly growing hole in the starry fabric of space, defined mainly by a sliver of white light around half its circumference.

"If they had survived," Riker went on, "they would surely have maintained an outpost here—at the gateway to their home system. But scanners show no installation of any kind on the planet's surface." He leaned back. "Only a couple of massive, blackened pits where installations could have been located."

Picard considered his first officer. "You sound disappointed."

Riker smiled. "Maybe a little. I mean, I certainly wasn't looking forward to a confrontation with the kind of people the Klah'kimmbri used to be. Not with their record for shooting first and asking questions later—if at all. But I was hoping that there was *something* left of them. A culture, maybe, that had learned its lesson after its clash with the Cantiliac. One that had found more peaceful means of existence . . ." His voice trailed off wistfully.

Picard nodded. "Yes. That would have been interesting. It seems, however, that for once the common wisdom has proven accurate. The Cantiliac offensive was of such a magnitude that the Klah'kimmbri were obliterated. That proud fleet of theirs must have been destroyed before it knew what was happening—and the rest of their civilization soon after."

The other man grunted. "It's like my grandfather used to say. No matter how big and tough you think you are, there's always someone bigger and tougher."

"A wise man, your grandfather." But the captain's mind was on neither the fate of the Klah'kimmbri nor Riker's homespun advisement. His thoughts had returned to their former course—to the research ship *Gregor Mendel* and the personal burden it represented.

It was quiet for a moment, the only sounds coming from the subtle hum of the impulse engines and a murmured conversation at the aft stations. The system's outermost planet gradually loomed larger.

"Of course," said Riker, "I'd like to keep the shields up—just in case. File it under Appearances Can Be Deceiving."

"By all means," said Picard. "Whatever you think best."

And then someone called for the first officer's help, and he was consuming the bridge again in those ground-eating strides of his.

Alone again, with Troi immersed in her search efforts,

Picard regarded the planet framed in the viewer. He found himself going over the statistics that he'd memorized in his preparation for Trilik'kon Mahk'ti.

One stuck in his brain. *Two billion four hundred thousand miles.* The average distance from this outermost world to its sun. No doubt, Data could have calculated a more precise number, but it was sufficient for the captain's present need.

Two billion four hundred thousand miles. Not a very big system. The last one they had combed was twice that size.

In a way, though, Picard wished it *were* big. Infinite, in fact. For if it were, he would never have to face the slowly unraveling truth.

Suddenly, he found he couldn't remain in his chair. He had an irresistible urge to get up, to move. To *do* something.

It took all of his willpower to stand up in a decorous manner, and to gradually approach the screen, hands clasped behind his back, until he was almost even with the forward consoles.

The planet was a bit closer now, a bit more fiery at the edges, but it remained dark and essentially featureless. Picard peered at it as if he could have spotted the *Mendel* just by looking hard enough—as if he could have outdone the *Enterprise*'s vast array of instruments, not to mention Troi's considerable abilities, by determination alone.

But of course, there was nothing to be seen. Even if the research ship was anywhere in orbit around this world, they were still too far away to be able to detect it.

The captain took a deep breath, let it out. It was all so damned . . . *frustrating.*

The doors to the turbolift whooshed open, providing Picard with a momentary distraction. He glanced over his shoulder in time to see one of Worf's security people come out onto the bridge. There was a brief *sotto voce* discussion with the Klingon, and then the man exited again.

The exchange aroused Picard's curiosity. What could the man have had to say that could not have been communicated over the intercom?

And then he realized what had just happened.

That security officer had been Worf's replacement. The Klingon's shift was over, and yet he had refused to abdicate his position on the bridge.

It was a breach of regulations, no matter how small or well-intentioned.

Picard traversed the bridge, leaving the expanding shape of the planet behind. As he approached the aft stations, Worf glanced at him and looked away again.

Surreptitious behavior, observed the captain. *He knows that I know.*

"Mister Worf," he said. "A word with you, please."

With obvious reluctance, the Klingon tore himself away from his place at one of the scanner monitors.

Picard headed for his ready room. The doors slid aside and he entered. Nor did they close again until Worf had followed him in.

Picard sat down behind his desk and watched his security chief take a seat on the other side of it. The Klingon didn't seem comfortable—and not just because the chair was a bit too small for him.

"I thought," said the captain, "that we had been through this already. Months ago."

Worf scowled, held his head up with what would have appeared to be defiance in a human. "Aye, sir," was all he said.

"Then why did you refuse to turn over your duties at the end of your shift?"

The Klingon shrugged his broad shoulders, eliciting a tiny *klink* from the metal honor band he wore across his chest. "It seemed the best course of action at the time."

Picard grunted. "I applaud your perseverance, Lieutenant. No one will ever call you a shirker. But all those selected for bridge duty are highly trained—as you well know, having provided the training yourself in some instances. What's more, we have finite shifts for a reason. Neither human nor Klingon—nor anyone else, for that matter—can maintain a peak level of performance indefinitely." He paused for effect. "Do I make myself clear?"

"Aye," rumbled Worf. He seemed as if he was about to say something more, but didn't.

"Is there anything else?" prodded the captain.

The security chief's scowl deepened, but he could not avoid answering the direct question. At least, not altogether.

"There is," he said finally.

"Elaborate," Picard instructed, having had the experience of having questioned his Klingon officer before. It was a laborious process, to say the least.

Worf's eyes narrowed. "You," he said.

The captain leaned forward, his curiosity piqued. "Me? What about me?"

"You are the reason I acted as I did—sir. It is apparent that this mission means a great deal to you. So I took it upon myself to become more . . . personally involved."

It was perhaps the longest speech Picard had ever heard him make. And it took him aback. Surprised him.

Not that Worf had seen through to his anxiety—but that he had been so wrong when he thought he'd masked it. That his judgment could have been so far off.

The captain cleared his throat. "Tell me," he said. "Have you shared this perception with the others?"

Worf nodded—a short, quick movement of his oversize head. "It was Mister La Forge who pointed it out to *me*—though I had already come to my own conclusion."

Picard considered that. "Mister La Forge," he echoed. "He also thinks I'm . . . agitated over the outcome of this mission?"

"Aye," said Worf. "Also Mister Crusher. And Commander Riker. And Counselor Troi, I believe, though she would not comment on the matter."

Picard found that his mouth was open. He closed it.

"Is that all?" he asked.

"No," said the Klingon. He went on to list the others.

"Really," said the captain. "And to what do you—all of you—attribute this agitation?"

Worf shrugged a second time. "That," he said, "is unknown. Except, of course, to you—sir."

Inwardly, Picard breathed a sigh of relief. At least *that* stone had remained unturned. He leaned forward over his desk.

"I must confess," he began, "that this mission does have a personal meaning for me—though I had hoped to keep that information from becoming common knowledge. And I *am* grateful for your concern." He consciously changed his tone. "But that still does not mean that bridge shifts need be altered. You will contact your replacement and have him up here on the double."

"Understood," said Worf. Was that a note of petulance in his voice? After all, Klingons hated to be lectured. "I will notify the others."

Picard looked at him. "Don't tell me," he said, "that the others have overstayed their shifts as well."

The expression that took shape on Worf's face was a new one on the captain. It seemed to partake of surprise and shame and a desire to escape, in more or less equal portions.

The Klingon's temples worked savagely as he tried to fashion an answer—one he could live with.

"Lieutenant?"

The security chief sighed. "Aye, sir. It is . . . as you say."

Picard felt a gobbet of anger rise in his throat. Not at his crew, but at *himself.* How far had he let things slip in his preoccupation with the *Gregor Mendel?*

Turning away from the Klingon abruptly, he punched a code into his computer terminal. A list sprang up on the screen. After taking a moment to digest the information, he erased it.

Worf still sat on the other side of the desk, looking miserable.

"You are dismissed," said Picard.

The Klingon rose. "Thank you, sir." He turned on his heel and exited—grateful to be gone, the captain thought.

So. Worf was not the only one who had breached this regulation. Almost a third of the bridge crew had done the same.

In a way, it was all very touching. Picard had never made an effort to be popular—only to be fair. It was gratifying to see the lengths to which his people had gone on his behalf.

But he couldn't allow it to continue.

Rising, he negotiated his way around his desk and crossed the cabin. A second later, the doors parted for him, revealing the bridge and its complement of scofflaws.

No one looked in his direction. It was almost comical.

Restraining a chuckle, Picard took up a position between the forward consoles and the main viewer. "Your attention," he said in his deep, resonating voice—just loud enough to be heard at the aft stations.

Suddenly, all eyes were on him.

"It appears," he went on, "that a number of you have overstayed your welcomes here. I expect that situation to be rectified immediately." It occurred to him to take matters a little farther—as a sort of backhanded recognition of their efforts. "What's more, all bridge crew not on duty are to take full advantage of the ship's recreational facilities. And that is *not* just a recommendation." He remembered Worf's mention of Geordi. "This applies to the engineering staff as well."

In the wake of Picard's announcement, glances were exchanged. Resigned glances, for the most part. Hardly jubilant. After all, these officers felt that their place was on the bridge. If they had wished to recreate on their own time, they certainly could have done so without an order from the captain.

Nonetheless, they complied. Calls for relief personnel were placed to a number of different sections.

Satisfied, Picard made his way back to his seat. As he

leaned back, he looked neither to his right nor his left. But he knew that he had the attention of both Riker and Troi.

"I am disappointed in you," he said in a low voice. "The two of you—but particularly in *you,* Number One. When I'm not here, I look to you to be my eyes and ears—not to lead the revolt."

He heard Troi muffle a chuckle with her hand. It was hard to feign annoyance with an empath around.

Riker, however, didn't seem to notice. He shifted his weight in his chair. "It was hardly a revolt, sir. I'd call it a demonstration of loyalty. Of some good, old-fashioned values."

"Perhaps. But you know as well as I that a crisis may be just around the bend—so to speak. I would prefer that my best people expend their excess exhuberance on emergencies—rather than on duties that can be handled equally well by others." He harumphed. "Some of our people were on their third and fourth shifts without a break. One can hardly remain sharp under those conditions."

Riker nodded. "I see. Then you would say that twenty-four hours or so is enough to dull one's edge?"

Picard looked at him. "Of course, Number One."

"And anyone up here on the bridge that long would do well to take a break?"

"Without question." The captain's eyes narrowed suspiciously as he scrutinized his first officer. But Riker was maintaining that poker face he had worked so hard to perfect. "What are you telling me, Will? That there's someone up here who's been at it that long—and failed to follow my order?"

Riker and Troi exchanged glances.

"Aha," said Picard. "There *is* such a person—isn't there?"

"Aye, sir," said the first officer.

"Then *out* with it, Number One. Who?"

Riker looked apologetic. *"You,* sir. By my count, you've been on the bridge for twenty-six hours now."

"Twenty-seven hours, thirty-nine minutes," said Data, "to be precise." He offered it rather matter-of-factly, looking back over his shoulder.

Picard felt himself frown. He wished that Data's sense of discretion was as acute as his other senses—hearing, for instance. Gathering himself, he turned back toward Riker.

"Thank you," he said, "for the imposition of perspective on the matter. You're on your own, Number One."

And with a nod of *adieu* to Troi, the captain joined the growing clot of officers at the turbo doors.

At first, Fredi figured it was only fatigue. After all, he was working overtime to catalog the geological data he had collected on Baldwin-McKean's Planet.

And not because he *had* to. Lord knew, there was very little that smacked of urgency in the professional life of a geologist. The Baldwin-McKean rocks had been around for a long time; they'd be around for a long time after he was gone. Nor would he be collecting any new ones until well after the search for the *Mendel* was concluded—one way or the other.

Even under normal circumstances, he wasn't the busiest of men. How often did the *Enterprise* stoop to such a mundane chore as planet survey? Very seldom. There were smaller, less capable vessels for that. Vessels like the *Mendel.*

In a sense, he was a luxury on the big ship. A component that only came into play when there was nothing really important going on.

When news of the research ship's disappearance came down, certain science subsections had sprung into action. Nucleonics. Quantum mechanics. He should have been used to watching his colleagues labor in double and triple shifts, shuttling up to the bridge and back, while he twiddled his thumbs. But he couldn't tolerate it—not this time.

He felt too hyper. Too full of energy. Thank God he still had the bulk of the Baldwin-McKean analyses ahead of him, or he might have exploded. As it was, he launched himself into them with the same fervor that drove the subsection search teams. Like them, he worked double duty, slept a little and chained himself to his workstation again.

What's more, it felt good. *Damned* good. Not that his work contributed anything to the problem at hand. But it was a fine thing to be working hard, swept up in the wave of purposefulness. He hadn't felt that way in many years— maybe since school, and that was a long time ago.

Then he had started to feel the weariness—in his fingers, in his back. The natural results, he told himself, of long hours spent hunched over a monitor, no matter how ergonomically it had been designed. And that had been explanation enough to set his mind at ease.

But things had gotten worse—and quickly. His fingers had become wooden, inflexible. The muscles in his lower back, in his legs, were cramping with the effort to hold him erect in his chair.

A break, he told himself. *I just need a break.*

It was only then that he got an inkling of how badly off he really was. Because when he rose to get something to drink, his knees buckled beneath him. And as if he'd had jelly in his legs instead of bones, he crumpled over on his side.

Damn. What's happening to me? he asked himself.

Even then, his impulse was to deny that there was anything seriously wrong with him. To chalk it up to blocked circulation after sitting in the same position for so long.

However, that sort of thing would have gone away after a few moments—and *this* wasn't going away. He half pulled himself up onto the back of his chair, but he couldn't seem to get his legs to support him. Soon, his arms got too tired to hold him up and he slithered back down to the ground.

"Computer," he called—or rather, *tried* to call, hoping that he could summon help. But the word had come out tangled and slurred—nothing like what he had intended.

Again he tried it—but with no better results. If anything, his plea was less intelligible than before.

His mouth felt thick, sluggish. As listless as his lower body.

Now he lay on the carpeted deck of the geology lab, panic starting to eat into his overlay of reason. There *was* something wrong with him. Something *very* wrong. And if he didn't get help soon, he was afraid of what might happen.

The door was just a few feet away. If he could reach it, he could trip the sensor . . .

The lab doors opened on a silent corridor, dimmed in accordance with the ship's "night" cycle. Fredi gripped the carpet with splayed fingers and pulled himself toward the exit. He was weaker than he had been even a few minutes ago. He was fading, fading fast.

It was insanely difficult to drag himself along, his legs barely able to provide any help. By the time he reached the corridor, he was sweating in rivulets, gasping for breath.

Gasping . . .

Was it just from exertion? Or were the muscles that enabled him to breathe getting as bad as all the rest?

His arms and shoulders still seemed to be holding out, but they hurt—as if someone were twisting small, sharp knives into them. His right calf muscle was spasming savagely.

How long before he couldn't move at all?

Fredi poked his head out, looked both ways down the curving passageway. Nothing and no one. And no sounds of approach, either.

"Help!" he cried—or at least made the attempt. But his speech was no longer just mangled—it had been pared down to nothing, not even a whisper.

Naturally, there was no response. Just the steady *thrum* of the ship's engines, felt through the deck.

The nucleonics lab was two doors down. Surely, there would be someone in there. There *had* to be.

Fredi dragged himself out into the corridor, despite the steadily mounting pain in his shoulders. His breath was coming harder and harder. He was wheezing, struggling for air.

Come on, he told himself. *Just a little farther.*

It became too difficult to hold his head up, so he just let it droop against the deck. It made it harder to move, but he couldn't help it.

Fighting, clawing, he passed the door to the astrophysics lab. At this hour, it would be empty—he was almost positive of that. And if he stopped to make sure, and there was no one home, he didn't think he'd be able to get going again.

So he ignored it, kept his eye on his original goal. Clenched his teeth together and jerked himself forward. Again. And again. Like a fish on dry land, pop-eyed, frantic. And dying for lack of a way to fill its lungs.

The sound of his breathing seemed to fill the corridor now. Like one long, terrible groan, rising and falling and rising a little less each time.

Fredi started to feel light-headed. There was a bitter taste in his mouth, a taste of metal.

The door to the nucleonics lab was just ahead. Just a few feet away. But he knew he wasn't going to make it. Eyes closing, he fell into a pit—a deep, black whirlpool that dragged him down and down and down . . .

Chapter Two

IT WAS DUSK. Outside the colonnades of the airy, open hall, beyond the orchards of pear and pomegranate and fig, there was a glorious profusion of color on the black and hilly horizon. Blushing reds, burnished orange golds and wistful greens, warring at angles in the fierce wake of the setting sun.

Geordi was glad he had programmed it that way. It was a fit scenario for Homer's performance; anything less would have paled by comparison.

He was also glad for the opportunity to experience it. As willing as he had been to endure multiple shifts in engineering, the captain was probably right. They *were* working too hard—all of them. A little rest and relaxation would make them more efficient in the long run.

And if it gave him a chance to try out this new holodeck simulation he'd put together . . . who was *he* to complain?

Not that it was the first time he had visited this hill-lord's palace in ancient Thessaly. Nor was it the first time he had lost himself in the imagery of Homer's verse. But it *was* the first time he had heard this particular passage—the story of the Trojan horse and how the Greeks used it to sack Troy—from . . . well, from the horse's mouth.

And it was even better than he had expected. Whoever had invented the holodeck was right up there on Geordi's list of mankind's greatest benefactors.

At the height of the celestial display, three young girls came out from another part of the house. They went around to the fancifully sculpted golden pedestals that were scattered about the place and, standing on tiptoe out of necessity, lit the torches of pitch pine that gave the pedestals their purpose. The flames climbed, struck light off the silver dogs that stood just inside the entranceway, and guttered in the cool breeze.

Everything seemed so real, right down to the finest detail. The smell of the carved meats that sat on trenchers beside each guest; the taste of the honeyed wine, the soft feel of the fleece that covered his chair. Even the appreciative murmuring at a particularly witty turn of phrase.

But none of it was more remarkable than Homer himself. His face was long and supple, his brow a jutting precipice that somehow complemented his thick thatch of a silvery beard.

He was more than a poet. He was a performer. If he had been born in another place and time, he might have been a great Shakespearean actor. Or a pillar of the short-lived Thespocracy on Roper's World.

That is, of course, if not for his blindness.

Geordi felt a light touch on his arm, glanced reluctantly at the man who sat in the chair beside him. Memnios leaned over and whispered in his ear.

"He's in rare form tonight. You see the gleam in Leokritor's eye? He doesn't weep easily, you know."

Homer had come to the part where Priam, Troy's king, was found dead by his daughter Cassandra. It was poor, troubled Cassandra who had stood on one of the city's watchtowers as her people dragged in the huge, wooden horse—supposedly a peace offering from the departed Greeks—and shrieked of impending disaster if the thing was not destroyed. But no one listened to her. And when the

Greeks worked their treachery, pouring out of the hollow horse to slit throats and open the Scaean Gates, Priam had become one of their first victims.

The bard treated the situation curiously. Cassandra, distracted and bedraggled on the watchtower, was transformed. Calm, almost detached in a rare moment of clarity, she neither mourned her father nor called down curses on his killers; there would be time for that later. For now, she was thankful—that Priam had not lived to see his city go up in flames. And she was still expressing her gratitude to the gods when the Greeks found her and took her into slavery.

It was *that* approach that had brought a tear to stalwart Leokritor's eye.

Too soon, the riotous sunset gave way to a starry darkness. And not much later, Homer brought his tale to an end. His signature was a certain bold chord; he plucked it now from the strings of his simple, wooden harp. It echoed, seeming to touch each enraptured face in the great room. Slowly, inexorably, it faded to silence.

"May the gods save me," said Akaythyr, their host. There was plain, unadorned admiration in his voice as he addressed Homer from his throne. "You were right, my friend. That country harp of yours has a more pleasing sound than all the fancy instruments I offered you. I feel like a fool now for having spoken so highly of them."

The poet laughed graciously. He had a naturally deep voice, and his laughter was easy to listen to. Like the music of a waterfall.

"You're no fool," he told Akaythyr. "You're a generous man, eager to share his wealth with others. How were you to know that the brightness of an instrument has nothing to do with the way it sounds?"

"Hah!" chortled Danike, one of Akaythyr's neighbors. "His wit never fails him. His harp may be plain wood, but his tongue is purest silver."

Homer smiled, laid his harp aside and stood. He was tall for his era—a couple of inches taller than Geordi, in fact.

17

"You are too kind," he said, smoothing out his robes. He took a deep breath, let it out. "The orchards smell perfectly wonderful. Would anyone care to help a sightless old man wend his way through them for a little while?"

Normally, that kind of honor would have fallen to the evening's host. But Akaythyr looked at Geordi instead.

"Why don't *you* accompany our guest?" he asked, grinning with all the generosity Homer had assigned to him. "After all, you come from so far away to hear him—or so you say."

This wasn't something Geordi had specifically programmed into the holodeck computer. It was a pleasant surprise.

"Well . . . sure," he stammered. "Absolutely. I'd be honored."

He stepped up to the long chair on which the bard had been sitting. Offering his arm, he placed Homer's hand on it.

"Thank you," said the bearded man. He allowed Geordi to lead him as they made their way around the chair and then past one of the torch pedestals. "I see you've had some experience with the sightless. You guide me well."

Sure, Geordi mused. *The blind leading the blind.*

"Some," he said, by way of a response.

As they left the hall through the space between two columns, the fragrance of the orchards became stronger, almost heady. There were four steps between the floor of the great room and the ground; they descended them.

"Watch out for the bottom step," said the poet. "There's a crack; don't catch your sandal in it."

Geordi looked down. Sure enough, there was a crack along which the stone had separated. He avoided it.

"I've been here at Akaythyr's many times," explained Homer. "I know my way around a bit."

"I see," said Geordi. It wasn't until after he had said it that he realized how it might have sounded—under the circumstances. "That wasn't a joke," he added.

The poet nodded. "I know. And don't worry—it happens all the time." A pause. "So—what is it about you, Geordi? You're different from the others, aren't you?"

They were walking up a dirt path that bisected the slope of a dark hill. On either side of the path, there were fig trees arranged in neat rows.

Geordi shrugged. "Not so different. I just come from . . . somewhere else."

"Somewhere far, I understand."

"You could say that."

"And yet you come to hear me sing. Don't they have bards where you come from?"

Geordi laughed. "Plenty of them. But none like you."

Homer grunted. "I appreciate the compliment. But there is more to it than that, isn't there? Something you want to ask me, perhaps?"

Had he put so much of himself into the program? Or was the computer just that good at extrapolation?

Geordi swallowed. "I guess I'm just . . . I don't know. Curious."

"As to how I do it? How I describe things I've never actually seen?"

"Something like that."

It was the bard's turn to shrug. "That's any storyteller's problem, whether he has the use of his eyes or not. To sing of the gods, who reveal themselves to no one—despite accounts to the contrary. Of heroes long dead. Of events that happened far away. Just because you've never witnessed them doesn't mean you can't *imagine* them."

Geordi had never thought about it quite that way. He said so.

"There are worse faculties to lose than your sight," said Homer.

"Such as?"

The poet sighed almost imperceptibly—a slight flaring of his nostrils. "Such as your ability to remember, my friend.

19

Memory. It's your life, your identity. Without it, who are you? *What* are you?"

Geordi watched the old man's face. Was that a hint of pain he saw in the regions around Homer's eyes? Was the bard of bards, in his latter years, starting to *forget* things?

It was certainly possible. In this era, senility was still a problem. Hell, that hadn't changed until the twenty-second or twenty-third century.

Geordi considered it for a moment—what it would be like to be Homer, the greatest bard of his age. To have all that knowledge, all that poetry and legend stored in his mind. And to know that it was gradually abandoning him. Not just his inner world, but his *only* world—because for blind Homer, the world outside was something forever beyond his reach.

Then he caught himself. *Wait a minute. This isn't Homer, not really. This is just a simulation generated by the holodeck computer. The real Homer died around 700 B.C., back on Earth. How can you feel sorry for someone who no longer exists?*

But when he looked at the sightless old gentleman walking alongside him through the fig orchards, it was hard to be quite so logical. Maybe it wasn't the fall of Troy, exactly—but it was a tragedy nonetheless.

"Is that pity?" asked Homer abruptly. "I can feel it coming through your pores."

Geordi swallowed. It was frightening just how perceptive this simulation appeared to be.

"Don't weep for Homer," said the poet. "Weep for Odysseus and Menelaos, Akhilleus and Hektor. When my memory dies, so do they."

Over the hills, the moon was just coming up. It was large, a pale and luminous shade of blue.

"I wouldn't worry," said Geordi. "I think you'll find that there will be others to take up the stories. Just as they were passed down to you."

Homer harumphed. "I wonder. Poeting isn't the honored

profession it once was. With so few new bards, our numbers dwindle all the time. In a generation or two, we may vanish entirely from the face of the earth."

"That won't happen," said Geordi. "Not ever."

"You sound so sure. No man can see the future."

Geordi couldn't help but smile. "Why's that? I thought it was a storyteller's job to see things that aren't there."

Homer laughed heartily. "You lift my spirits, Geordi." A pause. "Have you ever thought of becoming a bard yourself?"

Geordi shrugged. "Once or twice, I guess. When I was younger. But that's not really what I'm good at. I like . . . well, machines. Engines. Warp . . ." He stopped himself. "Things like that."

"Machines, eh? That is one of the ways I've always thought of Odysseus. An engineer, a builder of things mechanical. The horse, for instance, that carried the invaders into Troy."

"You know," said Geordi, "I've always been curious about that. I mean . . . didn't anyone at all think to look inside?"

"I have to admit," said Homer, "I've wondered about that myself." The moon pulled free of the hills as he thought about it. "My best guess is that Cassandra helped the Greeks without knowing it. Everyone considered the girl insane, you see. No one wanted to be associated with her. So when she warned them about the horse, everyone rushed forth to embrace it. To prove their sanity, as it were."

Geordi smiled. "That would explain it, I guess."

There were other questions he'd like to have asked. About the construction of the horse, for instance—an engineer's curiosity. But it occurred to him that his holodeck time was almost up, and he didn't want to be a pig about it.

"What's wrong, my friend?" Homer's brow had creased. "The muscles in your arm just tensed."

"Nothing," said Geordi. "Nothing really. It's just that it's time for me to go."

21

Homer nodded. "Back where you came from." It wasn't a question. "That faraway place."

"Yes. But I've still got time to walk you back to the house."

"Thank you," said the poet. "I am grateful."

"Don't mention it," said Geordi.

Commander William Riker felt as if he had done something wrong somehow. He said so.

"You shouldn't," said Troi. "You acted just as he would have expected—you put the welfare of the ship and its crew first."

They stood forward of the control consoles, dwarfed by the magnitude of the celestial tableau on the viewscreen. Her tone, like his, was confidential.

"Sure. But now that I think about it, the effect was a little humiliating—wasn't it? I mean, to be shooed from your own bridge like some kind of worn-out part . . . especially when your defenses are down, and you're vulnerable . . ."

"That's not the way it happened," she insisted. "Certainly, the captain could have remained if he had wanted to."

"You don't think I was too cavalier? Too flip?"

"On the contrary. You were really quite gentle. Quite diplomatic. And I'm sure the captain understands."

Riker sighed. "I hope so, Deanna. The last thing I want is for him to feel crowded by me. That's not why I'm here."

"Of course not," she said. "You know, it is funny. You are so solicitous of his feelings sometimes—much more so than you need be."

He shrugged. "I can't help but put myself in his position. The captain has been commanding starships for a long time and doing a damned fine job of it. Then I come along, maybe a little wet behind the ears—at least by *his* standards. Suddenly, he finds himself sharing some of his responsibilities—and some of his prerogatives as well."

"What's more," said Troi, "you're a constant reminder that he is closer to the end of his career than the beginning.

You're a younger man, one with aspirations to command—aspirations you have never bothered to conceal."

He looked at her, cleared his throat. "Exactly."

"But don't you think," added the empath, "that *he* occasionally puts himself in *your* position—just as you put yourself in his? That he knows how difficult it can be to remain in the background, when one is capable of commanding one's own ship? And how a first officer must walk a tightrope between saying too little and saying too much?"

Riker shook his head. "You make it sound so simple, Counselor. It's one thing to appreciate the situation intellectually—and quite another to actually . . ."

"Commander?"

He turned in response to the voice. Wesley Crusher was standing just to one side of Data's Ops console.

"Yes, Ensign?"

"I think we've got something, sir."

Riker shot a glance at Troi and followed Wesley up the ramp to the afterbridge. He could feel his pulse speed up with anticipation.

"Exactly what is it you've got?" he asked, even before they reached the young man's station.

"It may be that ion trail we've been looking for." Wesley leaned past his empty chair and pointed to the scanner screen.

Riker took a look. What he saw took some of the edge off his optimism. "I'm no expert," he said, "but it seems like a very low concentration. What makes you think it came from the research ship?"

"Well," said Wesley, "it *is* a low concentration. But it's all relative, sir. If we were in a sector with a lot of activity, natural or otherwise, I'd say that it meant very little. But this area's been so clean up until now, I've got to believe it's significant."

Riker bit his lip as he studied the monitor. "Do you have enough information to project where the trail might lead?"

Wesley nodded. "I think so, yes." He called up a representation of the Trilik'kon Mahk'ti system and it supplanted the ion data. "You see those two planets—fourth and fifth from the sun? The trail seems to lead somewhere in there."

The first officer frowned. "That is, if it's really a trail in the first place."

Wesley looked at him. "Have we got anything to lose?" he asked.

Riker had to smile. "Good point, Ensign. Advise Mister Sharif of the coordinates and I'll authorize a course change."

"We won't need much," said the youth, his brow furrowing slightly as he made some quick computations on the screen. "In fact," he added with a note of mild surprise, "a couple of degrees to starboard ought to do the . . ." He stopped himself, looked up. And saw how Riker's eyes had narrowed in mock reproach. "Sorry, sir."

"That's all right," said the older man. "But I think we'll let Mister Sharif perform those calculations. After all, it *is* his job."

"Aye, sir," said Wesley. "I'll pass the information on to the conn."

"Thank you," said the first officer. Leaving matters in the ensign's capable hands, he descended the ramp again.

When he reached the command center, Troi was already seated in her usual spot. Riker sat down in the central chair—where the captain would have sat if he had been present.

"Lay in a course change," he instructed Sharif. "Mister Crusher is sending the coordinates."

"Aye, Commander," came the answer. "I've already got them."

"All right, then. Full impulse."

"Aye—full impulse, sir."

The ship surged effortlessly ahead—its progress evident only in the subtle movement of the planets on their viewer.

Troi looked at him expectantly. "So?" she prodded.

"We may have found the *Mendel*'s ion trail," he said. "Though I'm not betting the farm on it. The evidence is very faint."

There was a pause in which the same question occurred to both of them. Troi was the one who finally voiced it.

"Are you going to let him know?" she asked.

Riker weighed the particulars of the situation. "No," he told her. Then, with more certainty, "Not quite yet. This mission obviously means a lot to him. Why raise his hopes just to dash them?"

Troi nodded but did not comment. Nor, having made up his mind, did he press her for her opinion.

Lieutenant Worf—*just* Worf, no compilation of wasteful syllables as was the custom among humans—set his teeth against the pain. It was terrible, excruciating. Like a flame that ate at him from within. At the corner of his mouth, a muscle twitched. With an effort, he forced it to stop.

After his unceremonious departure from the bridge, Worf had needed to burn off his frustration. It had never been easy for him to live among humans—to practice discipline, to observe the rules. *Always*, it seemed, there were rules, coming at him from every direction.

In this case, the rules had proven particularly onerous. He had acted out of loyalty and he had been publicly shamed for it. No doubt, the captain had believed he was practicing diplomacy. But then, really, he understood the Klingon mind and soul no better than anyone else.

So Worf had been on his way to the gym, and his locker here, even before Radzic and Pappas had walked in—discussing Picard's all-inclusive, no-exceptions recreation order. The Klingon took note of the fact that he was no longer alone in his expulsion—but it didn't serve to quench his fury any.

Only the rigors of *battle* could do that.

Worf glanced at the digital display he had programmed

into the gymnasium wall. It showed him that he had been at this for thirty-two minutes and five seconds, ship's time. *Six. Seven. Eight . . .*

The *eurakoi* that he held in front of him, extended at arm's length, weighed slightly more than thirteen pounds a piece. They were made of *shrogh,* a metal as common in the Klingon Empire as it was rare in the Federation territories.

This was not a source of envy on the part of the Federation, nor had it ever been so. *Shrogh* was a fairly useless metal, difficult to alloy and too heavy to be helpful in the construction of space vessels. In fact, it was only mined at all to be employed in the manufacture of *eurakoi.*

Worf had discovered this particular pair in a pawnshop on Starbase 13. At the time, he had had mixed emotions about them.

Of course, there had been an eagerness to rescue the *eurakoi* from their ignominious fate as curiosities in the shop's display window. To put them back in the hands of a Klingon, where they belonged.

But there had also been a feeling that the things were not his—could *never* be his. A Klingon was given the *eurakoi* by his mother's eldest brother—that was the tradition. Any other way of obtaining them was considered tainted. Not necessarily wrong, but not quite right.

In Worf's case, there had been no possibility of receiving the *eurakoi* in the prescribed manner. His immediate family was dead; he barely remembered them. Having been raised by humans on a Federation world, he had never even heard of *eurakoi* until they turned up in a cultural tape at Starfleet Academy.

He knew now that they had become a symbol for him then—of the extent to which he had been divorced from his Klingon heritage. Of the schism within him, across which his born-Klingon and raised-human selves constantly eyed one another with suspicion.

And so, for Worf—ironically, perhaps—the use of the *eurakoi* had a greater meaning than for others. It was not only his strength he put to the test, his ability to deny gravity its rightful prize; it was also the degree to which the Klingon in him had survived.

The display showed thirty-six minutes and twelve seconds. He could feel the pain mounting, shooting through his wrists, his shoulders, his neck. His muscles spasmed and cramped as he fought to keep them steady.

Unbidden, the thought came to him that he had only substituted one form of discipline for another—Klingon discipline for human discipline. But the Klingon brand was liberating for him, while the human kind was stifling.

A contradiction? Not to one who appreciated the subtleties of the Klingon psyche.

Thirty-seven minutes and fifty-seven seconds. Fifty-eight . . .

Once, a Vulcan classmate at the Academy had taught him a method of submerging physical discomfort. Of letting it sink to a level at which it could be managed—tamed. And finally ignored.

But that was not the Klingon way. The whole point of the *eurakoi* exercise was to experience the pain. To meet it head-on, to embrace it. And then to laugh in its ugly face.

Anything less would make his victory a hollow one.

Thirty-nine minutes and forty-four seconds. Forty-five . . .

It was agony now. Sheer, unadulterated agony. Even his breath was coming harder. Sweat ran down the sides of his face from his temples—and a Klingon did not perspire easily.

Worf glared at the *eurakoi* as he would have glared at a living enemy. He noted the humpbacked shape of them, the grisly carvings that depicted the violence of his people's earliest beginnings. The way the dull, dark metal seemed to absorb the light, giving off only the faintest of reflections.

His lips curled back from his teeth, wolflike. Deep in his throat, so deep it was audible only to him, he growled long and low.

He wanted very much to put the *eurakoi* down. He could not remember anything he had ever desired so fervently.

But he would not be defeated. He would not *allow* himself to be defeated.

Forty-one minutes and thirty seconds. *Only three and a half minutes to go . . .*

"Worf?"

The Klingon did not dare turn his head. But then, he didn't have to. The voice was a familiar one. And a moment or two later, he saw Data's approach out of the corner of his eye.

The android's head was tilted slightly to one side as he came up alongside Worf. His brow was slightly wrinkled, his golden eyes alight with curiosity.

The Klingon concentrated on the *eurakoi.*

"If I may ask," said Data, "what are you doing?"

"Exercising," snarled Worf.

The android thought about that for a second, then registered mild surprise.

"Really? That is very interesting. I had always thought that exercise involved movement. And yet, except for that trembling in your arms, you are hardly moving at all."

The Klingon's teeth ground together. "My arms . . . are not . . . trembling," he said.

Data looked closer. "It certainly looks as if they are trembling. Or perhaps 'trembling' is the wrong word. Would 'shuddering' be more to the point?"

"They . . . are   not . . . shuddering . . . either." Each word was an ordeal. But Worf could not allow himself to seem weak. Not even in front of Data.

The android regarded him with a strange expression. As if he had caught on that there was a discrepancy between his own perceptions and those of the Klingon. Or at least, a difference in their interpretations of the physical evidence.

And if he didn't quite know why that should be, he appeared to have the sense not to press the issue. Worf was grateful for that much.

Forty-two minutes and eighteen seconds.

"Would you prefer that I went away?" asked Data. "Until you finish . . . exercising?"

Worf would indeed have preferred that. But the android was his comrade—his fellow officer. He could not simply rebuff him—not as *he* had been rebuffed by Picard.

"No," Worf squeezed between clenched teeth. "You may . . . stay."

Data's face brightened. "Thank you," he said. And folding his arms across his chest, he continued to watch—as immobile as the Klingon would liked to have been.

But the android was right—despite Worf's denials. He saw that his massive, white-knuckled hands *were* beginning to tremble. The *eurakoi* each felt like many times their actual weight. He might have been holding up a whole shuttlecraft, the way his body screamed for relief.

Forty-three minutes and six seconds.

Not much longer to go—objectively speaking. But to Worf, it seemed like a lifetime. The pain was giving way now to a numbness—a lack of control that was infinitely harder to master. Slowly, the *eurakoi* started to sink from shoulder level.

The Klingon stifled a whimper. *No!*

But he couldn't help it. There was hardly any feeling left in his forearms or in his hands. The *shrogh* weights were getting the best of him.

"I see," said Data unexpectedly, "that you are about to fail at this exercise."

Worf glowered at him. Bile rose in his throat like liquid anger.

"But then," Data went on, "I did not believe you would succeed. After all, you are only flesh and blood. And flesh, as the saying goes, is weak."

Worf could not believe the android's insolence. It was more than mere naïveté—it was a direct and purposeful insult. The warrior inside him uncoiled, surged to the surface.

"Are you angry with me?" asked Data. "Do you wish to wring my neck?"

Worf's rage made him inarticulate. All he could do was sputter and hiss like a trapped animal.

The android grinned—*grinned!*—with satisfaction. "Good. I was afraid that my words would not have the desired effect."

Worf almost lost control—came within a hair, in fact, of lashing out at Data with the *eurakoi.*

And then he realized what the android was doing.

He looked up at the digital display.

Forty-four minutes and fifty-seven seconds. Fifty-eight. Fifty-nine . . .

Forty-five minutes.

With a howl of triumph, Worf knelt and let his hands—still holding the *eurakoi*—come crashing down to the padded deck. For a moment, he knelt there, savoring his accomplishment.

Then he peered up at Data.

"You did it," said the android, obviously pleased with himself. "And I helped."

"Yes," rumbled Worf. "You helped." But he couldn't keep a note of rancor out of his voice entirely.

In a sense, Data's intervention had cheapened his victory. It had distracted him, even as the Vulcan technique would have—and thereby eased the path to his goal.

But that was all history now. Challenges were things of the moment; what was past was past. And whatever might be said of Klingons, they did not bear grudges. Not unless they were big ones.

"You see," said Data, "once I came to understand the nature of your exercise, it was a simple matter to devise a ploy to spur you on. As the Klingon psyche does not respond significantly to encouragement, I chose to taunt you. To mock you. To question your abilities . . ."

"Yes," said Worf, cutting the android off. "It is clear to me now."

Data's smile faded a little. "I hope I was not . . . what is the expression? Out of line?" He regarded the Klingon. "Perhaps it was presumptuous of me to interfere."

Worf scowled, shook his head. What could one say to someone like Data? "No," he assured him. "You did not overstep your bounds."

The android's smile came back with renewed enthusiasm. "I am glad, then, to have been of service."

Leaving the *eurakoi* on the floor, Worf stood. He towered over Data by half a head.

"What are you doing in the gym anyway? I thought you had no need of physical education."

"True," said Data. "No more than I have need of other forms of diversion. But the captain ordered us to recreate, and he did not make my case an exception." He paused. "I had thought to spend some time on a holodeck, but they all seem to be in use. Nor was there anyone I knew in Ten Forward, so . . . here I am."

Worf grunted. "Here you are."

The android glanced around at the various activity areas, shrugged. "Would you care for a game of Ping-Pong?"

"Ping-Pong?" said Worf.

"Yes. I have seen it played in tapes. And if I am not mistaken, the Ping-Pong table Commander Riker created is still right over *there.*"

The Klingon eyed the table, snorted. "No," he said. "Thank you." And stooping to pick up his *eurakoi,* he went to replace them in his locker.

Doctor Katherine Pulaski sat on the hard edge of a lab table, her arms folded across her chest, considering the sleeping form of Giancarlo Fredi through the transparent wall of the critical care area.

He was a lucky man. If one of Worf's security people hadn't found him when she did, he would no doubt have died in that lonely science-section corridor.

The doctor consulted the monitor on Fredi's biobed, saw

that everything was more or less stable—except for one thing. The toxin in his bloodstream was gradually building up again.

Maybe lucky wasn't quite the right word after all.

Initially, Pulaski had gone with the obvious hypothesis: that the geologist had been exposed to the poison during his away duty on Baldwin-McKean's Planet. However, his exposure had taken place weeks ago, and that was a long time for even a slow-acting toxin to make its presence felt. What's more, if the problem were a simple poisoning, the blood purifier would have taken care of it—and it hadn't. Minutes after the purging process was complete, the toxin was evident again. And a second purge hadn't managed to get rid of it either—not permanently.

Which added up to one thing—the toxin was being manufactured by something in Fredi's system. An alien bacterium had taken hold inside him—in quantities small enough to have gotten past the transporter sensors, which meant *really* small—and then, given time, had multiplied to the point where it could generate a significant level of toxin.

It *sounded* good. Unfortunately, there *was* no alien bacterium—or at least none she could find. But if a bacterium wasn't responsible . . . then where in blazes was the poison coming from? *Something* had to be producing it. It couldn't very well be materializing out of thin air.

Fredi stirred and turned his head toward her. For a moment, his eyes blinked, as if at a bright light. Then he fell asleep again.

It brought her maternal instinct to the surface. The man was only a couple of years her junior, but that didn't matter. In a sense, all doctors felt like mothers to their patients.

She bit her lip. Enough romanticizing. She had some work ahead of her.

Fredi himself would be all right for a while. As long as his blood was purified every so often, his symptoms wouldn't get any worse. As for the rest of the crew . . . well, that was another story.

Those who had been part of the Baldwin-McKean away team were naturally at risk. They would have to be tested for evidence of the toxin. And even if they tested negative, they'd have to be watched closely for a while—in case the ailment took even longer to develop in their cases.

What's more, in the weeks since they'd left Baldwin-McKean, there had been plenty of time for Fredi to pass on the disease—assuming, of course, that it was contagious.

The fact that Fredi's case was the only one she'd encountered so far was encouraging—but hardly conclusive. Until Pulaski knew exactly what this ailment was, she had to entertain all possibilities.

Hence, the quarantine order. Not only for Fredi, but also for the other Baldwin-McKean away team members, once they were identified and brought to sickbay.

The thing to do now was to inform the captain—even before she rounded up the others who'd participated in the Baldwin-McKean survey. If the disease *did* prove to be communicable, she didn't want Picard caught by surprise.

Not that there would be anything he could do about it. That responsibility would come to rest squarely on *her* shoulders.

Chapter Three

RIKER HEARD the last of Pulaski's report. He nodded as if she were standing there in front of him, rather than communicating from her office in sickbay.

"Thank you, Doctor," he told her. "Need any help corralling the rest of the survey team?"

"I can do that myself," said Pulaski. "I know how quickly you bureaucrats roll into action."

Riker chuckled. "All right," he said. "Have it your way."

As luck would have it, he had missed that rather uneventful away mission, having entrusted it to Ensign Pappas. "Is there anything *else* I can do for you?" he asked.

"No," said the chief medical officer. "That will be all— for now."

Having gotten what she wanted, Pulaski terminated the exchange. Again, Riker couldn't help but be a little amused. The doctor was so *brusque* sometimes. But then, in a perverse way, that was part of her charm.

Right now, of course, he was glad that the conversation hadn't drawn on. There were more important matters with which to contend.

Like the strange-looking planet dead ahead, the one to

which the ion trail had finally led them after a wild and woolly chase throughout the system. It seemed that the *Mendel* had regained a semblance of its impulse power—if only for a little while. It had been long enough, however, for the ship to keep from getting snared in the gravitational fields of the fifth and sixth planets. Some effort had been made to turn the *Mendel* around, to leave Trilik'kon Mahk'ti the way it had come in. Then the engines had all but conked out again—leaving the ship headed for the world on their viewscreen.

The *Enterprise*'s first officer had seen his share of unusual planets. But he had never seen one like this one. It looked like a perfect golden ball hanging in space—not just golden in color, but also in its ability to reflect the light of the sun.

"Confirmation, Mister Fong?"

Above and behind him, at tactical, the assistant security chief was still seeking the information Riker had asked for entire minutes ago, when the planet had been a lot farther off. He could hear him mutter something under his breath, then drum his fingers on the console.

"Not yet, sir. I . . . wait a second. I think I've got it." A pause while he called up yet another reference file, scanned it. "Yes—here it is, sir. In an academic treatise partly devoted to the Klah'kimmbri: This people refers to its homeworld as A'klah. Our best guess is that it is the fourth planet from Trilik'kon Mahk'ti."

Riker leaned back in his command chair, eyed the golden sphere with redoubled curiosity—and wariness. "Thank you," he told Fong.

He could almost hear Troi asking him that question again: *Are you going to tell him?* She was off duty, in accordance with the captain's order, but his response would still have been the same.

Before he contacted Picard, he would make certain that this was where the *Mendel* finally wound up. Maybe Troi was right. Maybe he *was* too solicitous of the captain's feelings sometimes. But the man damned well didn't need to

35

be dragged out of a holodeck or Ten Forward or wherever he was—wherever he'd found some peace, some distraction— unless their search was really over, one way or another.

"Sir?"

It was Wesley, now at the conn. He was facing Riker, having swiveled around in his seat.

"What is it, Mister Crusher?"

"We've got some readings now on the planet. But I'm not sure what to make of them."

The first officer eyed him. "What do you mean, Ensign? Be a little more specific."

Wesley frowned. He looked puzzled—rare for him. "Sensors indicate that there's a planet-size mass up ahead all right—but it's not nearly as large as the planet we're looking at. This world has some sort of mantle around it—a low-level energy field that makes it appear to be bigger than it really is."

Riker turned back to the screen and the shiny, golden sphere. "Interesting," he said. "Could this be a natural phenomenon?"

Wesley's eyes narrowed in thought. "It's possible, I suppose. But the field is amazingly uniform. And if it were natural, I don't think that would be the case."

The first officer considered that. "What about the planet beneath it?"

The ensign swung around again to face the conn monitor. "Can't tell much about it, sir. Density and such, but that's about it. The field is playing havoc with the scanners."

"Life signs?" pressed Riker.

"Inconclusive," said Wesley.

"But if you're right, and that mantle's artificial—then there has got to be someone down there. Someone with a rather advanced level of technology. And since at least one source cites this as the homeworld of the Klah'kimmbri . . . I'd say the Cantiliac weren't as thorough as we figured."

Fong cleared his throat to get the first officer's attention.

"Suggest we practice caution, sir. If this world can generate a field like that one, it may also have some pretty fierce weaponry."

"Noted," said Riker. He was glad now that he'd opted to keep the shields up, that he'd been prepared for any eventuality from the start—even if it had seemed like *over*-preparation just a few hours ago. "Mister Crusher, continue to scan. If the *Mendel*'s in there, we've got to find it somehow. Maybe as we get closer, the mantle will become a little more penetrable."

"Aye, sir," said Wesley.

The first officer stroked his beard with thumb and forefinger. As they approached the golden ball, questions came to him. Some easy to answer, some not so easy.

What was that energy field all about?

That was one of the easy ones. Obviously, the Klah'kimmbri wanted some privacy from prying eyes.

Why? What was it they wanted to keep private?

That was a little harder.

Was it simply a matter of defense? If so, why were there no working outposts? No satellites or ships or other, simpler ways of keeping intruders at arm's length?

A harder one still.

And what would the Klah'kimmbri be defending against? Or more to the point, *who?* Was there a new aggressor in this sector—one they should be aware of?

He couldn't even guess.

But as they approached A'klah—and very likely, the end of their mission—he wished he had more answers. He had a feeling they might come in handy.

Picard could not begin to count the number of orders he had followed in the course of his career with Starfleet. Apparently, he had followed them well enough, or he would never have been placed in command of a ship like the *Enterprise*.

It was ironic, then, that he should have so much trouble following his *own* directives. Perhaps familiarity *did* breed contempt.

Here he had instructed his command staff to relax during their off-duty hours. But instead of heading for a recreational area, he had come directly to his quarters. And too contrary-minded to even get some sleep, he had paced the length and breadth of them—which is just what he would have done if he'd remained on the bridge.

This is getting you nowhere, he told himself. *Nor is it any help to Dani.*

Picard had met Abraham Orbutu more than twenty years ago. They were assigned to the same colonization team on Cassiopeia Gamma Four—he as Starfleet liaison, Orbutu as survey zoologist. The two of them hit it off right from the start—and no wonder. Picard had always had an interest in zoology—had in fact considered it as his life's pursuit after his initial failure to get into Starfleet Academy. In a similar vein, Orbutu would gladly have traded his zoologist's credentials for a chance to serve aboard a starship—were it not for a rare brain dysfunction that caused him to black out under duress.

What's more, Orbutu spoke fluent French, having been educated in Tangiers back on Earth. It was rare to find someone with whom Picard could converse in his mother tongue, much less someone as jovial and entertaining as big, broad-shouldered Orbutu.

The stint on Cassiopeia Gamma Four had lasted only a few months, but their friendship went on long after that. Orbutu eventually married and had a family, and finally— after an incident in a Glorgothan jungle during which his dysfunction almost claimed his life—grudgingly returned to Earth to teach at his alma mater.

It was shortly after that that Orbutu's daughter followed in his footsteps. A bright and pretty young woman with her father's sense of humor, Dani began corresponding with Picard on her own after her first assignment in space. Once, they had even managed to cross paths on Starbase 19—she making a transfer en route to a zoology conference, he in for the *Enterprise*'s scheduled maintenance check. They had spent a delightful few hours there, trading stories about the elder Orbutu and discussing Dani's future with the Survey Service.

He remembered how eager she had been to join a research mission out of Starbase 84—one that was headed out beyond the pall of Federation space. Months later, he learned that she had gotten the berth she wanted—zoologist and second medical officer—thanks in some part to his recommendation.

Now that research vessel was lost, and Dani along with it. Probably, she would have earned herself a spot on the *Gregor Mendel* even without Picard's help. But he couldn't help but wonder.

Was it so surprising, then, that he had campaigned to have the *Enterprise* designated as the search-and-rescue ship? Or that he had taken this mission so much to heart?

Picard found that his cabin was closing in around him. He yearned to go back to the bridge, where he at least had some illusion of control over Dani Orbutu's fate. Frowning, he quelled the impulse.

Get a grip on yourself, Jean-Luc. You're driving yourself to distraction. Do as you've told the others to do: relax. Go down to the gym. Pick up an epee, work the kinks out. Yes?

Yes, he told himself.

But he did not go. He stayed in his quarters and continued to pace.

It was as Riker had hoped. The energy mantle was less effective at close range. Only a *touch* less effective—but enough to yield the treasure they'd been seeking for so long.

The Ops monitor held the computer-enhanced silhouette of the *Mendel* within its electronic grasp. Emerald green shadows against a blacker-than-black field.

Up on the main viewer, there was nothing but gold and

glitter from pole to pole. But then, Riker had given up looking at the big screen some time ago.

"No question about it?" he asked.

Still making adjustments, Wesley shook his head. "No question, sir. It's an Icarus-class vessel, model Four. That fits the description of the *Gregor Mendel* to a tee."

"And there are no life-sign readings? None at all?"

Wesley shook his head again, sighed. "I can't pick anything up, Commander. But . . . that *could* be the fault of the field."

True. The energy mantle might have entirely blanked out that aspect of their sensor capability. But what were the odds of that? Not good.

More likely, the sensors *were* getting through—and there just wasn't anything alive to pick up.

The first officer straightened, still glaring at the monitor. He had hoped to have better news when he finally contacted the captain. But like it or not, it was time to bring him in on this.

"Bridge to Picard," he called out. It took a few moments for the captain to respond.

"Yes, Number One?"

Could it be that he had sensed the substance of what Riker had to tell him? And was that reluctant to hear it?

The observation gave the younger man new insight. *Geordi was right all along,* he told himself. *Someone the captain cares about is on the* Mendel. *Someone he cares about a lot.*

Riker swallowed. "We've located the research ship, sir." He didn't have to say any more at this point, but he didn't want to keep the captain guessing. "Unfortunately, we've failed to pick up any life-signs."

Again, that bottomless pause. "I'll be right there," said Picard, his voice flat and devoid of emotion.

Chapter Four

PICARD CHEWED the inside of his cheek, regarded the dazzling energy display on the viewscreen and mulled it all over silently—while Riker and Troi sat on either side of him and waited.

All the evidence supported the thesis that the *Mendel*'s crew was dead. The sensors spoke eloquently of it. So did the communications silence, which persisted despite Worf's repeated efforts to establish contact.

Even Troi had been unable to find a conscious mind on the research vessel with which to link up.

It cast a pall over the captain, forced a part of him to start mourning. But another part had no time for such luxuries. Even if he were to admit that Dani had been killed—along with her crew mates—a bigger question still loomed.

How?

As badly as the Murasaki disturbance had burned the *Mendel*'s hull, it was apparently intact. Had the life-support systems simply failed without warning? Had a radiation leak gone undetected until it was too late?

If they had discovered the research vessel in the lonely

depths of space, he might have put more trust in these possibilities. But the *Mendel* being where it was, he couldn't ignore a more obvious conclusion—that the Klah'kimmbri had played some role in this. After all, they had once been known for their aggressive tendencies. And even if their defenses were somewhat unorthodox, it appeared that their level of technology hadn't slipped any.

On the other hand, he couldn't just assume the Klah'kimmbri were guilty of something. He had to know more before he could make any accusations.

Accusations? He rebuked himself even for his choice of words.

Aren't you letting your personal feelings—your all-too-human need for a scapegoat—cloud your perceptions, Jean-Luc? The Klah'kimmbri may be completely innocent. Who knows? They may even have tried to help.

At the very least, they might have received some communication from the research ship—some information that would shed some light on how Dani and the others had perished.

If they had perished. That had yet to be substantiated.

"Mister Worf," he called, "open hailing frequencies. Try to raise someone on the planet's surface."

"Opening hailing frequencies," said the Klingon.

It was comforting, Picard had to admit, to have his most capable personnel around him—regardless of what shift they were supposed to be on. He could feel their sharpness, their precision. If the Klah'kimmbri *were* responsible, and it came to blows, this was the complement he wanted at the controls.

Was he feeling resentful that Riker had waited so long to contact him? To let him know about the ion trail—and about A'klah? Perhaps, yes. But he understood the man's motives well enough. And besides, the first officer was more than a fixture. He had carried out his duties exactly as he should have.

In the final analysis, it had been a judgment call—on both levels, professional and personal. Not worth mentioning again on either level.

"Any response, Mister Worf?"

"Nothing yet, sir."

"Isn't it possible," offered Riker, "that this mantle *precludes* long-range communications? I mean, if it can prevent our sensors from penetrating all the way to the planet's surface . . ."

Picard nodded. "Certainly, it's possible. But I'm betting that the Klah'kimmbri have found a way to defy their own invention. After all, this mantle isn't much of a protection if it blinds them as much as it blinds us."

The first officer chewed that one over. "A polarized field then? One which lets radiation in, but not out?"

"That's my guess," said the captain.

"Still no response," reported Worf.

Picard regarded the whiplash dance of yellow golden light on the viewscreen. "Keep trying," he said.

The Klingon worked at his communications board for a good half hour. A certain tension built up on the deck; the captain felt it like a weight on his brow, growing heavier and more painful by the moment.

Finally, he had had enough.

When Sam Burtin heard the cry that came out of Pulaski's office, his first thought was that his superior had injured herself somehow. Then, as he came marching down the hallway to investigate, he saw that she was doubled over by her desk.

Immediately, his training took over. He swung past the threshold and dropped down beside her. "Doctor? Are you all right?"

Pulaski looked up at him, a wistful expression on her face. "*I* am, yes. But *this* thing has seen better days."

She held up two pieces of her Mondrifahlian good-luck

charm, the one he had given her as a gift. The ceramic statuette had split into fragments, each fiery red on the outside and a dull beige on the inside. One piece, the largest, sported three snakelike appendages and a slender eyestalk.

But that was the only casualty. Pulaski was fine.

Of course she is, he told himself. *What did you expect? This isn't Vega Antilles, Sam. You're not on the frontier anymore. Even when there is an emergency—like poor Fredi out there—you've got the hardware to keep it under control.*

"Damn," said Pulaski, replacing the shards on her desk. "I really liked that little fellow." She smiled. "Oh well. I guess I'll have to make my own luck for a while."

And what a nice smile it was. The stories about Pulaski had been patently untrue. She wasn't nearly the iron-handed ogre she'd been made out to be. In fact, she was more pleasant than most of the medical chiefs under which he'd served—and certainly a damned sight more attractive. He couldn't help but notice that.

Not that he'd ever make any advances toward her. Not even now, when her ice blue eyes were just inches from his. He was too much of a professional for that. And maybe too much of a coward as well.

"When I heard you scream," said Burtin, "I thought there was something wrong."

Pulaski chuckled. "Wrong? Quite the contrary. Everything is remarkably right." She got to her feet, then came around her desk and plunked down into her chair. "Have a seat."

Burtin rose too, then, and took the chair on the other side of the desk. He didn't have to ask for an explanation—she'd already embarked on one before he could say a thing.

"We have been looking," she told him, "for the wrong kind of bacterium. We've been assuming that the thing that's afflicted Fredi—that's releasing the toxins into his system—is something foreign. Something alien."

Burtin shrugged. "What else can it be?"

Pulaski leaned forward across her desk, brushing against

one of the luck-charm fragments. Her expression had intensified; the skin between her brows was pinched together.

"Picture this," she said. "Fredi encounters an unfamiliar bacterium on Baldwin-McKean's Planet—a bacterium that produces the toxin we've been purging him of. It gets inside his tissues and lives for some finite period of time. But it's only present in trace quantities—and it doesn't replicate very quickly, so it can't produce much of the poison. Therefore, there are no obvious effects. Eventually, the bacterium finds something about its new environment intolerable. Maybe it's already dead by the time Fredi beams up; maybe not. In any case, it has expired long before he displays any symptoms.

"But before it keels over, it has an effect on one of the body's normal bacterial residents. It *translocates* some of its genetic makeup—don't ask me how—to that resident. One gene, say, for production of a toxin that happens to cause paralysis in humans. Another for a stimulant that tickles the adrenal gland—causing the energy spurt that Fredi described to me. You know, that period of unusual efficiency before his muscles began to lock up on him?"

Burtin nodded.

"In effect," she went on, "a hybrid is created. A bacterium that looks and acts like one that we know—except that it has an alarming propensity to produce an alien toxin."

He grunted. It was *theoretically* possible. Viruses communicated genetic material to other viruses. Why not bacteria to other bacteria?

And of course, she *was* Kate Pulaski. It was difficult not to take her seriously.

"You seem a little skeptical," she observed.

He smiled. "A little."

"Well," she said, "there's only one way to prove me wrong. Let's see if we can't isolate the affected resident." She leaned back from her desk now. "But I have to warn you—I've got a good feeling about this one."

Burtin looked at her—purely as a colleague now, doctor

to doctor. "Tell me one thing," he said. "How the hell did you come up with this?"

She shook her head. "I don't know. I was sitting here, racking my brain for a new angle—and it just hit me. Out of the blue, as it were." She blushed a little—but just a little. "That's when I let out with that victory cry. And knocked over my good-luck charm."

Ruefully, Pulaski considered the shattered souvenir. "A small price to pay," she concluded, "in the scheme of things."

Burtin was about to agree when her monitor beeped. She swiveled it around to face her and answered, suddenly all business.

"Pulaski here."

"I'm convening the command staff in the lounge." It was the captain's voice, though Burtin couldn't see his face. "Five minutes, Doctor."

"I have a rather serious case here in sickbay," said Pulaski. "Crewman Fredi, as I . . ."

"*None*theless," said the captain, his voice charged with impatience, "I expect to see you in the lounge. That is all."

And the communication ended.

The chief medical officer appeared a little startled. It wasn't an expression that became her.

"Well," she said, looking up at Burtin, "I can hardly refuse when he asks so nicely. I guess it's up to you to run the isolation patterns."

"No problem," he told her.

Pulaski met his gaze. "Good. I like the sound of that. Now if you'll excuse me, I have a meeting to attend."

Outside the observation lounge, stars and planets alike were only points of light. Neither Trilik'kon Mahk'ti nor A'klah's golden presence were visible to Picard as he took his seat.

Just as well, he thought. They would only be distractions.

He waited for the others to file in and find their places.

First Troi, then Riker, Worf and Data. A moment later, Geordi. And finally, Doctor Pulaski.

The captain leaned his elbows on the long conference table, placed his palms together to make a wedge of his hands.

"Mister Riker," he said, "would you bring Mister La Forge and the good doctor up to speed?"

His first officer nodded and gave an account of what had transpired on the bridge. It was short and to the point.

"Thank you, Number One." Picard sat back in his chair. "So, though the Klah'kimmbri are not proving very helpful, we must nonetheless find out what happened to those on the *Mendel*. The only way to do that is to board the vessel." He looked from one face to the next. "However, as I understand it, there are some obstacles to be overcome in such an endeavor." He looked to his chief engineer.

Geordi nodded. "That energy mantle makes beaming over a real can of worms . . ."

Picard couldn't help but notice how Data's face screwed up at that. Holding up a hand to stop Geordi, he asked: "Is there a problem, Commander?"

The android seemed startled by the sudden attention. "Sorry, sir," he said, "but the reference eludes me. Can . . . of worms?"

"A set of difficulties," explained Riker.

"Right," said Geordi. "My apologies, Data."

"That is all right," said the android good-naturedly. "I understand now."

"In other words," said the chief engineer, addressing all of them again, "it may not be possible to teleport onto the *Mendel*—at least, not with positive results. If our sensor capabilities are hampered by the energy field, who knows what obstacles it'll present to our transporter technology?"

"Even at close range?" asked Riker. "What if we were to bring the ships almost hull to hull?"

"I would not recommend it," said Worf. "That would place the *Enterprise* inside the mantle." He shook his head slowly from side to side, frowning. "What if the energy level is raised suddenly? We could find ourselves trapped. Or worse."

"Noted," said Picard. "But if we were to approach the very limits of the mantle—without actually entering it— what would that do to our chances for a successful teleport?"

Geordi shrugged. "It'd improve them significantly. But the results would still be uncertain."

"What about a tractor beam?"

The question came from an unlikely source: Doctor Pulaski.

"Why can't we just drag the ship out of there? And *then* beam aboard?"

"We've already tried that," said Worf. "To no avail. The tractor beam is adversely affected by the field as well."

"I see," said Pulaski.

"Good try, Doctor," remarked Picard.

"Of course," said Riker, "we *could* board the *Mendel* physically—but that would mean having to cut our way inside."

"Exactly," confirmed Geordi. "And without knowing how volatile those engines might be, or what kinds of gasses might be loose, we'd stand a good chance of blowing the ship up before we got very far. Even if nothing exploded, we'd still have the problem of keeping things from getting sucked out of our entrance hole." He paused. "Just imagine if we're wrong about those people being dead, and we let out all their oxygen. I wouldn't want to be the one to take responsibility for *that*."

Picard looked around. "Any other ideas?"

No one seemed to have any. Out of habit, he turned to Troi. It wasn't unusual for her to remain silent until the very last, though her insights were often what tipped the scales.

But not this time. Like Pulaski, she was a little out of her element.

Then Worf spoke up. "If we are to beam aboard," he said, "we must do it one at a time. To minimize the chances of something going wrong." His Klingon eyes narrowed. "And I will go first. In case the results are . . ." He glanced at Geordi. ". . . *not* positive."

Picard saw Geordi's Adam's apple move up and down at the image. He sympathized.

"No," said Riker. He met the Klingon's gaze. "If anyone goes first, it'll be me." He managed a smile. "Why do you think they call me the *first* officer?"

Worf scowled. A couple of the others chuckled.

Picard waited a moment before he went on. He wanted Riker's jibe to be forgotten before he broke the news to him. It would be embarrassing to the younger man in any case—no need to rub it in.

"All right, then. It seems that the transporter route is our only viable option. Nor is there any reason to delay. Mister Data, maneuver us to the boundaries of the mantle. We will beam over in, say, twenty minutes. Full containment suits and life-support gear."

Riker was looking at him, the smile long gone. "*We,* sir?"

He returned the look with equanimity. "Yes, Number One. I'm taking charge of this away team."

His first officer flushed slightly, but he didn't press the issue. It was the wrong time and place.

"Mister Worf," said Picard, "I'd like you to accompany me. Also, two of your people. Mister La Forge, the same."

"Aye, sir," said the Klingon. Geordi nodded.

Finally, Picard addressed Pulaski. "You and I will round out the group, Doctor."

She didn't look too happy about that. Less happy, in fact, than she had been about attending this meeting in the first place.

"Captain," said Pulaski, "I have a sick man to attend to."

"A task," said Picard, "which I'm sure is well within the

49

capabilities of your staff. Whereas our investigation of the research ship calls for the highest level of expertise we can muster. And since you *are* my chief medical officer . . ."

Seeing that he would not budge on this matter, the doctor swallowed her pride. For the second time in the last hour, the captain noted.

"As you wish," she said. "Sir."

When she first came to the *Enterprise,* Pulaski wouldn't have hesitated to make a scene over something like this. He was grateful that they understood each other a little better now.

"Good," said Picard. "Then everyone is dismissed—except for you, Number One. I believe we have something to discuss."

He could have put Riker in the position of having to request a private meeting. But why postpone the inevitable?

Once out on the bridge, with the lounge doors safely closed behind them, Geordi turned to Data. "Boy," he said, "I'll bet there'll be some fireworks in *there.*"

The android stopped and tilted his head to one side. "Fireworks?" Comprehension seemed to dawn a moment later. "Ah. *Fireworks.* Pyrotechnics. An incendiary display for the purpose of entertainment." He paused, suddenly at a loss again. "But why would the captain and Commander Riker engage in . . . ?"

He cut himself short when he saw Geordi shaking his head.

"I am being too literal again," Data concluded.

"Yes," said the chief engineer. "What I meant is that Commander Riker may have some harsh words for Captain Picard. And I can't say I blame him."

"Harsh words?" echoed the android. "For what reason?"

Geordi began to explain, then thought better of it. He didn't want to be standing out here when one or both of his superiors came storming out.

"Tell you what," he said to Data. "I'll explain when I get back."

"Sir . . ."

"You need not say it, Will. I know. Of all personnel, the captain is the least dispensable. It is the role of the first officer to act as the captain's surrogate in situations that appear dangerous or unpredictable."

Riker frowned. "That's right." His voice was even, but it had an edge to it. "And from where I stand, this situation is both. An entire crew died on that vessel. I'll be damned if I'm going to let you expose yourself to whatever it is that killed them."

Picard felt the other man's emotion as if it were something tangible. Riker wasn't just doing his duty. He *meant* it.

The captain grunted. "I didn't expect you to let me go without a fight. But I must remind you—the choice is ultimately mine."

His first officer leaned forward. "Sir, I can see that you've taken this search-and-rescue to heart—whatever your reasons. But in the end, it's like any other mission. And logic demands that I lead the away team."

The captain regarded him. "Yes—perhaps you're right. Logic *does* demand it. But then, logic must sometimes take a backseat to other considerations."

And he went on to speak of his friendship with Orbutu. Of Dani's berth on the research ship, and his role in getting it for her. Before he was finished, Riker's expression had changed. The air of forcefulness had receded, giving way to understanding.

"So you see," said Picard, "I must do this myself. If I am to face my friend again, I must be able to say I did everything I could—with my own hands, my own eyes. This is not my duty as captain of the *Enterprise,* I grant you. But it *is* my duty as a man."

Riker took a deep breath, let it out slowly. "Officially," he said, "that doesn't change things. It still makes more sense for *me* to go."

Picard nodded once. "Duly noted. And unofficially?"

Riker shrugged. "A man must do what a man must do."

The captain smiled. "Thank you for your support, Number One. Unofficially, of course."

His first officer smiled back—though his heart wasn't quite in it. "Just don't make me regret it, sir."

"I assure you," said Picard, "that is not my intention."

Chapter Five

WORF WENT FIRST—fortunately, without incident. As soon as that fact was established, the rest of the away team came over one by one, starting with the captain.

He materialized in the research vessel's common room—a space big enough to hold them all, and a central location from which they could fan out. As he joined the hulking figure of the Klingon, their containment suits glittering like ruby skins in the low light from the overhead panels, Picard took a look around.

There wasn't much in the way of amenities here. Some tables and chairs, a few scattered pieces of artwork on the walls. Long, narrow windows, curved to conform to the shape of the hull, showed the golden dazzle of the surrounding energy mantle in brilliant sections.

No bodies—not here, anyway. The captain noted that with some relief. But there was *something* here—something curious. On one table, a game of *flaga'gri*—the Rhadamanthan equivalent of chess—stood undisturbed.

Picard knelt beside it. He had never taken the time to really familiarize himself with *flaga'gri*, but he understood the basic principles. It seemed to him that this game was still only in its first stages.

Would someone have started a *flaga'gri* match while the *Mendel* skittered through unknown space? Possibly. A number of crewmembers—life sciences people, primarily—would have found themselves of little or no help. Why not seek out a distraction—find a way to pass the time, to stave off outright panic?

On the other hand, would someone have begun this game knowing that death was imminent? Not likely. Not unless that person had a remarkably overdeveloped sense of fatalism. So—whatever happened to the crew of the *Mendel,* it probably caught the players and everyone else by surprise.

Picard frowned, looked up at Worf. Their eyes met through their transparent faceplates. Apparently, the Klingon had come to much the same conclusion.

As the captain got to his feet, they were joined by Doctor Pulaski. She became solid with a look of extreme discomfort on her face, but it didn't last long. Not when she saw that she was being observed.

Pulaski's loathing for the teleportation process was common knowledge. Normally, Picard would have brought someone else along—but these circumstances were far from normal.

Instantly, the doctor took a tricorder reading. She peered at the results for a moment.

"Interesting," she announced. Her voice was something of a shock, a pebble dropped into the tomblike silence. "This air is eminently breathable. Gases all in the proper proportion, and none that shouldn't be here." A second reading. "Nothing significant in the way of radiation either."

Another figure reformatted itself on the other side of the cabin. The captain recognized Palazzo, one of Worf's security officers.

"Of course," Pulaski went on, "that's just in this part of

the ship. Conditions might be radically different elsewhere, so let's not get lax."

"I second that," said Picard, remembering his pledge to Riker. He could still feel the heat of his first officer's glare back there in the lounge.

They all watched as a fifth member of the party took on substance. Geordi's VISOR was unmistakable, even before the molecular stabilization process was complete.

The Klingon tapped the communicator beneath his containment suit. "Lieutenant Worf to transporter room. You may beam down the remainder of the team as a group."

The answer was somewhat garbled, thanks to the blanketing effect of the energy field. But a moment later, the transporter chief indicated his understanding another way: by depositing the last three members of the team in the space between Pulaski and Geordi.

"All right," said the captain, as each of them got his or her bearings. "Lieutenant La Forge, you and your people will inspect the engineering section. Start with the engines; after that, life-support and whatever else you have time for. Lieutenant Worf, take Mister Palazzo and search Deck Two—laboratories, cargo areas, sickbay. Doctor Pulaski and Mister Badnajian will investigate personal quarters."

Worf looked at him. "And you, sir?"

"The bridge," said Picard. "I'm going to see if I can wring anything out of ship's computer."

The Klingon scowled but didn't protest. No doubt, he knew it would do him no good.

"Questions?" asked the captain. There weren't any. "Then let's get cracking."

Riker was starting to get antsy. As much as he understood and sympathized with Picard's motives in this case, he couldn't help but feel that his place was with the away team.

Don't be a mother hen, he told himself. They're all big boys and girls. They can take care of themselves.

Then again, the crew of the *Mendel* had been a capable bunch as well. And look what had happened to *them*.

What was worse, he couldn't even keep tabs on the away team through the monitoring function of their communicators. Thanks to the energy field, the signals were weak and sometimes disappeared altogether.

"Mister Fong," said Riker. "Contact the captain for me."

"Aye, sir."

A moment later, Picard's distinctive voice broke like a wave over the calm of the bridge. The considerable static caused by the energy mantle rendered it necessary to turn up the volume—making the captain sound even more commanding than usual.

"Can you hear me?" asked the first officer.

"Barely, Number One. Is something wrong?"

"I just wanted to know how things were going." Even as he said it, Riker realized how foolish it sounded. "Anything I should know about?"

A pause. "Nothing yet. However, I'm on my way to the bridge now. Perhaps I'll find something there."

"You're alone, sir?"

Picard confirmed that he was, indeed, alone. "We've split up," he explained, "to go over the ship more quickly."

Of course. That's what Riker would have done in the captain's place. But the idea still made the hairs on the back of his neck prickle a bit.

"Objections, Number One?"

"No," said the first officer, feeling the heat climb into his face. "Carry on, sir."

He had barely uttered the last word when the connection died. Just like that—no sign-off on Picard's part, as custom and courtesy dictated.

Was it the captain's way of telling him he was getting in the way? Maybe—though Picard was usually the model of Starfleet etiquette.

More likely, the energy field had become particularly unruly at that moment. Yes, he decided. That had to be it.

In any case, he'd found out what he wanted to know. There was no point in reestablishing contact—and making himself an even bigger pain in the butt.

Since the moment she'd set foot in the transporter room, something had been gnawing at Pulaski. She'd done her best to concentrate on the task at hand, but she couldn't shake the feeling that she'd left some job undone. Forgotten something—something *important*.

The feeling plagued her as she inspected the first three cabins she came to—none of which yielded any answers. Or, for that matter, any evidence of tragedy. As in the common room, all was in perfect order, undisturbed. Life-support systems functioning, beds made, tapes neatly filed away.

Still, she thought, the bodies of the crew had to be *somewhere*. It was just a matter of time before one of the searchers found them.

And then, as she pored over the fourth cabin . . . it *came* to her. Descended on her, really, like a small avalanche.

Her thesis about Fredi's disease—it *hadn't* sprung from her fertile mind fully formed, as the goddess Athena was reputed to have sprung from that of Zeus. She had *heard* of such a disorder—a long time ago, when she was an intern back on Chaquafar.

Of course, the Chaquafar'ath version had never been officially recorded in Federation medical annals. Chaquafar was an advanced but iconoclastic world, one that was still spurning Federation membership to this day.

Some thirty years ago, Chaquafar's scientific community had been convinced to share its technologies with Pulaski and her colleagues—but the natives had played it rather close to the vest when it came to medical history. Apparently, it was inextricably entwined with cultural practices the Chaquafar'u would rather have forgotten.

Only Perrapataat—the elderly physician who'd taken a liking to a young and eager Katherine Pulaski—had been willing to speak of his people's ancient afflictions. Among them had been an illness—she remembered the name now—called *stirianaa*.

A disease that turned on an unusual translocation of certain genes—and therefore certain capabilities—from a foreign bacterium to a familiar one. A disease that . . .

Suddenly, Pulaski felt cold all over.

Oh my god.

The Chaquafar'ath disease had killed hundreds of thousands before it was stopped. And why? Because early on, about the time the medical community thought it might have discovered a cure . . . the hybrid bacterium had mutated.

Of course, mutation was something any doctor had to expect—on Chaquafar or anywhere else. It could have been triggered by almost anything at all that was hostile to the hybrid bug—a drug, a change in diet, a rise in temperature. Even natural selection, over time.

But this mutation had transformed the disease from something non-communicable to something contagious— *highly* contagious. And naturally, because of the change, the antibiotic devised by the Chaquafar'u was no longer effective. The organism had become much hardier, much tougher to kill.

By the time they came up with a second cure, the disease had ravaged two continents. *All those lives* . . .

Pulaski's heart was hammering against her ribs. With an effort, she calmed herself—enough to think clearly, anyway.

"The captain," she murmured. "I've got to tell the captain."

Pressing the communicator beneath her containment suit, she said: "Pulaski to Captain Picard."

There was no answer.

She tried it again.

Still nothing.

"Damn it," she whispered. For some reason, the communicators weren't working. Did it have something to do with the energy mantle?

Then she definitely wouldn't be able to get word back to the ship. Nonetheless, she made an attempt to contact the bridge.

"Riker here," came the somewhat mangled reply.

Pulaski breathed a deep sigh of relief. For the moment, she put aside the fact that she'd been unable to raise the captain. The vagaries of communicator technology weren't exactly her field of expertise.

"Commander, something serious has come up. I need to get back to the ship immediately."

She could hear the tension in the first officer's response, though his words tried to rise above it. "Has something happened over there? Someone hurt?"

"No," she said. "Nothing like that. It's the—"

"Doctor?"

She turned at the sound of the voice just behind her—in time to see Badnajian's bulk fill the open doorway.

"Not now," she told him. "I'm—"

"There's something wrong," he interrupted a second time. "No one's answering my security checks."

"I know," she told him. "I had some trouble, too. But I've managed to contact the ship. Now . . ."

She was completely unprepared for what happened next. First, a web of slender green filaments came out of nowhere. Then it closed down around Badnajian. Finally, man and web just vanished.

All in the space of a heartbeat, maybe less.

Pulaski felt light-headed. She clutched at a bulkhead for support.

"Doctor Pulaski?" It was Riker's voice again, strident with alarm now. "Doctor, what's going on there?"

"Badnajian just disappeared." She swallowed, understanding for the first time what might have happened to the crew of the *Mendel*. "And he may not be alone in that regard."

"I'm beaming you back," said Riker. "All of you. Stand by."

"No," she told him, recalling the reason she'd contacted him in the first place. "Listen. There may not be time. You've got to get word to Doctor Burtin. Tell him that . . ."

But she never finished her sentence.

"Transporter room—report!"

The hesitation in Chief O'Brien's voice told Riker all he needed to know. His teeth grated together as he tried to control the anger building up inside him.

And it was only himself he had to be angry with. For letting the captain go in the first place. For not following up when Picard signed off so abruptly. Most of all, for not seeing what was coming . . . until now, when it was obviously too late.

"I . . . I don't know what happened," said O'Brien finally. "First, I could only record two of our people within the parameters of the *Mendel*. And then, just as I tried to bring those two back . . . they vanished, sir. They're gone—and I don't know where."

The first officer cursed beneath his breath.

"Sir?" asked the transporter chief.

He took a deep breath, let it out slowly. "If you had to guess," asked Riker, "what would you say happened to them?"

A pause. "It almost seemed as if someone else just got to them first, sir. Teleported them, I mean, just as we were about to."

"Thank you," said Riker.

He tried to think. To ignore the challenge he couldn't help but see in the midst of the viewscreen's golden chaos.

"The Klah'kimmbri," said Troi, at his side. "The captain was right, wasn't he?"

She was still a little shaky, barely recovered from the turbulent, desperate emotions she'd experienced as she probed the away team before its sudden disappearance.

However, she was a lot more composed than she had been even moments ago.

Riker nodded in answer to her question. "But it's not just a matter of polarization, apparently. They seem to be able to penetrate the mantle in either direction—send as well as receive. That's the only way they could have established the coordinates they needed to beam down our away team. Or, for that matter, the crew of the *Mendel.*"

"It was the one possibility we didn't consider," said the empath. "That the research people could have been *teleported* off their ship."

"And for good reason," said Riker. "It just didn't make any sense. Still doesn't. Why would the Klah'kimmbri develop a special transporter beam—one which can ignore the mantle—when it would be useless against any real aggressor? Obviously, it can't penetrate a high-energy shield, or we'd have seen some disappearances on the *Enterprise* as well. The only crews vulnerable to forced teleportation would be those on primitive vessels without sophisticated shield technology—or crippled ships like the *Mendel,* where . . ."

He stopped himself.

Troi regarded him. "What's the matter?"

Riker glanced at the screen again. "I wonder," he said. "Could they have been *waiting* for a ship like the *Mendel* to come along? A crippled vessel, without any shields to protect it?" He licked his lips. "Maybe we've been looking at this the wrong way. What if the Klah'kimmbri aren't on the defensive after all? What if their real objective is to, say, *kidnap* the crews of unprotected vessels?"

Troi's delicate, dark brows came together. "But . . . ?" Her unspoken question seemed to hang in the air.

The first officer finished it for her. *"Why* would the Klah'kimmbri want to do such a thing?" He shook his head. "I don't know, Deanna." Resolve stiffened in him. "But I'm damned well going to find out."

Chapter Six

STARFLEET OFFICERS weren't supposed to take things personally. Will Riker *did*. It was evident in the way he leaned forward out of his seat, elbows dug into his knees, hands locked together like primordial creatures engaged in a death struggle. It could be seen in the way his eyes narrowed as he considered the splendid turmoil on the main viewer—the nearest thing he had to a real antagonist.

Deanna Troi didn't have to open her mind to read the combative emotions seething in the first officer. As a trained psychologist, she could glean all she had to through visual observation alone.

Amazing, she mused briefly, how the primitive hunter-defender still survives in the human psyche—even after all those centuries of so-called civilization. *Sometimes I think humans and Klingons have more in common than either race would like to admit.*

On the other hand, as involved as Riker got, he didn't let it affect his decisions. That's one reason it was taking him so long to make this one—knowing how confrontational he could be when the ship or its crew was threatened, he wanted to be absolutely sure he had distanced himself from his feelings.

Finally, he decided that he'd weighed the options long enough. Leaning back in his seat, he noticed her scrutiny.

"Taking the measure of my emotional stability?" he asked, keeping his voice down.

"It's my job," she reminded him in the same tone.

"And?" he asked. "Do I seem confident?"

She thought about it for a second or so. "Yes," she decided. "You do."

His chuckle was a little drier than usual. "Shows what *you* know."

She smiled. "But you *have* come to a decision."

Riker nodded. "Have you ever heard that expression the captain uses? 'If the mountain won't come to Mohammed . . .'"

She *had* heard it. "'Then Mohammed must go to the mountain.'"

"Exactly," he said. "And that's what we're going to do." He raised his voice to the necessary level: "Mister Data, I want you to drop us down into the closest orbit possible. How far can the ship descend before we get into trouble?"

The android turned away from his console and shot him a querulous look.

The first officer amended his question. "Before either gravity or atmospheric friction starts to present a danger to us?"

Data gave a quick little nod to show he understood. "It is difficult to say, Commander. The energy mantle makes my readings somewhat unreliable. But at sixty kilometers of altitude, we should still have sufficient margin for error."

"All right," said Riker. "Then take us down that far—at half impulse. Mister Fong, let me know how the shields hold up."

"Aye, sir," said Fong, busy at the tactical board.

"Engineering," called the first officer.

Modiano, Geordi's second-in-command, responded after a moment or two.

"We're taking the ship down into the planet's upper atmosphere," advised Riker. "Be prepared for some stress on the engines."

"Aye, sir," said Modiano. "We'll be ready."

Under Data's expert touch, the feeling of descent was imperceptible. But Troi felt it nonetheless, the way one feels a wall when approaching it in the dark. After all, in a very real sense, the energy mantle had made blind men out of all of them.

"Well," she said, *"this* ought to get their attention."

"That's the idea," said Riker. "Of course, it's possible that the mantle will dissipate at a certain depth, and we'll be able to finally see what we're up against. But I'm not counting on that. All I really want to do is give them the idea that we're going to land in their backyard. Then—maybe—they'll be moved to open communications."

She nodded. "I see. And if it comes to a battle first?"

The first officer frowned. "That's something else again. I can't fight a whole planet—not this one, anyway. But with any luck, it won't come to that."

"One hundred kilometers," announced Data. "And closing."

"Some strain on the deflector shields," said Fong. "But hull temperatures well within normal limits."

"Thank you," said the first officer. "Steady as she goes."

Troi recalled what Worf had said about bringing the *Enterprise* into the energy field: *What if the energy level is raised suddenly? We could find ourselves trapped. Or worse.*

It wasn't a reassuring thought. The idea of the ship being caught like an insect in a spider's web . . .

No doubt, Riker had considered that possibility—and decided it was a risk worth taking. So far, circumstances had yet to prove him wrong.

"Eighty kilometers," called Data.

"The burden on the shields is increasing," Fong reported.

"At this point, it's a geometric progression. But we've still got everything under control."

"Good," said Riker. "Let's keep it that way."

Where was the Klah'kimmbri response? Surely, by now, they would have noted the ship's approach.

Or had they recognized the move for the bluff that it was? And decided to maintain communications silence?

From where Troi sat, she could see the muscles in Riker's jaw rippling now beneath his beard. *Was that what he was thinking too?*

"Sixty kilometers," said Data. "We have reached the safety threshold."

"Shields are buckling," warned Fong. "The friction is too much." And then, almost in the same breath, "Shield Number One is gone, sir."

Riker's eyes took on a noticeably harder cast. He shifted in his seat. "Continue to descend," he ordered. "Maintain speed."

Not one of them balked. They continued to do their jobs as if nothing unusual were going on. As if there were no danger at all.

Troi herself resisted glancing at the first officer. She looked straight ahead, her hands composed in her lap—the picture of confidence, even if her feelings were in direct contrast.

"Come on," said Riker. "Come out from under your rock, you slimy—"

"Shield Number Two is gone," said Fong. "The hull is beginning to heat up, sir."

"Fifty kilometers," noted Data. "Still no break in the energy field."

Was it Troi's imagination, or was the bridge starting to feel warm? She could feel the perspiration beading up on her brow.

"Forty-five kilometers," marked the android. "And—"

"All right," Riker cut in. "That's enough. Arrest descent, Data. Take her back up."

It wasn't an order that had come easy to him, Troi knew. But what choice did he have?

"Descent arrested, sir. Preparing to—"

"Commander!" cried Fong. "I'm receiving a hailing signal—from the planet's surface."

Riker pounded his fist on his armrest. *Triumph,* the empath told herself. Standing, the first officer turned to address Fong.

"Can we maintain this position?" he asked the security officer.

Fong frowned. "For a little while—but not long. We're down to our last shield. And if the Klah'kimmbri should decide to fire on us—"

He was interrupted by a disembodied intercom voice. After a moment, Troi recognized it as Modiano's.

"The engines are laboring pretty badly, sir. If we don't get out of here soon, we may not get out of here at all."

"Noted," said Riker. "Nurse them just a little longer, Mister Modiano." Then, to Fong: "Answer their hail. Let's see what these Klah'kimmbri have to say for themselves."

"This is the High Council of A'klah," said one of the seven enthroned figures. "Who dares disturb our perfect peace?"

Riker, standing before the viewscreen, was prepared with a response. But before he could bring himself to say the words, he was struck by the Council's appearance. With those narrow faces, that pale skin and those golden eyes, they were dead ringers for . . .

He shook off his surprise. "I am William Riker, first officer in command of the Federation starship *Enterprise.* It is not our intention to disturb your peace, but to obtain information—concerning the smaller vessel in orbit around your world."

"We have been aware of it," said the same figure who spoke earlier. "But we have no information concerning it."

Riker darted a glance at Troi, standing over by a bulkhead

—where she was not likely to be noticed. She shook her head subtly from side to side: *they are lying.*

Well, at least they'd established *that.*

But he couldn't confront this Council with it. It would gain him nothing—and it might cost him the chance to learn something about Picard and the others.

Fine. The indirect approach, then . . .

"We sent an away team to the ship just a little while ago," Riker went on. "Shortly thereafter, it disappeared. We thought you might be able to shed some light on the disappearance."

"I told you," said the councillor, "we have no information concerning that vessel. Nor do we have information regarding what you call your *away team.* Finally, we wonder if this professed need for information is your real reason for disturbing us. In any case, you are not welcome here."

"Am I to understand," asked Riker, "that you will not help us in our investigation? Even though our comrades' lives may be at stake?"

"This is correct."

"Perhaps, then, you can drop your energy field— temporarily. So that we may conduct our own investigation."

"That is impossible—for security reasons. What's more, if you do not depart immediately, we will be forced to defend ourselves against your presence. This is the end of our communication."

A moment later, the image on the viewscreen blinked out, to be replaced by the mantle's now familiar interference field.

"They've terminated their signal," reported Fong, underlining the obvious.

Riker bit his lip. The Klah'kimmbri were playing their role to the hilt.

But he'd be jeopardizing the ship and its crew if he stayed here. The engines were already being pushed to their limits. It was the wrong time to get involved in an exchange of fire.

"Mister Data, take us back to our former position."

"Aye, Commander."

Riker was halfway back to the command center when he had a brainstorm.

"No—check that, Data. Heading—let's see . . . seven four four mark nine one. Half-impulse until we break free of A'klah's atmosphere."

"Acknowledged," said the android.

With only the slightest of tremors, the ship started to ascend. The golden light of the mantle continued to whip from one end of the viewscreen to the other. But soon it would begin to thin out.

Riker took the captain's seat. "Mister Fong," he said, "given the conditions in this system, what do you estimate our maximum scanning range to be?"

Fong gave him a figure. It was actually a little greater than he had expected, considering the amount of debris in the vicinity.

"When we reach that distance from A'klah," he told Data, "I want you to stop and hold us steady."

"Will do, sir," said the android.

Riker felt Troi's gaze on him. He returned it.

The empath was looking at him with a little half smile, tempered only by her concern for the away team. Obviously, she'd figured out what he was up to.

He acknowledged her with a curt nod.

Sometimes, he told himself, Mohammed must withdraw to another mountain.

The post of Preparation Overseer seldom involved any serious decisions. That was fine with Lean'druc—he hated making them.

However, this time he could not avoid it.

"You see the problem?" said his undertechnician—one named Cafar'ris. "It is some sort of prosthetic device. Without it, he is blind."

Lean'druc considered the prone form of the one who wore

the prosthesis. Unconscious, he had no idea what had happened to him—nor, for that matter, that he was the subject of this discussion.

Of course, the conscripts were supposed to be stripped of *everything*—all garb, all forms of equipment. But this case was a little different, wasn't it? Without the device, the alien could not see. And if he could not see, how could he truly participate?

"What was his aptitude level?"

"Quite high," said Cafar'ris. "And he is otherwise in perfect health." The undertechnician glanced at Lean'druc. "If I may say so, Overseer, it would be a shame to release him without the device. He would not survive for very long—nor would his death be—"

Lean'druc held up his hand for silence. It was hardly an undertechnician's place to give *him* advice.

Nonetheless, Cafar'ris had a point. Able-bodied participants were increasingly few and far between, it seemed. Why waste one for the sake of a rather arbitrary regulation?

"All right," he said. "Let him keep the device."

Cafar'ris seemed pleased with the decision. "As you wish, Overseer."

Lean'druc scanned the other aliens—all prone like this one, all oblivious to the fate that awaited them.

There was still much to do before their preparation was complete, and the Fulfillment Facilitator did not like to hear of tardiness.

"Now, get to work," snapped Lean'druc. "I want them ready for teleport by day's end—*all* of them."

The undertechnician moved crisply to comply.

Chapter Seven

FOR A TIME, he struggled as if submerged in a nightmare—plagued by a wild dance of indistinct and vaguely disturbing images, circling him, whirling about his head and hands like a school of tiny predators. Shadowy things, real and yet unreal.

He tried to claw his way to the surface, but the things confused him—disoriented him. His chest began to hurt with the effort of holding his breath. His arms and legs lost their strength; they felt leaden, useless, like parts of someone else's body.

Finally, lungs near to bursting, muscles shrieking with effort, he broke through.

And came up gasping for air, staring into an expanse of pale violet sky. All about him was a landscape of pits and crags and impossible-looking upthrusts of rock—peopled by a scurrying assortment of humanoid and near-humanoid forms. Each of them seemed to have a purpose, a sense of urgency.

He tried to catch his breath, to calm himself, and finally succeeded. But he had a more difficult time getting his bearings. He seemed unable to put everything in the right order somehow. His head felt as if it had been packed with mud.

The wind rose, bringing with it a slight chill. Instinctively, he hunkered down lower into the shelter of his rough-spun cloak. Underneath, he noticed, he wore a tunic of the same material, belted at the waist. There were boots on his feet constructed of something sturdier—animal skin, he decided, and not without a slight feeling of revulsion.

Someone bent down over him—someone big and dark and oily looking, with a knobby head and a wide, mobile mouth. The being's lidless eyes gave it a queer, startled expression.

"Come," it said, extending a thick articulated limb with three stubby fingers on the end of it. "It's time." There was an edge of anxiety in its voice. "Here—I will help you."

He moved to accept the help, then stopped himself. "Time for what?" he asked.

"Hurry now," said the being. It gestured—a sweep of its limb—to indicate a stretch of terrain that ended abruptly in a jagged cliff. On the other side of what appeared to be a ravine there was a similar cliff. "There is work to be done."

This time, he accepted the proferred help. Felt the strange, wormlike fingers wrap themselves around his hand and pull him up. But he needed more of an answer. As the being released him and started to move away, he called out after it. "What kind of work?" he asked.

It turned back, regarded him. "We are building a bridge." It seemed to think that this was explanation enough

He was about to tell it that bridge-building was not his function. That he did not belong here—in fact, had never seen this place before now.

And then a pit seemed to open up in his stomach. A great, yawning hole into which he could feel himself falling end over end.

For if he didn't belong *here* . . . then where *did* he belong? And if he was not a bridge-builder . . . then what *was* he? Blazes . . .

Who was he? A name emerged echoing from the depths of the pit. *Geordi.* Yes—that was his name. But *who was Geordi?*

He didn't know.

Surely, he had known that *once*. Before . . . before he came here. When he was . . . *where?* Damn! Why couldn't he remember anything?

The knobby-headed one was still looking at him. But it didn't appear that he would remain that way for long. The being seemed to be straining at an invisible leash—eager to get about its business, yet reluctant to leave him where he was.

"Something is wrong," he told it. "Something is *very* wrong. I . . . I can't remember who I am, or how I got here, or . . ."

"Don't try," it said. "You are not supposed to remember any of those things." It regarded him with a bizarre rippling of the skin under its eyes. "It is part of your punishment. Accept it, and it will become more tolerable."

"Punishment?" he repeated dumbly. "For what?"

The being's voice changed suddenly. It became more of a bark.

But the answer was still clear enough. "For your crimes."

And then, as if it could not wait another fraction of a second, the being lumbered away with all the haste its awkward body allowed it.

Geordi felt a wind on his bare skin as he shivered. Wrapping his cloak more tightly about himself, he hurried after his benefactor.

"Wait," he said. "You've got to tell me more than that." If he had committed crimes, what had they been? Like so much else, they'd been stripped from him.

The being glanced over its shoulder as before, but this time it kept on moving. Climbing over a rise, it disappeared.

Geordi, however, was right behind it. And as he negotiated the rise himself, he got a better view of what was going on here—literally.

From his vantage point, he could see how the ravine he'd noticed earlier actually curled around the jut of land that he and the others occupied—served to define it, to separate it from the rolling, gentler terrain on the other side.

At the ravine's narrowest point, there was a ruined thing hanging from the opposite cliff—a thing of wood and some sort of thick, vegetable fiber, twisting against the bare rock in the drafts that came up from below. It seemed to Geordi that it might once have been a rudimentary bridge.

Was this the task his benefactor had been talking about? Were they building a new bridge to replace the old one?

Then he noticed something else—something dark, hovering in midair over the far side of the ravine. It was small—maybe a meter in height, though it was hard to judge at this distance—and it had a disc near the top of it that reflected the light when it turned just so.

He had the feeling, somehow, that the thing was watching them. Was it the eyelike appearance of the disc? Or something about its attitude as it hung there?

Just beneath him, not far from the brink, there were streams and eddies of activity. Huge coils of the vegetable fiber and long, scaly logs were being dragged down from higher ground off to the right.

Geordi picked out the figure of the knobby-headed one as it bent to help with the log hauling. Careful not to lose his footing on the pebble-strewn incline, he came down alongside it.

His benefactor tried to ignore his presence, but Geordi saw through the deception. He laid a hand on the being's shoulder, covered with rough-spun like his own.

"Please," he said. "Tell me what's happening here. Why are we building this bridge? Who is it for?"

The being looked at him, though it dared not pause in its efforts. For a moment, it looked as if it would say something. Then it looked away again.

Geordi watched it labor at a job it was obviously not well equipped for. Despite all its bulk, despite the thickness of its limbs, it didn't appear to be very strong. As it toiled, it made huffing sounds.

There were others here, too, who were bending under the strain. Fragile-looking beings, some of them without the proper appendages for this sort of work.

As they struggled past him, they regarded Geordi with expressions he could only guess at. Alien expressions, fashioned out of loose, sickly white flesh and jewellike orbs and mouths that seemed to harbor swarms of tiny tentacles. But he knew what *he* would think of someone who just stood by while he broke his back trying to get something done.

He was still confused. Confused and scared and sorely in need of answers.

But these beings needed help, and it was in his power to give it to them. Besides—they were building a bridge, and bridges were useful things. Helpful things. Could it hurt to pitch in? He could still use the time to observe. To think.

Slipping into the line of laborers, he took hold of the log in both hands and added his efforts to those of the others.

As he approached the inner doors of the Council Chamber and the guards that stood to either side of them, Dan'nor ordered the features of his too-broad face. He would not let on how desperately his heart was pounding against his rib cage. He would *not*.

It was bad enough that he had allowed the error to occur in the first place. It would only compound his difficulties if he were to *look* guilty as well.

Appearance was everything. Every First Caster knew that. And if Dan'nor was not exactly pure First Caste, he had trained himself to act like one.

So he kept his composure. Even when one of the ceremonial guards—his peer by rank—gave him that pitying look. As if Dan'nor had damaged himself and his career worse than he'd originally imagined.

He stopped as the guards pulled the doors open, exposing the elaborately military design of the Council Chamber within. Monstrous, stylized birds of prey seemed to hover within the shadows of the high, vaulted ceiling. Earthbound hunting animals appeared to slink behind the Seven Thrones, their jeweled eyes glinting in the light of a hundred smoking torches.

Dan'nor had seen this place only once before—at a reception for the new Conflict Commander. But then, the thrones had been empty.

This time, the thrones were occupied; the Council awaited in their military finery, no less elaborate and awe-inspiring than the chamber itself. Dan'nor swallowed once and walked inside.

He stopped at an appropriate distance, dropped to one knee and averted his eyes. For a time, no one spoke. There were only small sounds—a clearing of someone's throat, a scrape of boot on the polished floor—but in the vast, echoing space, even such small items sounded great and portentous.

"Rise, Dan'nor Tir'dainia."

He got up, regarded the one who had finally spoken. It was Councillor Eliek'tos—a good sign. Of all of them, Eliek'tos was reputed to be the most lenient, and it was he who seemed to have taken the lead in this matter.

"Most honored Councillor," responded Dan'nor. "I came as soon as you sent for me."

"Of course," said Eliek'tos. "But let us get to the point now. I have heard reports; I wish to hear *yours.*"

Eliek'tos was the epitome of First Caste dispassion—as befit one who served on the Council. His golden eyes betrayed nothing; likewise, his voice. Dan'nor envied him his pale, perfect skin, his mane of red hair drawn back into a warrior's knot.

If his nose had been as straight as Eliek'tos's, if his lips had been as thin and his face as narrow—he would never have been given the lowly post of Fulfillment Facilitator. He would never have had the opportunity to make the mistake he had made.

If.

It was a bitter fruit of a word. If his father, a pureblood, had mated with one of his own kind instead of a mixed-blood woman, many things might have been different—for his father even more than for himself. After all, mating downcaste was an unofficial crime, punishable by ouster. His military career destroyed, Trien'nor Tir'dainia had had to accept menial labor in one of the factories.

All for love. To Dan'nor, it was inconceivable.

Considering his family history, he had done well to rise even as far as he had. To gain a place in the military. To have a function, no matter how simple, and a command, no matter how small.

Once, he had aspired to more. He had hoped to garner respect for the efficient performance of his duties—to earn himself a promotion to field service, where he would participate directly in the Conflicts.

Now, however, that dream was in jeopardy—and perhaps much more than the dream. Dan'nor recalled the guardsman's look of pity, blinked it away.

"Did you hear me, Tir'dainia?"

Dan'nor inclined his head before speaking. "My apologies, revered Councillor. I was gathering my thoughts, so as to present them in the most concise way possible."

One of the other councillors snorted in derision. Dan'nor didn't look to see which one—it would have been an act of discourtesy to Eliek'tos, and he could ill afford *that*.

"Are your thoughts ordered now?" asked Eliek'tos.

"They are," said Dan'nor.

"Then proceed," said the councillor.

Dan'nor was tempted to blame it all on those who reported to him. Nor would it be far from the truth. It was they who had failed to maintain the computer; ultimately, the fault was theirs.

But he did not think the Council would take kindly to such a tactic. An officer was *always* responsible for whatever his underlings did—or failed to do.

So, with no better option available, he told the truth.

"When I came on duty," he said, "I did as I always do—I checked the log of the previous shift. Naturally, I was eager to see how the conscription procedure had been carried out by my predecessor."

"Your predecessor was not available to tell you himself?"

Dan'nor turned to the councillor who had asked. Since he had been addressed by another, it could no longer have been construed as an affront to Eliek'tos.

"No, Councillor. He had already left the station." He recognized the man as Fidel'lic, the youngest one on the Council. And the cruelest, if there was any truth to the rumors.

"But if both of you were on schedule, that would not have happened. Correct?"

"Correct, Councillor."

"Then which of you was taking liberties—you or he?"

Dan'nor didn't hesitate. "*He* was, Councillor. He left before he was scheduled to."

Fidel'lic turned to Eliek'tos. "Is this true?"

Eliek'tos nodded.

"And what about his crew?" asked Fidel'lic, still addressing his fellow councillor. "They left early as well?"

Eliek'tos nodded again.

"It was not unusual," offered Dan'nor, recognizing the other facilitator's laxity as a way out. Of course, he could never have raised the issue himself—for the same reason he couldn't have blamed his own crew. But since the Council had brought it up, it was a different matter entirely. "They often take it upon themselves to . . ."

Fidel'lic turned his gaze in Dan'nor's direction. He stopped in mid-sentence.

"You will speak," said the councillor, "when you are given leave to do so."

The Fulfillment Facilitator felt himself flush with the rebuke.

"Once again," said Eliek'tos, as if the interruption had

never occurred, "the record bears this out. Despite the fact that a conscription had been completed in the course of their shift, the day crew left before the proper time."

Fidel'lic sat back in his seat. "Amazing." He turned to Dan'nor again. "And you have never reported this before now?"

"But I have," protested Dan'nor.

"Once again," said Eliek'tos, "true." He waited a moment, in case Fidel'lic had any more questions. When it was plain he did not, he gestured for Dan'nor to resume his account.

Despite his indiscretion, he went on with a little more confidence. After all, he had survived the first volley.

"The log told me that the conscripted vessel had been emptied of all useful occupants. But when I consulted with the computer, it showed that the vessel was still intact. Moreover, I had life-sign readings. Eight individuals still aboard."

"And what did you make of this?" asked Eliek'tos.

"My best guess," said Dan'nor, "was that these eight had gone undetected in our initial scan—something that has happened before, when one of the alien alloys used in a ship's construction serves to shield occupants from our sensors. Instances of this should also be in your records."

"Go on," said Eliek'tos—with perhaps a touch of impatience.

"That seemed to explain why the ship had not yet been disposed of. The computer had detected additional conscriptable life-forms after the initial transport procedure was complete. This triggered the contingency protocol, which in turn prevented the vessel's destruction."

"And believing this," said Eliek'tos, "you beamed down the eight occupants."

"That is correct, Councillor." Dan'nor's mouth felt dry, as dry as dust—but he resisted the impulse to lick his lips.

Again, that derisive snort. "Then you were never aware of

the larger ship? The one those eight *occupants* apparently came from?"

The question had come from Orian'tuc. He was easily the eldest of the councillors, and the only one whose pale, narrow countenance showed any signs of aging.

It was a crucial question. If Dan'nor had been derelict in anything, it was in this: that he had never thought to check for other vessels. It would have been so simple to widen the preset scan parameters—and yet it never occurred to him. He had been too preoccupied with the existence of these seemingly undetected occupants.

Nor, to be fair, had anyone from Central Defense thought to inform him that there was an armed and capable ship in his sector. With its appearance so close on the heels of the recent conscription, one might have expected that Fulfillment would be notified.

"Councillor, I was not apprised of the larger ship's existence—not until well after the damage had been done."

Orian'tuc's eyes narrowed the slightest bit. "Surely, however, your superior knew of it. Didn't you think to contact him—before you did anything?"

"No, Councillor. It is my duty to make speedy work of conscription. Recruits must not be lost to either the failure of their life-support systems or external threats to the ships themselves. Those are my orders."

Orian'tuc glanced at Fidel'lic, who was seated beside him. But he said nothing more.

"When did you realize your error?" asked Eliek'tos.

Your error. Inwardly, Dan'nor cringed at the phrasing.

"I thought that there might be a problem, Councillor, when the computer remained incapable of destroying the ship. A second scan revealed no newly detected life-forms. So I ordered a check of the computer."

"And it revealed," said Eliek'tos, "a malfunction, which was responsible for the ship's never having been eliminated."

"As you say, Councillor." Dan'nor heard the slight tremor in his voice and hoped it had escaped the notice of the Council. He sensed that this hearing was coming to a close, and he still had no sense of where he stood.

"Are you saying, then," asked a fourth councillor, "that we have a computer to blame for all of this? A simple malfunction has brought down this plague of a . . . what is it called? *Enterprise?*"

A trick question. Blaming the incident on the computer would have been the worst strategy of all. After all, a machine was only as good as the people in charge of it.

"No, Councillor. With all respect, I am not saying that."

Orian'tuc looked at him. "No? Then where would *you* say the blame lies?"

He had no choice. There was only one avenue open to him.

"It lies with *me,* Councillor. I was in command when the error was made. I gave the order to conscript the eight occupants. Nor did I check for a malfunction until it was too late."

There. He had said it. But with any luck, they would give more weight to other things he had said. For instance, his information about the other facilitator, which Eliek'tos had confirmed. And they would direct their anger at him instead of Dan'nor.

He didn't dare look for his fate in their faces because Orian'tuc was still in eye contact with him. And even if he could have glanced around, he would probably have learned nothing. Councillors were not likely to give their conclusions away so easily.

"Are there any more questions?" asked Eliek'tos.

No one spoke.

"Then you are free to go, Dan'nor Tir'dainia."

The Fulfillment Facilitator bent his neck again. "Thank you, Councillor." He took two steps back, out of respect. Then, as crisply as he could, he turned and left the chamber.

Dan'nor didn't bother to sneak a look at the guardsman

again—to see if his expression had changed any. He just kept walking, listening to the sharp *click* of his heels against the intricately patterned paving stones of the corridor . . . to the *clang* of the doors as they closed in his wake.

He walked through shafts of sunlight projected by the windows set high in the southern wall. On his other flank, ancient tapestries depicting great and bloody battles found new glory in the red gold light.

He might have done better, he decided. He might have been a little less nervous. A little quicker with his answers, a little more to the point . . .

Gradually, the sound of another set of footfalls invaded his reverie. He looked up.

And saw his superior, Conscription Master Boron'bak, approaching from the opposite end of the corridor.

As they drew closer to one another, their eyes met. And locked.

Each knew that the other was a potential source of danger. An enemy, in fact, for as long as the investigation went on. Each knew that the other would gladly sacrifice him if it meant saving his own skin.

Dan'nor had already made trouble for Boron'bak—if indirectly. The other facilitator's schedule violations would not reflect favorably on the superior who had allowed them to continue. Nor would his own oversights and miscalculations. Just as he had had to assume responsibility for his crew, Boron'bak would have to take responsibility for him.

A couple of seconds before they passed each other, the Conscription Master's mouth pulled up at the corners. As if to say, "Nothing personal."

Then he was gone, and Dan'nor tried not to think of what he might tell the Council.

How much time had passed since her awakening? Since her emergence into this . . . she had no words for this place, no way of truly knowing how long she had been here. It had been a while since she'd had a chance to think about her own problems. Lately, she'd been occupied with a more urgent matter—namely, the flood of damaged beings that had suddenly poured into the med enclosure, carried by other beings only slightly less damaged. In the light of the overhead cylinders, they all looked a pale and ghastly shade of blue.

As hideous as their wounds were, most of the victims might have been saved—*if* there had been enough meds to go around. Unfortunately, there weren't. For every two victims they got to, a third lay dying in agony.

It was hard work. Heartbreaking work. There were the faces that went slack even as she shouted encouragements at them. The circulatory organs that refused to respond to the desperate pummeling of her fists.

But Pulaski couldn't cry over them. There was no time. Because after the first deluge, there were others. Before long, her arms were bathed to the elbows in three different colors of blood.

Where were they all coming from? she asked herself again. Obviously, there was an armed conflict somewhere nearby —she deduced as much from the armor and the nature of the wounds. But a conflict with whom? And over what?

Somewhere between the second wave and the third, the flying machine entered the enclosure. It was about a meter tall, with a distinctly insectlike body made of a dark, non-reflective material. About two-thirds of the way up, a round and slightly convex glass surface protruded like the eye of a living creature.

The machine flitted throughout the enclosure, occasionally coming to hover over one patient or another. Always, it seemed to pick out the most severe cases—but only as long as the screaming went on. As soon as the patient succumbed to death, unconsciousness or an anesthetic, the thing appeared to lose interest.

Pulaski tried to ignore the flying device, but she found she couldn't. It was like some sort of scavenger, feeding on the miseries of others. Of course, it was only a machine—it could have no such hungers. More likely, she decided, it was recording the suffering on behalf of some living intelligence. But that conclusion only made the thing seem more ghastly than before.

It annoyed her for another reason as well: the level of technology it represented. A certain sophistication was required to build something that could fly at all—much less with the grace and stability that *this* machine exhibited.

That same sophistication could have been applied to their med facilities. It could have gone toward saving more of these lives. Perhaps she couldn't remember how she'd wound up here or where she'd come from, but she knew *one* thing: she had been trained to work with equipment a whole lot more advanced than what was available here in the enclosure.

On the other hand, no one else seemed to be bothered by the flying device. Was it just that they'd gotten used to it? Or was she unique in her resentment of it?

The last straw fell as she was struggling to close a vicious gash in a patient's gut—*before* the poor bastard bled to death. It was a race, and a close one. The victim, a large and scaly specimen, was too weak to cry out—but even so, it took three other meds to keep his powerful arms and legs from jerking while Pulaski, only guessing at the locations of his internal organs, tried to stitch the wound without doing any additional damage.

And then, just as she was about to finish up, the flying machine homed in on the scaly one—an attempt to obtain a closer appreciation of his agony. In the process, it brushed against her shoulder. There was something about its ghoulish eagerness, its cold, metallic touch . . .

Seized by revulsion, she couldn't help herself. She lashed out, battering the thing aside with her clenched fist. It was lighter than it looked—her swipe sent it bobbling halfway across the enclosure, glancing off a metal support before it could stabilize itself. A little puff of white smoke rose from its casing, and it seemed to drop a couple of inches toward the floor. Then, like a whipped house pet, it wove its way out of the enclosure.

Pulaski felt a rush of satisfaction.

But it was short-lived. She had a patient to attend to—one who actually had a decent chance at survival.

Willing her tired fingers to perform the necessary maneuvers, she tied off another stitch.

Chapter Eight

IT HAD WORKED.

Not at first, of course. Riker had had to wait two ship's days and more before there was any sign that he had guessed right.

And then, just like that, the mantle disappeared—revealing your average Class M planet in all its cloud-swaddled glory.

A cheer went up on the bridge. The first officer felt a tension go out of him that he hadn't realized was there in the first place. *Was I really screwed up that tight?* he asked himself.

"Congratulations," said Troi, meaning every syllable of it. Her smile was inexpressibly lovely.

Nor could he suppress a grin himself. But that was quite all right. Hell, he'd earned it, hadn't he?

Of course, in retrospect, it only made sense that the energy field couldn't have been maintained indefinitely. It had to take enormous amounts of power to keep something that vast in operation.

But when he had first decided to try his little ploy—to make it look as though they'd turned tail, abandoning their comrades in the face of the Council's threat . . . at that point, it had still seemed like an iffy proposition.

For one thing, the Klah'kimmbri's methods of energy generation might have been a good deal more efficient than he'd anticipated. Or, as unlikely as it appeared, the mantle might have been a natural phenomenon after all.

Finally—and this had been his main cause for concern—the Klah'kimmbri might not have fallen for his act. They might instead have opted for a sophisticated game of chicken, waiting to see which gave out first—their energy-production or Riker's patience.

Without any encouragement that the mantle would eventually lapse, he would have had to try something else. But in two-plus days of racking his brain, he hadn't come up with an alternative plan that he could live with.

Now, he realized gratefully, he would no longer have to.

"Mister Crusher," he said, "initiate long-range sensor scan. The first order of business is a population distribution profile. Then we can make some educated guesses as to where our people are being held."

"Aye, sir," came the eager response. Wesley was as excited as anyone that the waiting game was behind them.

"Mister Fong," said the first officer. "See what you can find in the way of surface communications."

"Will do," said Fong. "Initiating monitor sequences now."

"Thank you. Mister Data?"

The android peered at Riker over his shoulder. "Sir?"

"I want you to take charge of correlating and interpreting whatever information we dig up. We need a point man, and it appears you're the best equipped."

Data swiveled in his chair. He looked a little confused. *"Point man,* sir?"

"Coordinator," suggested Riker. If he hadn't been stretched so thin, he would have thought twice before using slang with his android officer.

"Ah," said Data. "Yes. Of course. I should have deduced as much from the context."

"No," said the first officer. "It was *my* fault." In the next breath, he arranged for a relief officer at the Ops console, so the android could move back to Science One. Then he gave the necessary orders to Fong and Wesley, so that Data could access the information they gathered as soon as it came in.

Finally, he sat back.

They weren't out of the woods yet. Not by a long shot.

But they were making progress.

The day after his interrogation by the Council, Conscription Master Boron'bak was transferred to Civil Service. Worse, he was demoted. He would be in charge of the police post at Tengla'var, one of the factory towns upriver from the capital.

To Dan'nor, it was neither a good sign nor a bad one. The Council might have been satisfied with a taste of Boron'bak's blood. Or it might simply have whet their appetites.

The following day, another high-ranking officer was toppled—the Central Defense liaison assigned to Fulfillment. Apparently, he'd been held accountable after all. And like Boron'bak, he was relegated to an obscure position with Civil Service.

Finally, Dan'nor's counterpart on the day shift was replaced. One night when he reported for duty, he found a new man finishing up. He said he didn't know what had happened to his predecessor.

After all that, Dan'nor thought that he would certainly be next. Strictly speaking, it was *his* mistake that caused all the trouble. The others had only laid the groundwork for it.

Nor did the passage of time do much to ease his insecurity. After a full five days had gone by, and nothing had happened to him, someone else might have believed the danger past. But not Dan'nor. He felt as if there were an ax dangling over his head, and the rope that held it there was slowly unraveling.

Then it came—the audience with his new superior. Normally, a simple computer memo would have been sufficient to announce a change in command. A personal audience could mean only one thing—the ax was about to fall.

In a way, it was a relief. The sooner he was transferred, the sooner he could work on getting his career back on track. With any luck, he'd get himself out of Civil Service after only a few years—maybe less.

But Dan'nor's expectations didn't take into account the identity of the new Conscription Master.

"You look surprised," said the man who had been the Fulfillment Facilitator on the day shift. "You expected, perhaps, that I'd been transferred out of Conscription? Rather than made Master of it?"

Dan'nor murmured a denial. But it didn't sound very convincing—not even to him.

"Come now," said the man. "I left early every evening and shirked my duty—ultimately contributing to your unfortunate error. And yet here I've been promoted, while everyone else associated with this fiasco has been banished to the factory towns. You're baffled—admit it."

Dan'nor frowned. "All right. I admit it."

The man smiled. He had coarse features for an officer—even coarser than Dan'nor's. But the compromising of his bloodline probably dated so far back that no one paid attention to it anymore. Recent impurities were considered much more despicable.

"It's really very simple, Tir'dainia. One of my relatives is . . . shall we say *intimate* with one of the councillors?"

Dan'nor grunted. "Very interesting." It also explained the man's ability to flaunt regulations with impunity. Why had he not suspected something like this before? "But," he added, "it is hardly any of my business."

The new Conscription Master learned forward. "Actually, it's very much your business. Without it, you wouldn't understand what I am about to tell you. You see, Tir'dainia, the Council was inclined to be lenient with you—at least by *their* standards. However, my relative's paramour swayed them toward a more severe punishment."

Dan'nor felt a sudden surge of anger—but he suppressed it. A confrontation with this man would only make things worse for him.

The Conscription Master leaned back again into his chair. "The reason? Because you *reported* me, Tir'dainia. Everyone else was willing to overlook my transgressions—but not you." He paused. "Perhaps I was foolish to take such chances. I can see that now. Without my ally on the Council, I would have been severely disciplined—which is what you must have expected when you made that report. Or didn't you give much thought to *my* fate?"

"I . . . I was only protecting myself," said Dan'nor. "Surely, you can understand that."

"Perfectly. And I trust that *you* will also understand—when I tell you the Council's decision." Again, a pause. "You're not going to Civil Service, Tir'dainia. You're being ousted from the Military altogether."

Dan'nor felt numb suddenly. The words seemed to hang in the air like smoke, incomprehensible and without meaning.

He thought he had been prepared for the worst. But this was a much more hideous turn than he ever could have foreseen.

"Why?" he finally asked—though it was little more than a rasping sound in his throat.

"Because a stint in Civil Service is only a minor setback for a clever lad like you. You might have wriggled your way back into the *real* Military someday—and resurrected the issue of my irresponsible behavior. By then, my relative might have fallen from her councillor's favor—and he might not have been inclined to protect me anymore. But with you out of the way, I will need no protection. There will be no one around with a reason to bring up the past."

Dan'nor licked his lips. "I won't bring it up either."

"Of course not. You won't have an opportunity."

"Don't do this to me," he begged.

The Conscription Master looked at him. "You mean . . . have pity?"

Dan'nor swallowed. "Yes. Pity."

The man's smile returned. "The same kind of pity you had for *me*—when you reported me?"

Dan'nor's throat was so tight it hurt. "Please," he said. "I'll do anything."

The Conscription Master looked away. "That will be all, Tir'dainia."

A strange thing happened then. Dan'nor's desperation seemed to harden into something else. And without thinking, he flung himself over the desk that separated them.

But he had only a second or two to vent his fury before the guards came in to restrain him.

When Commander Riker originally called Burtin up to the bridge, just about five days ago, he hadn't sugar-coated the situation. Not one bit.

"We're doing everything we can, Doctor. And there's still a good chance that we'll be successful. But for the time being, you're going to have to operate on the assumption that Doctor Pulaski isn't coming back." An eerie pause. *"In the meantime, what's the status of Fredi's case?"*

At the time, Burtin hadn't had much to report. Just that they were proceeding on the basis of Pulaski's hypothesis, trying to isolate the hybrid bacterium—if there *was* one.

Now, however, he had quite a bit to report. He wished only that Pulaski could be present to hear it too.

"Commander?"

"Is that you, Doctor?"

Riker sounded a damned sight better than he had the last

time they spoke. Of course, that had been before the Klah'kimmbri dropped their energy mantle.

"It's me, all right. And I've got some good news. I found the bacterium that's afflicting our friend Fredi."

"Glad to hear it," said the first officer.

Burtin had expected a little more excitement—something along the lines of what he himself was experiencing. Then again, Riker no doubt had other things on his mind. Even with the mantle down, they still had to find the away team. And bring it back.

"Now," said the doctor, "we've just got to make sure that the antibiotic we *usually* use on this bacterium also works against the altered version. But my preliminary analyses indicate that it will."

"So Fredi's all but cured?" concluded Riker.

"It looks that way," said Burtin. "Also, I don't see any reason to hold the other survey team members any longer. They still show no signs of the disease—I'm going to lift their quarantine."

"Good news, Doctor. But don't let me keep you. I know you've still got a lot of work ahead of you."

It was a polite way of saying "go away," and Burtin took the hint—without taking offense as well. What the hell, he thought. On the frontier, that message would have come across in much less delicate terms.

"Burtin out," he said, making it official. His duty done, he decided to get back to the lab. See how the accelerated cultures were doing.

As he traveled the short corridor that led past Pulaski's office, he hit something with the toe of his boot. It ricocheted off the bulkhead and came to rest on the soft deck-covering right in front of him.

Curious, he picked it up. It took a moment before he recognized what it was.

A fragment of the Mondrifahlian good-luck charm—the one Pulaski had shattered shortly before she beamed over to the *Mendel*. Apparently, it had eluded her clean-up effort.

Burtin turned it over in his hand. A superstitious Mondrifahlian might have called the statuette's destruction an omen. A harbinger of evil to come.

But doctors weren't supposed to believe in omens. Halfway to the lab, he deposited the shard in a waste disposal unit.

Chapter Nine

THE WAGON LURCHED, sliding him halfway across the board that served as a driver's seat. With a tug on the reins, he convinced the burden-beasts up ahead to make the necessary adjustment.

A couple of moments later, the wagon righted itself and he slid back to his original spot. "Careful up here," he cried, the sheer walls of the pass raining echoes upon him.

A cry from behind him: the next driver acknowledging his warning. As the echoes of that sound devolved on him too, he turned inward again. Dragged out his questions as if they were prized possessions, poring over them with undiminished zeal.

Was he a criminal? He certainly didn't feel like one. But then, that was *now*. How could he know what he was like *before*?

And was his name really Picard—or was that just a name that had been assigned to him? There was no way of figuring it out. He'd decided that some time ago.

It seemed to him that he should be able to reason his way out of the darkness—the oblivion into which fate had cast him. But to do that, he had to have a starting point. He had to have *one* thing he knew for the truth—just one.

Unfortunately, even that was denied him. All was speculation, conjecture—built on the speculation and conjecture of those around him, and theirs on that of others before *them*. There was no basis of certainty, no bedrock on which to build a viable hypothesis.

Such was the nature of their prison. Stronger than any wall, broader and taller than any tangible barrier to freedom. For without one's memory, how could one escape? Where would one go—in which direction? And how could it be determined that escape was even possible?

Picard had a sense, of course, that there were other places than this. Not actual memories, but vague impressions of more pleasant surroundings. That made sense; how could he think of *this* place as desolate unless he had something with which to compare it?

But where *were* these other places? Nearby? A couple of days' journey? Or too far away to even think about?

His meditation was interrupted again—this time by the sight of the silhouette that hung against the pale clouds up ahead, suspended between the dark jaws of the pass. Not one of those mechanical things; it was the wrong shape.

A marshal, then. He felt his spine straighten at the thought.

He had seen sky riders like this one only twice before—both times at a distance. The first one had paced the supply train only for a while and abruptly taken off. The second one had stayed somewhat longer—long enough, anyway, to torture the hindmost driver for his laggardness.

Picard had been too far up the line to really see what happened—much less do anything about it. There was a rippling effect—for a couple of seconds, no more. An anguished cry that lasted much longer than the assault itself, forced out as if through clenched teeth.

He hadn't seen the victim for some time after that; the

example had spurred the other drivers to new levels of efficiency. And considering their position on a narrow ledge beside a steep drop, Picard couldn't help but be pushed along. But after dark, when they'd unshackled the burden-beasts and made camp, he searched the ranks of his companions until he'd found the object of the marshal's attention.

The being, small and wiry with a light brown fur over much of its body, was sitting with its knees clutched to its chest. Still shuddering, still staring as if its eyelids had been propped open. Nor did it look as if it would have welcomed an attempt at conversation—so he made none.

And that, he mused now, was *another* reason that escape was so difficult to contemplate.

As he neared the end of the pass, the sky opened up. And the marshal loomed closer—his sleek black sled glinting in the cloud-filtered sunlight.

Despite the awkward angle and the interposing bulk of the sled itself, Picard was able to get his first good look at a sky rider. All he'd been able to discern up until this point was that they were basically humanoid—and that they wore their hair long, tied up in a pigtail.

Now he could see how, in many ways, they resembled his own species. Two eyes, a nose, a proper mouth; long, narrow features set in a pale complexion beneath that dark, drawn-back hair.

Suddenly, he felt that he'd seen that face before—or one very much like it. Where? In his former life?

Was that a clue, then? Something he could trace back to his own identity?

He set his mind to it, never taking his eyes off the marshal—not even as his wagon passed beneath the sled. But try as he might, he could recall nothing more.

Damn.

As he emerged from the pass—the first to do so—Picard saw that they had their work cut out for them. The long, winding ascent up the lee side of the mountain and the slow, careful progress through the pass had been only a prelude . . . to the *difficult* part of the journey.

What stretched before them was a long series of terraced ledges descending from left to right. Like a gargantuan set of stairs, seen from the side.

Each ledge was narrow—though some were narrower than others. And in every case, there was a considerable drop from a given stairstep to the one below it.

The wind howled out there, savage and unfettered. Picard slowed his beasts to a halt as he considered his options.

He'd been a little surprised at the way his companions had gradually deferred to him—selected him as their de facto leader. Nor had the former leader—an angular individual with an angry red, leathery sort of skin—been reluctant to give up the position. Quite the contrary.

There were no benefits to being the first driver in the line—other than the knowledge that one had the trust of one's peers. Mostly, it was a burden.

But Picard had taken it up without hesitation. It gave him a measure of control over what happened to him. If he couldn't dredge up his past, at least he could take an active part in preserving his chance for a future.

In short, he felt safer abiding by his own decisions than someone else's.

The situation at hand was a good example. Of the three paths accessible to them, the most obvious choice was the one straight ahead. However, that one appeared to lose too much breadth just before it disappeared around the flank of the mountain.

The ledge immediately above it would give them more latitude, but it seemed to pitch this way and that, making the going tricky. If a driver was caught unaware when the path chose to tilt down slope . . .

The lowermost trail, on the other hand, started out fairly narrow. But it remained the same width as it went on—at least for as far as he could see—and the pitch was about as good as one could hope for. What's more, it was remarkably free of the detritus that popped up from time to time on the other ledges.

The only problem with the low trail was that some skill was required to get to it. The ground between this spot and the beginning of the ledge was steep and littered with loose stones.

Nonetheless, he concluded that it was worth the risk. Spurring his beasts on again with a flick of the reins, Picard concentrated on the terrain before him.

And tried to ignore the sky-riding marshal for the time being.

The wind was cold, cutting through his cloak as if it didn't exist. But as he left the sheltering pass behind, and the other wagons moved out to follow, the howling he'd heard at first seemed to dissipate—to become a sound like that of rushing water, felt in the bones as much as heard.

It took some time to negotiate the open slope, but it went well enough. *Exercising caution,* Picard told himself, *even the least proficient driver among us ought to be able to handle it.*

Finally, he was on the ledge, and the ride became much gentler. He was able to pick up the pace just a bit, despite the proximity of the precipice to his right. Then, after the first twist in the trail, he caught sight of what figured to be their ultimate destination: a squat, dark edifice that seemed to lurk in the folds of a particularly stark mountainside. Picard could barely make out tiny figures moving along the walls that girded the inner keep.

A sense of foreboding gripped him. Perhaps it was just the look of the place—so severe, so unadorned. But then, what had he expected in the midst of this wilderness?

Or was it more than the place's appearance? Something about the figures on the walls?

What were they watching out for, anyway? The supply train?

Or something *else?*

He would have plenty of time to ponder that. The edifice was a good day and a half away—maybe more, depending on how long it took to skirt the intervening vault of a valley.

The wind scoured the terraces, blowing a fine grit about in the air. Picard had to shield his eyes from it.

Worse, it seemed to infuriate the burden-beasts. They stabbed at the air with their long, majestic horns and shrieked in that ear-shattering pitch Picard had become familiar with.

Farther back, he could hear some of the other teams shrilling like his own. The drivers were no doubt doing their best to restore calm, but if anything the noises were growing louder.

Picard set his teeth. This was hardly the time and place for the beasts to become rambunctious. Not with the cliff so near and the drop so far . . .

Suddenly, the wind's rush was punctured by more than animal screams. There was a bellow from a throat that couldn't have been too different from his own—followed by the *crack* of splintering wood.

He whirled just in time to see one of the wagons flip halfway over in the direction of the precipice. The driver was thrown out into space with a strange, agonizing slowness—along with much of his cargo. But somehow he managed to hang on to the reins. Nor did he let go as his frenzied team tried to pull free of their twisted harness, dragging the wagon forward and scraping the driver along the cliff's edge.

Half a heartbeat later, Picard saw through a rising cloud of grit how the driver could be so tenacious: his arm was entangled in the reins. But for that, he would have been dead already, crushed against the next ledge below.

There were no second thoughts for Picard—only the fact of danger to someone who had followed him into these straits. Not that it had been his fault—nor did he blame himself, exactly. It was just that he had assumed responsibility for the others—and he didn't take that responsibility lightly.

Vaulting down from his wooden seat, he made his way past two other wagons, hugging the mountainside in order to avoid both the cliff's edge and the raging burden-beasts. By the time he'd reached the upended vehicle and come around it, he saw that others had beaten him to the spot.

But no one was doing anything, not even leaning over to lend a hand. In fact, they were backing off from the brink—before the weapon-wielding figure of the marshal, who was fighting the winds on his bucking sled.

"Out of my way," Picard shouted, shouldering past the other drivers. His eyes met those of the sky rider—briefly. Then, with determination flooding through him like an elixir, he knelt at the edge of the cliff and peered over.

The entangled driver couldn't look back up at him. He was struggling too hard to free himself from his bonds, which had cut deep into his arm. Every twist of the reins brought forth a strangled whimper.

"Back off!" cried the sky rider, struggling with the winds. His pigtail whipping behind him, he aimed his blaster at Picard. "You hear me? Leave him be!"

And without warning, he pulled the trigger. But at the very last moment, he turned his weapon aside—and instead of hitting the human, the ripple stream splattered against the frantic animals still harnessed to the overturned wagon.

Instantly, the beasts stopped shrieking. They collapsed—and Picard had the feeling that they would never get up again. He realized then and there that the blaster had more than just a pain setting.

"Dispose of those animals," shouted the marshal, looking back to Picard. "Salvage what you can of the wagon's supplies—and get this train moving again!"

"Certainly," cried the human, containing his anger at the beasts' unnecessary destruction. *"After* we get our comrade back up."

Without waiting for a response, he lowered himself carefully over the edge, using the twisted reins for support. Finding a foothold, he pushed himself out from the cliff face and reached down for the tortured driver.

The victim saw him but didn't dare reach up. If he let go of the reins with his free hand, all his weight would depend from his mutilated arm—and he couldn't endure that prospect.

Picard understood. It meant that he would have to lower himself a little further, grab the driver by his tunic or something. He began to work his way farther down.

Suddenly, there was another blast of that strange, light-bending beam. Picard couldn't help but flinch at it, and that almost cost him his hold on the reins. As it was, he lost his foothold. Desperately, he scrambled to find another while vertigo gripped him like an iron fist, threatening to squeeze the breath out of him.

Finally, he caught hold—steadied himself. And got his bearings enough to see what had happened. The driver below him was still dangling from his ensnared arm—but now he was limp, lifeless. His eyes stared up at the sky.

Picard found the marshal, glared at him with all the force of his boiling hatred. "Damn you!" he cried. "What kind of barbarian *are* you?"

He could see a crooked smile take shape on the sky rider's face. Then, abruptly, it disappeared.

"Climb," he said. *"Now.* Or you'll join your friend."

However, Picard was too caught up in the wave of his anger. "Answer me," he roared, the wind snatching at his words. "Answer me, you heathen!"

Coolly, the marshal leveled his blaster at him—again. But this time, Picard knew, the weapon wouldn't be turned aside.

Releasing the reins suddenly, he dropped. The blast hit nothing but the rock above his head as Picard snared the reins again, stopping himself a meter or so below his original position.

He and the corpse at the end of his life-rope spun dizzily together in the wind, the cliff face finally coming up hard against his shoulder. He fought for balance, tried to find the marshal again so he could attempt to dodge the next volley.

But when he located his antagonist, he saw that the sky rider's attention had shifted. Picard looked up and saw someone descending after him—just as *he* had descended after the one who was now dead.

The marshal's visage had become a mask of rage. Now he pointed his weapon at the newcomer.

"Get back!" shouted the sky rider. "All of you—get back!"

But Picard's rescuer kept coming. For a moment, he thought the marshal would destroy *both* of them—send them plummeting to a grisly end.

Then, with a voluble curse, he holstered the weapon. And veered off on his sled, describing an arc as he used the winds to achieve height—and distance.

Picard stared after the sky rider for a moment, then sought the face of the one who'd saved his life—at the risk of his own. When he saw it, it startled him a little.

He hadn't expected it to look so much like the face behind the blaster.

Abruptly, he realized why the sky rider's countenance had seemed familiar to him. There was a definite racial resemblance between the two—though the marshal's dark hair, so different from the driver's reddish locks, had distracted him from seeing it.

Picard took the offered hand, felt himself being pulled up. He did his best to aid in the process. And when it came time to use the other driver for a ladder, he did so as delicately as possible.

Once the human was at eye level with the ledge, his comrades raised him the rest of the way. A few seconds later, his rescuer received the same treatment.

As the two of them sat there getting their breath, Picard

placed his hand on the other driver's shoulder. "Thank you," he said.

The golden-eyed one just nodded.

"Pardon me," said Picard, raising his voice a little to be heard better over the wind, "but I've forgotten your name."

The driver smiled a little. "Ralak'kai," he said.

Picard smiled a little too. "Ralak'kai."

Their conversation was interrupted as the overturned wagon and its assorted burdens were pushed off the ledge— sent crashing down the terraces of stone so the train could move again.

Before another tragedy had a chance to befall them.

At first, Dan'nor didn't want to watch the Conflicts again. They reminded him too much of what he might have done—what he might have been. They were salt, ground hard into his still-open wounds.

His former quarters had had no videoscreen. Officers were unofficially discouraged from viewership, under the theory that it would make their brains soft. Particularly field officers—those who created the Conflicts in the first place.

However, he had a videoscreen now. And if he left it off indefinitely, the Viewership Service would eventually catch on to him. In a Lower Caster who'd spent his life in the factories, a disinterest in the Conflicts would have prompted the scrutiny of the authorities. After all, non-viewership was a sign of disenchantment. And disenchantment often led to antisocial behavior.

In someone who *knew* that videoscreen use was monitored, a failure to at least tune in would be seen as something more extreme: a conscious and perhaps even flagrant decision to rebel. The scrutiny stage would be bypassed and sanctions imposed—subtle at first, and then less so if non-viewership persisted.

And then, of course, there was always the possibility—no matter how remote—that model behavior would be rewarded with a second chance. An opportunity to pick up the pieces of his career and go on.

So he tuned in. He thought he would just let the damned thing play, doing his best to ignore it. Then he found out that he couldn't.

Once, the Conflicts had intrigued him—he'd forgotten that somehow. Of course, he had been just a boy back then—taking apart each strategy in his mind, bit by bit, until he could see why the successful ones had worked and the unsuccessful ones hadn't. And all the while, his Lower Caste playmates were reveling in the blood and glory, miniature versions of the viewers they were to become.

Before long, all that came back to him, and the old intrigue snared him once more. He found, ironically, that the only way to escape the bitterness of his fate was to immerse himself in the very source of that bitterness. To play again at being the field officer he had hoped to become in reality.

This time, however, he saw more deeply into the strategies. He saw beyond the level of winning and losing to the underlying dynamics: the rise and fall of action, the thwarting or satisfaction of expectation—all of which served to enthrall the viewer.

It was far from a revelation. He had known for a long time, of course, that the purpose of the Conflicts was to distract the Lower Castes from the tedium of their lives—from the fact of their servitude. But now he saw *how* it was done—and that there was more skill involved than he had first believed.

In one sequence, for example, the video alternated between two hostile reconnaissance parties—unknowingly about to meet head-on. Long shots established the relative positions of the groups, while closer shots showed their respective difficulties in negotiating the mountainous terrain. When the screen filled with one or another unsuspecting face, Dan'nor had an impulse to shout out a warning. To curse him for a fool. But at the same time, it gave him a sense of power to know something the participant did not.

The anticipation mounted steadily, culminating in a desperate and deadly encounter. Here again, certain warriors were singled out for special scrutiny—a most effective technique indeed. The expressions of the participants, seen up close, were fascinating—despite the headgear that obscured much of their faces, despite even their alienness.

One combatant in particular aroused Dan'nor's interest —though at first, he couldn't say why. Upon reflection, he decided that it was the warrior's *efficiency* that was so impressive. While others flailed wildly, caught up in a bloodthirsty frenzy, this one seemed to measure each blow with expert care—to use only as much force as was necessary and no more.

That was one reason he was still standing, while most of his comrades lay maimed or destroyed. He was more than a killer. He was, truly, a warrior.

Dan'nor would have liked to watch him longer. But in the middle of an especially fearsome exchange, the scene shifted to some other place entirely—another battle, this one just beginning, and another set of combatants.

It was a little too abrupt a transition for Dan'nor's taste. But he soon forgot about it as he lost himself in the drama of the new confrontation.

Worf brought his mace up to block his opponent's downstroke. He held fast beneath the impact of the blow, then turned loose one of his own. It caught the other warrior in the ribs, sent him staggering in a cloud of churned-up dust.

The Klingon advanced, peering at his adversary through the eye slits of his headgear, feeling his armor abrade newly healed skin. Not that he wasn't grateful for it—it had already saved his life more times than he cared to admit.

Others had not been so fortunate. Death was all around him in this narrow mountain pass, where his recon party had been surprised by the enemy. The clangor of clashing weapons and the cries of the wounded had blended by now into a single, maddening drone. The scent of blood—some of it his own—was thick and intoxicating in his nostrils.

His opponent—helmeted and armored even as he was—feigned an ax stroke at his knees. But Worf only snarled at the ploy and circled to his left.

The beast in his gut was rearing its head again, whipped into a frenzy by the atmosphere of unrelenting violence. He could feel it unwinding, serpentlike—glorious.

He yearned to crush his opponent under the weight of his mace—just as any of his comrades would have done, and without a second thought.

Worf didn't know what made him different from the others. Certainly, he shared their ferocity, their physical capacity for destruction—even their love of combat. Yet he could not bring himself to complete the critical act of war—the slaying of his enemy. Quickly and surely, as each of them deserved.

Somehow, at the last, the serpent in him turned back. Strangled on its own fury, leaving him cold and empty at the prospect of killing.

So painful had it been, this *inability,* that Worf had tried to refrain from battle altogether. His reward had been a blasting from the marshals.

Even now, he knew, they were hovering somewhere nearby. Ready to inflict agony if they caught him dragging his feet again.

But they would not catch him doing that. He had gotten too skillful at masquerading as a killer. At hiding his shame.

His adversary of the moment feinted again—but this time, he followed it up with the real thing. Worf leapt back and the ax missed.

"Run," he growled, too low for anyone but them to hear.

The warrior cocked his head. He seemed unable to believe his ears.

"Run," repeated Worf. "Now. While you still can." If he could pretend to show pity, rather than reveal his awful truth . . .

The warrior's response was muffled by his headgear. But it sounded enough like a laugh to start a boiling in Worf's blood.

Trying to ignore it, he pressed his case. "Look around— there aren't enough of you left to win this fight. Nor will your wounds permit you to endure much longer. Go now— before the others notice."

The warrior brandished his weapon. *"You* go—straight to hell."

Then Worf heard the whine of a marshal's sled, and the opportunity was lost.

With a deep-throated roar, he struck at his adversary's armor-encased head—holding back despite himself, allowing the warrior just enough time to move away. As it happened, however, his reaction was just a hair slower than Worf had expected. His ax came up and deflected the attack—but not before his helmet had taken the brunt of it.

At first, Worf believed he had done the very thing of which he had previously been incapable. His enemy reeled and came up short against a rocky outcropping. His headgear hung at an awkward angle, its hinges having cracked, and there was blood trickling down his partly exposed neck.

But when the Klingon came closer, his heart pounding with an apprehension he despised, the still form stirred. The warrior pushed himself off the rock, groaning, pulling the remains of his helm away so that he could see to fight. Spitting red ruin, he glared at his tormentor.

Since the hour Worf had woken, bereft of memory, he had seen all manner of faces. Faces of comrades and enemies, the living and the dead. But never had he seen a face that so closely mimicked his own.

Until now.

But for the scars, the cragginess that seemed to suggest age, that exposed visage might have been his—or a kinsman's. It occurred to him that this warrior might be able to *tell* him something—something about the time *before* he woke in the barracks, sweating and struggling against his restraints.

It was obvious that they were of the same race—and that that race was a minority here. Perhaps they had known each other once—even collaborated on whatever crime had earned them this fate.

He didn't dare question him now, of course. But this one had to live—so that he could find him again, when the marshals weren't looking, and pick his brain for some clue to the past.

Thinking this, Worf dropped his guard. Just for a moment, no more. But that was all the time his enemy needed.

With a speed he should no longer have been able to muster, the helmless one lashed out. Fortunately, his accuracy didn't match his quickness—all he could manage was a glancing blow.

It was enough, however, to send Worf spinning away, his arm a numb and nerveless thing. His mace fell from unfeeling fingers, raised dust where it hit the ground.

A second blow fell, and Worf barely eluded it. The third came closer, caused him to slip on a patch of gravel, lose his footing and come crashing to earth.

Immediately, his adversary was on top of him, his knee hammering into Worf's chest. It knocked the wind out of him, forced him to struggle to remain conscious.

His good hand groped, found his opponent's throat. Kept him at arm's length. But he was helpless to prevent the ax from being raised. It loomed against the sky like something gigantic.

Then it fell, and Worf felt a terrible impact in his bones. But a moment later, the ax lay beside him in the dirt and his head was still in one piece.

He wished he could say the same for his adversary. The man's corpse lay slumped beside him.

Another warrior stood over them—one of Worf's comrades. His expression was concealed behind his headgear—but there was disdain in the way he wiped off his truncheon on his armored leg.

Worf sensed that there was something he had to do. He reached out for his enemy's slack-jawed visage . . .

But it was too late. The last vestige of life had ebbed away, leaving only a cold and empty husk.

Worf felt cheated—and in more ways than one. This one might have helped him *remember*. He was filled with rage—with blind, unyielding fury.

Scrambling to his feet, he went after the warrior who had killed his enemy. Took him down from behind, eliciting a cry of surprise. The truncheon flew out of his hand and they rolled together in the dirt.

Somehow, Worf came out on top. With all the savage strength he could command, he smashed his mailed fist into the man's face.

Again.

And again.

Suddenly, the world was flattened in a blast of barely visible force. Worf felt as if something had taken hold of his insides and was tearing him apart. He had felt such pain only once before.

Rolling up into a ball, he withstood it as best he could. But every now and then, despite his best efforts, a whimper escaped his tightly clenched teeth.

Finally, it stopped. For a little while, he just lay there, shuddering. Then he looked up and hissed curses at the marshal on his airborne sled.

The marshal, too far away to hear, only smiled.

Chapter Ten

As soon as the antibiotic was injected into Fredi's system, the man showed signs of progress. Before the day was out, Burtin had made the decision to take his patient off the blood purifier. By the following morning—ship's time, of course—he had expected to be able to take him out of quarantine.

Unfortunately, it didn't quite work out that way.

"I don't understand," said Fredi. He was lying prone on the biobed—not so much because of his physical turn for the worse, but so the machine could make its analyses. "I thought I was getting *better.*"

There was just the slightest hint of hysteria in the geologist's voice. Burtin tried to ignore it as he pondered the figures on the monitor display above the bed.

The poison was evident again—no question about it. And it was slowly increasing its presence. Just as if they'd never found the bacteriological culprit, as if they'd never introduced the antibiotic at all.

"Doctor? You're not answering me."

He sighed. "I won't lie to you. I fully expected that we'd licked this thing." His words were picked up by the intercom, funneled into the quarantine area. "But it's nothing to worry about. The recuperation process often has peaks and valleys. This may just be one of the valleys."

Even from here, he could see the deepening of the worry lines in Fredi's face. The geologist wasn't buying what he had to sell—not entirely.

"Unfortunately," he continued, "I'm going to have to put you back on the purifier. We can't just let the poison build up again, right?"

Fredi chuckled, but it was a dry, dead sound. There wasn't any humor in it. "Right," he echoed.

Burtin tore himself away from the barrier. He wasn't accomplishing anything by standing here and reassuring the geologist. If he was going to figure out what had gone wrong, it would be in the lab.

As he headed there now, he passed Vanderventer in the hallway. The big nurse was responding to the call Burtin had put in a couple of minutes ago.

"Hi, Doc. Some kind of setback?"

"Looks like it," said Burtin. "Just hook up that purifier again and try to keep him calm."

"No problem, sir. Fredi and I are old friends by now."

Then Vanderventer was past him, eager to be about his duties. Whistling, in fact.

No doubt, Vanderventer would do much to improve Fredi's frame of mind. Burtin had no worries in that regard.

It was the *rest* of the geologist he was concerned about.

The lab was on the other side of sickbay, set apart from the patient care areas. When the doctor walked in, there was only one technician on duty—a pretty brunette named Arguellos.

She looked up from her computer terminal. "Need some help, sir?"

Burtin nodded. "Those cultures we made of Fredi's bacteria. I need to see the latest data."

"Right," said Arguellos. She saved the project she'd been working on and filed it, then called up the requested information. "You look grim," she told Burtin. "What's the matter?"

"Fredi's toxin level is up again."

"Oh, no."

"I'm afraid so."

"Any idea why?" she asked.

He shrugged. "That's why I'm here. To find out."

"Right. Ah—here are the culture analyses."

He came around to stand behind her. Placing a hand on the back of her chair, Burtin leaned toward the screen to get a better look.

Arguellos pointed. "What's *that?*"

Burtin knew the answer immediately. After all, it had been the most likely conclusion all along.

"The bacterium has mutated," he told her. "This is a new strain—one that's impervious to our antibiotic." He shook his head. "Look at that replication rate. No wonder Fredi's showing a high level of toxin again—the same thing is happening in *him.*"

Arguellos leaned back. A whistle escaped between her teeth.

"The ironic thing," said Burtin, "is that the original strain must have been dying off—due to some environmental change—even before we introduced the medicine. Or else the new strain couldn't have proliferated."

The technician shook her head. "So it's back to square one."

"At *least,*" he said.

"What do you mean?"

He patted her on the shoulder. "Nothing. It's just the pessimist in me coming out."

On the other hand, he told himself, *your pessimism might be justified in this case.* If the organism had mutated once, it could mutate again. Square one might become a very familiar place.

Then, suddenly, he felt silly. Unprofessional, even. *Don't make this any more complicated than it has to be,* he advised himself. *Remember—you're on the* Enterprise. *Vega Antilles is a long way away.*

Taking a deep breath, he thanked Arguellos and headed for the critical care area. At least he could tell his patient that he'd figured out what had happened. That would make Fredi feel a *little* better.

Winter was approaching. The air was getting cooler, the days shorter. Over the jagged profile of the factory district, the sun was already setting in a mighty blaze. Red flecks of cloud, scattered about the sky, seemed stymied in their attempts to escape the conflagration.

Dan'nor poured out of the shoe works with the rest of the laborers, maneuvering his way through the press. He spoke to no one and no one spoke to him. Perhaps they sensed his disgust at being lowered to their station. It didn't matter—he wasn't looking for their friendship.

The shoe plant was located at the top of a hill. It made his walk home considerably shorter than his walk to work. On the way down, he passed the refinery and then the plastics plant, and a little while later he came to the river.

There were shops along the water—all owned, of course, by someone or other in the Military. Probably not Council members, though—they didn't get involved in such piddling operations. Not directly, anyway.

Normally, Dan'nor didn't stop at any of these places. Eager to get home and view the Conflicts, he seldom even took note of what they were selling. This evening, however, he felt a little curious. Maybe because the Conflicts had been less engaging for him lately. They were beginning to take on a sameness; he was seldom surprised anymore.

One shop in particular caught his eye. No, not a shop—a small tavern. And taverns, he'd heard, were rare in this town. On an impulse, he opened the wooden door and walked inside.

It was quite crowded, and he hated crowds. They reminded him too much of the shoe factory. The sight of all those bodies pressed together in the dim light, the loud sounds and the smell almost drove him back out the door. Then he saw what had attracted the crowd in the first place, and he forced himself to stay.

It was a videoscreen, not much larger than the one he had at home. There was nothing unusual on it, just another clash outside the walls of some fortress. Probably K'trellan—they had been featuring that one a lot lately.

The fighting was fierce, but it didn't hold Dan'nor's interest for long. The siege sequences were always the least artistic—just a lot of bodies sweating and grunting and trying to hack other bodies to pieces.

On the other hand, the crowd seemed to love it. They were roaring and raising their drinks and pounding their fists on the occasional table. It was almost as if they themselves were on the battlefield.

It occurred to him that he had never seen people watching the Conflicts en masse. Perhaps in two and threes at someone's home, but never in such a large group. And never in a place like this.

It made it something strange, something unfamiliar. There was an electricity in the air. A sense of involvement, of importance. Of magnitude.

Dan'nor wanted to learn more about it. Skirting the thickest part of the crowd, he worked his way to a spot in the corner. He could barely see the screen, but he had a good view of the onlookers. Finding a surprisingly empty chair, he sat down.

A moment later, he found out why the chair had been available. It was rickety. But by leaning back against the wall, he got it to bear his weight.

The screen generated a bright, flickering light, illuminating faces for him. It showed him the wild passion in their eyes, the way their mouths curled around their cheers and their curses. He had the feeling that they might whirl as one at any time and turn that murderous passion on *him*.

Until now, he realized, he had never fully appreciated the

impact of the Conflicts—the extent to which they could capture the hearts and minds of the masses. He had thought he understood, but his understanding had been a superficial thing. A cold and distant observation.

Now he was seeing it for himself—the eruption of violence for which there was no other outlet in Lower Caste society; the sharing in that violence that bound one man to another and all of them to the warriors on the screen. Now he *truly* understood.

"Can I get you something, Brother?"

Dan'nor looked up, a little startled. He found himself staring into the hovering face of a serving woman.

"What?" he asked dumbly.

"A drink," she explained. "This *is* a tavern, you know."

He frowned. "I'm aware of that. Yes, I'll have a drink. *M'tsila*, I think."

She smiled wearily. "Sure. I'll have some sent right over from the estate of Councillor Orian'tuc. Now what do you really want?"

He was surprised. It hadn't occurred to him that the liqueur wouldn't be available to everyone. In the Military, it was a common libation. As he cast about for another choice, he noticed another serving maid heading into a narrow hallway off the main room. She had a tray full of drinks and one of them looked like beer.

"How about a beer?" he suggested.

"Absolutely," she said. "A fine choice." There was still a hint of mockery in her tone, and it annoyed him—though he knew it wasn't meant to. That was just the way Lower Casters spoke to one another. Not like in the Military, where words were always carefully chosen. "Something to chew on with that?"

The thought of eating in this place repulsed him. "No," he said. "Nothing."

With a shrug, she turned sideways and disappeared into the crowd. Dan'nor was glad to have gotten rid of her.

But when he resumed his study of the viewers, he saw that their mood had changed. Their raucous calls were complaints now rather than encouragements. It seemed that the scene had switched from the battlefield to a construction site. Some participants were building a bridge.

Of course, this was only a prelude to something else. More than likely, a raiding party would swoop down out of the hills, destroy the bridge and take the builders captive. Or a counterforce would intervene and destroy the raiding party. Dan'nor had seen variations on the theme a dozen times or more in the weeks since he became a civilian.

As he was thinking this, he saw the other serving maid emerge from the hallway. Her tray was now empty.

It piqued his curiosity. To whom had she brought the drinks? And why weren't they in this room, which contained what was supposed to be the main attraction?

He eyed the hallway, even more dimly lit than the rest of the place. Could there be a gambling den back there? He had heard that such things were becoming more popular, though no one he knew had actually seen one. Of course, until recently, everyone he knew had been in the Military—and since gambling was illegal, they would hardly have been invited to attend.

Dan'nor decided to investigate—to see for himself. If there *was* a gambling operation here, and he helped the authorities break it up, it might bode well for his reinstatement.

Leaning forward, he rose carefully from his untrustworthy chair. He looked around, but his serving woman was still nowhere to be seen.

Should I wait for her to return—and then *slip into the hallway? Or should I make sure my prey doesn't elude me—and make use of what time I have now?*

His impatience got the better of him. He chose the latter option.

The hallway was longer than he thought—and darker,

once he got past the part that adjoined the main room. What's more, it took a left turn before he saw any doors. One was on his immediate right, just past the turning. And it was ajar.

He peered inside. It took his eyes a moment to penetrate the shadows. And when they did, there was nothing to see. Only some kegs of beer, some mops, a bucket. And a shelf full of cleaning supplies.

The other door, farther down the corridor and on the opposite side, was closed. But as he padded closer to it—grateful for the soft soles of his civilian shoes—he heard sounds from within.

Voices.

He crept even closer. The voices became more distinct. There were a number of them, some louder than others. He put his ear to the door and listened.

"That can't be, Ma'alor. History shows . . ."

"The hell with history. They're desperate, Brother. Can't you see that?"

"And besides, they've already gotten away with it. There have been no repercussions due to Ralak'kai's appearance —no widespread objections at all. And that opens the door for others to be used like Ralak'kai."

"Damn them. Can you imagine if they took all of those who've been imprisoned and . . ."

"It won't happen, I tell you. Perhaps they can get away with Ralak'kai, even one or two others. But if they were to conscript many more like him, the results would be catastrophic for them. The people would rise up—just as they've feared all along."

"You are too much the idealist, Zanc'cov. If the people were capable of rising up, they would have done so long before . . ."

Dan'nor never heard the rest. A hand gripped his shoulder, spun him around. And before he could protect himself, something slammed into the side of his head.

The next thing he knew, he was lying facedown on the

floor, looking at a circle of shoes. The taste of blood was strong in his mouth.

"He's a spy," said one of his antagonists. "A damned Military spy."

"Is he armed?"

Someone rifled the pockets of his coat. He didn't move to stop them.

"No. I don't think so."

"What do we do with him?"

"Kill him. What else can we do?"

Dan'nor didn't like the sound of that. It was obvious that he had stumbled onto something worse than a gambling den—*much* worse. If he didn't escape now, he told himself, he might never have another chance.

Scrambling halfway to his feet, he tried to bull his way through the circle. But his captors caught him and drove him back. They forced him down against the floor again and held him there—despite his struggles.

"Let me go," he snarled, his words muffled by the pressure of the floor against his mouth. "You're making a mistake."

"It's you who made a mistake," said one of them.

"I'm not Military," he growled. "I work in the shoe factory."

"He's lying. I can hear a Military accent a mile away. Get my knife—it's in my jacket."

That gave Dan'nor reason to struggle even harder—but it gained him nothing. There were too damned many of them.

"I don't like this," said another voice. "Insurrection is one thing. But murder . . ."

"You must have known it would lead to this, Zanc'cov. How could it have led anywhere else?"

"Here it is, Ma'alor."

Dan'nor saw the glint of the knife, fought with renewed intensity.

"All right. Hold him steady now, and I'll make a quick end of . . ."

"Wait!"

They all seemed to freeze at the cry. Whoever was holding Dan'nor's head down grew lax and he was able to twist it around. To look up, to see who had cried out.

But when he saw, he couldn't believe it.

"Let him go. I can vouch for him."

"What do you mean? He's a spy."

"I'm not," said Dan'nor. "I thought this was a gambling den. I swear it."

"No—he was listening at the door. I caught him."

"Out of curiosity," argued Dan'nor. "Nothing more."

"What's the difference? He found us out. We can't just let him go."

"We can—and we will."

"Why? Just because you say so?"

"Because we must trust one another. Without that, we might as well cease to exist."

"I trust *you,* Tir'dainia. But why should I trust *him?"*

The man who had interceded on Dan'nor's behalf looked around at the others. "Because he's a Tir'dainia too. He's my son."

There were looks exchanged. Mostly surprise, but also suspicion. Only one of the men exhibited relief. "There," he said. "You see? We need not kill him after all."

"Zanc'cov's right. Put the knife away, Ma'alor."

The one called Ma'alor eyed Dan'nor's father. "I hope you are certain about this, Tir'dainia. *Very* certain. Because if you're wrong, we will all pay dearly for it."

"I'm certain, Brother. Now let him up."

Gradually, Dan'nor felt himself released. The weight of bodies lifted off him. He got to his feet, wiped the blood from his mouth.

And noticed that they had formed that circle around him again. Were they having second thoughts now about letting him go? Surely, that was true of Ma'alor. It was evident in his face, in the way he held the knife.

But before the debate could be renewed, Dan'nor's father

came forward and embraced him. Then, his arm still wrapped around Dan'nor's shoulders, he escorted him between Ma'alor and another man. Through the circle—to freedom.

No one moved to stop them. When they reached the door, the elder Tir'dainia opened it.

"Go now," he said. "We'll talk later."

Dan'nor didn't have to be told twice.

"You should have seen it," said Marcroft, pushing some pasta around on his plate. "The poor bastard stood there for almost an hour, holding these damned weights at arm's length. Can you imagine? I can't even do that with my hands empty."

Vanderventer grunted, looked about the lounge. He had an urge to get up, to run, to burn off some energy. But that was crazy, wasn't it? He'd been dragging his rear end after that last shift, and the meal he'd just finished—big even by *his* standards—should have settled him into a nice, mellow lethargy.

But it hadn't. Quite the opposite, in fact. Maybe the food processing unit had taken some liberties with his Peking Duck recipe. After all, it was programmed to make substitutions when the requested ingredients weren't in its repertoire—and there was no telling how some of those ingredients might affect a given individual.

"Damn it, Hans, you're not even listening to me." Marcroft tilted his head to catch Vanderventer's eye. "Are you?"

"What can I say?" the big Dutchman returned, finally picking up the thread of the conversation. "You're just not a Klingon."

"Oh," said his companion. "I see. Thanks for telling me. Now I know why I'm not partial to raw meat." He shook his head, made a *tsk-tsk*ing sound. "I wasn't *looking* for an explanation. I was just expressing my admiration."

Vanderventer grunted again. But he couldn't seem to

make his body want to stay put. He felt as if each and every one of his atoms were vibrating, trying to burst free.

"Sorry," he said. "It's just that I feel so . . . so *jumpy*. Must have been something wrong with that duck I ate."

Marcroft leaned a little closer and peered at his friend. "Come to think of it," he said, "you *do* look a little flushed." He cracked a tentative smile. "You didn't by any chance sneak a little Maratekkan brandy into that recipe, did you?"

Vanderventer frowned. "No, of course not. I . . ."

Suddenly, his feeling of anxiety eased. It was gone—without a trace. And in its wake, he felt the lazy contentedness he'd expected after a big meal.

"You what?"

"Nothing," said Vanderventer. He sounded surprised, even to himself. "I mean, I feel better all of a sudden. For a while there, I was really zipping along—but now I'm okay again."

Marcroft's expression of concern hadn't quite disappeared. "You sure? You still look a little funny. Funnier than usual, that is."

The Dutchman took stock of himself, shrugged. "No, I'm fine." He shivered a little. "Boy, if that wasn't the *weirdest* sensation I've ever . . ."

The fork dropped from his hand, clattered on the table.

"Don't go losing your silverware over it," said Marcroft.

Vanderventer tried to pick up the fork, to replace it on his tray. But he couldn't. His fingers seemed thick and unwieldy. As if they'd forgotten what they were supposed to do.

He looked up at his companion, attempted to control the panic that was rearing up in his gut. The weirdness wasn't over—it had undergone only a change. "Something's wrong with me, Mick. Something's definitely wrong."

Marcroft returned the look as Vanderventer flexed his fingers—first those of his right hand, then those of his left. "What now?" he asked.

"My fingers," said Vanderventer, swallowing. "They feel stiff. I can't get them to move."

"Hey," said Marcroft, "maybe they're just tired. You wore them out with all that spaghetti-twirling."

"No," said the Dutchman. "This is serious. Oh, man—I've got to get to sickbay."

"Sickbay?" echoed Marcroft. "But—I mean, is it really that bad?"

Even as his friend asked the question, Vanderventer was figuring out the answer. He could feel his back muscles becoming soft, spongy. It hurt now just to sit up.

These were Fredi's symptoms, weren't they? The very same things Fredi felt before he collapsed down there in that science corridor.

But the disease wasn't supposed to be contagious. Their tests had shown them that.

So why was he feeling what he was feeling? Why were his legs starting to tremble as he tried to hold himself steady in his chair?

Did it have anything to do with Fredi's relapse?

It was getting more difficult to breathe. He forced his lungs to work harder, but it hurt like the devil. And he knew that he could keep it up for only so long.

"Sickbay," he insisted. *"Now."*

And to underline the urgency of his request, he lurched out of his seat—tried to get himself moving toward the door. But his legs refused to support his weight, and he had to throw his upper body onto the table to keep from falling down.

"Damn!" cried Marcroft, coming around the table as quickly as he could. Just as Vanderventer was about to slide off, his hands unable to find purchase on the smooth dining surface, his friend caught him around the waist.

"Mick . . ."

"It's okay, Hans. I've got you."

Slowly, Marcroft let the bigger man down, until he was

kneeling on the floor. Then he looked up at the intercom grid and called for a link to sickbay.

Vanderventer tried to relax, to ignore the fact that his muscles were betraying him. But when he stopped pumping air in and out, everything started to get gray and fuzzy—so he gritted his teeth and started making like a bellows again.

"They're coming, Hans. Hang in there, buddy."

The Dutchman nodded.

Chapter Eleven

THE TALL, SLENDER FIGURE had come into the med enclosure without her noticing it. She had been too busy attending to one of her patients—Toc'tu, the big one with all the scales. And too foggy as well, perhaps, from fatigue and lack of sleep.

Then the newcomer began giving orders, and Pulaski whirled at the sound of them. There was something about the tone of that voice she didn't like—even before she saw whose it was. It had an air of disdain, of imperiousness. As if it were used to being obeyed.

Also, a very definite ring of violence. Like the clashing of weapons in a confined space.

Her suspicions were confirmed when she saw the intruder —dressed in a uniform as proud as he was, festooned with military-looking insignia—point a gloved finger at one of her charges. The being, whose wounded arm was only half-healed, swiveled himself off his cot and stood.

"Wait a minute," she said, striding across the enclosure. "What's going on here?"

The lordly one only glanced at her as she approached.

"Mistress—no!" called Toc'tu, his voice just strong enough to carry. But she ignored the warning. The newcomer was continuing to point, and others of her patients were starting to get up.

Deftly skirting an operating table, Pulaski placed herself in the intruder's path. He fixed her with his golden eyes, paused to consider her. Intrigued, a little, by her behavior? Or just amused?

"I asked you a question," she said, ignoring his impudence. "What are you doing with my patients?"

"Restoring them to the battlefield," he told her. "What business is it of yours?"

"They're *my* patients," said Pulaski. "That *makes* it my business. And since they haven't recovered from their wounds yet, you've got no right putting them back on a battlefield." An addendum occurred to her: "Even assuming you had any right to put them there in the first place."

The intruder's mouth pulled up at the corners. He looked about at the other meds.

"Is she insane?" he asked.

No one answered. No one even met his gaze.

He looked back at her. "I suggest," he said, "that you get out of my way. I have a job to do here." The smile with which he'd been flirting vanished suddenly.

But Pulaski didn't flinch. "I have a job too. It's to see that these people get well again. If that wasn't important, what was the point of bringing them here at all?"

The lordly one's eyes seemed to darken a shade. "What you do here," he said, "is *very* important. But it is not up to you to decide when a warrior is healed."

"The hell it isn't," she told him. "I'm—"

Suddenly, she found herself on the floor, one side of her face slowly awakening to the pain of the blow she had never seen coming. Her mouth was filling with the warm, metallic taste of blood.

The intruder was standing above her, looking down.

Flexing the fingers of his right hand—the one he'd used to strike her.

Somewhere off in the enclosure, there were cries and the sounds of a scuffle. Pulaski propped herself up on one arm to get an idea of what was happening. What she saw wrenched at her stomach.

Toc'tu. He had gotten up from his cot—no doubt, to come to her aid. But a couple of his burly fellow patients were holding him back, keeping him from going after her assailant. And in his weakened state, he couldn't shake them loose. Finally, exhausted, he slumped back against his cot.

"Now, then," said the lordly one, walking past Pulaski as if she were part of the furniture. "Let us proceed without further delay." He surveyed the ranks of the wounded, selected half a dozen more. Obediently, they rose and fell into line.

Nor did anyone else offer opposition. The meds were as docile as the patients.

But why? Pulaski asked herself. There are so many of us, and only one of *him*. Why does he inspire such fear?

She caught sight of the holster on the intruder's hip, and the pommel that protruded from it. Instinct told her it was a weapon.

Was *that* the reason no one wanted to move against him?

She licked her lips, which were starting to swell up on the side where she'd been hit. The lordly one was standing with his back to her now; she could see the braid of dark hair that fell halfway to his belt.

If she moved fast enough, she told herself, she could *get* that weapon.

But if she didn't . . .

The idea scared the hell out of her. It made her stomach tighten into a small, painful knot. And yet, *someone* had to do something. These wounded wouldn't stand a chance under the rigors of combat. And she had worked too hard to save them to see them sacrificed now.

Slowly, she gathered herself, got to her feet. En route to the exit, some of the warriors she'd tried to protect filed past her—a couple of them limping, another cradling a wounded arm.

Pulaski waited until they were past, made sure the intruder was still looking in the other direction. Holding her breath, she focused on her target and lunged.

But the lordly one was too fast for her. Whirling with a flash of golden eyes, he grabbed her wrist before her fingers could close on the pommel. Then, twisting hard, he flung her onto an empty cot.

The pain in her wrist was excruciating—but after a moment, it began to subside. When he glared at her, she was able to return the expression in kind.

"You never give up," he said. "Do you?"

She didn't give him the satisfaction of a reply.

"Be thankful," he told her, "that your hands are so skilled, and your skills are so necessary. Otherwise, I'd make sure you never had the use of them again."

With that, he gestured, and the remainder of those he'd selected left the enclosure. He waited until the last one was gone, then—with one last look at the strange, defiant med—he followed the warriors through the opening.

After that, there was silence for a time. No one seemed to want to move, not even to breathe. Was that shame that hung so thick in the air?

Finally, one of the other meds came over to her. It was a female, the one with the plume of pale yellow feathers on her otherwise bald skull.

"Come," she said. "Let's see to that wrist."

A little grudgingly, Pulaski allowed her to tend to it.

Will Riker sat bolt upright in his bed, the darkness swimming all around him. It took him a moment to clear his head of sleep—and as sleep ebbed, the events of the last several days rushed in to fill the breach.

Vaguely, he remembered giving in to Troi's admonishments. Swearing to himself that he'd only take a short nap and be back on the bridge again in a few hours. But as he lay in bed now, staring at the ceiling, he knew it had been no short nap.

"Computer—what time is it?"

A velvety female voice delivered the response: "Oh-eight-hundred hours, thirty-two minutes."

Great. He'd far exceeded the time he'd had in mind. Apparently, he'd forgotten to program his wake-up call.

Riker yawned—just as another memory popped to the surface, bobbed there insistently. Was that a beeping he'd heard before? Was *that* what had woken him up—or had he only dreamed it?

Then it went off again—indisputably real this time—and reflex took over. Flipping the blanket aside, he swiveled around and stood up, mother-naked. Immediately, the coolness of his cabin—a preference that went back to his Alaskan upbringing—shivered him the rest of the way to wakefulness.

"Lights," he called out, and blinked against the sudden illumination. As his eyes adjusted, he padded across the floor, got his robe out of the closet and wrapped the thing around him.

What could it be? he wondered. Something wrong with the ship? All they needed now was a malfunction—as if they didn't have enough problems.

And why had someone come in person? Wouldn't it have been quicker to raise him on the intercom?

Of course, if it was bad news . . . No one liked to communicate that over a monitor. Was that it? Bad news about the captain—and the others?

Shrugging off a growing sense of dread, Riker called out again: "Come." Then wondered a little at his choice of words. Wasn't that Picard's line?

The door slid aside and Data entered from the corridor. He had a portable hologram generator tucked under one arm.

"What is it?" asked the first officer. "What's wrong?"

Data cocked his head and looked at him. "Wrong?" he echoed.

"Wrong," said Riker, realizing with a flood of relief that his worst fears had been unfounded. "I mean, you must have had a reason for waking me—didn't you?"

The android seemed to notice the human's mode of dress for the first time. "Oh. I see. I have interrupted your slumber. I did not realize." He frowned ever so slightly. "It is just that I thought you would want to see this immediately."

Sometimes Riker wanted to shake him. This was one of those times.

"See *what*, Data?"

The android indicated an empty table between two chairs. "May I?" he asked.

"Yes. Of course. Go ahead."

"Thank you."

Crossing the cabin, Data placed the hologram generator on the table. Then he pulled out one of the chairs and sat down.

Riker deposited himself in the other one, watched as the android activated the device and established a link with ship's computer. Once that was done, a couple of taps on the undersized keyboard was all it took to call up an image.

And what an image it was.

A battle scene straight out of Earth's Middle Ages. Maces and double-headed axes, swords and suits of body armor. Brutal, violent—yet for all of that, somehow compelling.

It was only then that he noticed that the image was two-dimensional. He had been so intent on the subject matter, he'd completely overlooked its format.

He looked up at Data. "Where did you get this? And what is it?"

"In accordance with your orders," said the android, "we have been monitoring all broadcast communications on A'klah. This is one of the images we recorded. As for what it represents . . ." His voice trailed off uncharacteristically. "At first, I speculated that the images were computer-simulations—perhaps of historical events, which would have explained the use of primitive weapons and tactics. Then I used our scanners to monitor activity in the areas where the broadcasts originated. It soon became apparent that they were transmissions of real events—as they were happening."

The scene shifted to the battlements of a stone fortress. There was no fighting here—only a sense of vigilance. But once again, all the figures depicted wore full suits of armor.

"It then occurred to me," said Data, "that these broadcasts might be journalistic in nature. Coverage of actual and ongoing border disputes—a theory supported by scenes such as this one, wherein territory is watched and defended. After all, it is not uncommon for neo- and post-nuclear cultures to turn to pre-nuclear forms of warfare—usually to settle territorial quarrels among various geopolitical entities."

"But?" prodded Riker, sensing that the android was about to list examples.

"There was evidence to the contrary. To begin with, the mode of warfare was a little *too* primitive. Beyond that, the forces in each conflict zone were employed haphazardly. I could detect no concerted efforts to achieve victory over opposing forces. Only isolated skirmishes, which ultimately achieved nothing. Finally, there was the manner in which events were recorded—as if the agency charged with recording them could *predict* their eventual outcome."

The android tapped in a new code and the image changed again. Now they were watching some sort of ambush-in-the-making. One group lay belly-down on a cliff, waiting for another group to pass beneath it.

"In this instance," said Data, "we have by turns followed the adventures of both groups—long before we knew that they would meet. Yet to concentrate on these two parties, out of all the possible subjects in the zone, those directing the broadcast must have known the outcome ahead of time."

Riker nodded. "And the reason no one warns the party about to be ambushed—no general, or anything like that—is because it's meant to happen. Is that what you're saying? That it's staged, in some sense?" He snapped his fingers. "Like . . . like a theatrical event?"

"Precisely," said the android. "At one time, possibly, these Conflicts represented real disputes. Then they came to serve this other purpose, and their original intent became secondary—if, indeed, it is still of any importance at all."

The first officer paused to digest it all. "All right," he said finally. "It all seems to fit—except for the soldiers themselves. What's their incentive? Not patriotism, obviously. Who would want to risk their life in an entertainment?" He massaged his temple with a forefinger, then answered his own question. "Money, then. The combatants must be mercenaries. Or slaves—fighting for their freedom? That's the way it worked in ancient Rome."

Data waited patiently for him to finish. His amber eyes seemed to take on a strange cast—one Riker couldn't decipher, not even after all the time they'd spent together since the human joined the *Enterprise*.

"I too considered these possibilities," said the android. "Until I saw *this*."

Tap. Tap tap. His long, slender fingers worked the keyboard of the hologram generator.

The tableau that materialized was one of pure carnage. The aftermath of a bloody encounter.

There was one figure in the foreground—a corpse. A corpse with its helm torn away, its eyes staring at infinity.

A Klingon corpse.

So unprepared was Riker for that sight, so shocked, that he heard his strangled denial even before he knew he'd voiced it.

Then he had time to see the projection more clearly, and

his stomach muscles unclenched. He lowered himself back into his chair.

"I know," said Data. "At first glance, I also feared that it was Worf. Then I realized—as you have, sir—that it was not." He gazed at the hang-jaw-dead visage, and Riker thought he understood now the hardness in the android's eyes. "Nonetheless, this told me something—that at least *some* of the combatants are not native to A'klah. Of course, I have since discovered this to be a gross underestimation. In all the hours of broadcasts I observed, I saw not a single native A'klahn."

Riker grunted. Then that was it—that was the answer.

"Our people," he said, "have been pressed into service— *drafted*. To provide a diversion for the Klah'kimmbri."

Data nodded. "So it would seem."

Riker's throat constricted. He felt his cheeks growing hot.

"The arrogance of these people," he muttered. "The *damned* arrogance. To whisk unoffending crews off their own ships . . ." He found himself unable to express what he was feeling. Anger? Resentment? Embarrassment? All of the above?

The dead Klingon just stared at him.

Data went on. "However, this knowledge only clouded the issue of motivation for me. If it was difficult to understand why the Klah'kimmbri would want to participate in these events . . . it was even more difficult to understand why our *own* people would do it."

Tap tap. Tap. Mercifully, the image of the Klingon fled. It was replaced by that of a small, sledlike hovervehicle. It had but one occupant—a Klah'kimmbri in rather elaborate military garb. Almost as elaborate, in fact, as that worn by the High Councillors themselves. Nor did the sled rider display a single stitch of armor.

Arrogance, thought Riker. It's in everything they do.

"These individuals serve as a sort of police force," said Data. "They seek out individuals who have deviated from

131

prescribed behavior—and use weapons not unlike our own phaser pistols to inflict punishment. On more than one occasion, I have seen this punishment extended to the point of death."

The first officer tried to appraise the figure dispassionately, but it wasn't easy. "You say this is only part of the answer?"

"Yes, sir."

The sled and its rider gradually grew smaller as the perspective expanded—none of Data's doing, but rather that of the device that originally recorded the action. Now Riker could see what the Klah'kimmbri was hovering over—some sort of supply train, made up of primitive wagons drawn by A'klahn burden-beasts. Each wagon was guided by a driver.

"It appears," said the android, "that a significant number of the conscripts are employed in nonaggressive activities. Such as this one—food supply. Similarly, there are medical personnel, bridge-building crews and the like. All support systems, if you will, for the actual combatants. And all engaged in what must seem—to *them*—to be innocuous, even humanitarian pursuits."

Riker watched the wagons trundle down a mountain path. There were no signs of resistance on the parts of the drivers.

"In other words," he said, "they don't know what they're supporting? They don't actually get to see the combats?"

"The medical groups, of course, have an inkling of what is happening—though they can hardly refuse to help when they are presented with the wounded. The others, for the most part, have no idea. On occasion, a support group will be set upon by an enemy raiding party—and the noncombatants are exposed to the central experience of these conflicts. However, such incidents yield few survivors; the general support population remains essentially ignorant of the bloodshed it makes possible."

For the time being, this particular supply train was safe.

There was no sign of impending disaster. But that didn't mean it wasn't lurking around the next bend.

"As for the combatants themselves," said Data, "they are generally representatives of traditionally belligerent races. I have noted the presence, for example, of Gorn, Pandrilites, Dra'al . . ."

"And Klingons," said Riker, again encouraging brevity.

The android returned his gaze. "Yes. And Klingons. The point, sir, is that only those with a predisposition toward violent confrontation are placed in the role of warrior. Those who would take to the task most naturally."

Riker mulled it over. It would have made for an intriguing case study, if he'd been back at the Academy studying xenology. But this wasn't a chapter in some text—this was *real*. Somewhere down there, his crew mates were in *real* danger.

And anyway, it occurred to him that there was still a piece missing. He said so.

"Let's say," Riker posited, "that all your speculations jibe with what's actually happening down there. That the offworlders find their options limited by these airborne enforcers. And that they're ignorant of what it is they're supporting with their labor, so there's no moral imperative to defy authority. Still—wouldn't a member of a spacefaring culture—and presumably, that covers every off-worlder involved in this thing—place a premium on his or her *freedom?* I mean, even if A'klah were a garden of delights, wouldn't the participants eventually rebel? Make an attempt to escape, to return to the lives they led before the Klah'kimmbri plucked them off their ships?"

He shook his head. "I just don't see how a system like this one could go on for very long. Even threats of pain and death aren't enough to keep so many people in line for very long. At least, not in the history tapes *I've* seen."

Data looked at him. "There may be another factor," he offered.

Riker returned the look. "Such as?"

"A behavioral anomaly that I have noted in the course of my research. But its significance has thus far eluded me. I cannot seem to put my thumb on it."

For the first time since the android had barged in on him, Riker smiled.

"No," he said. "Not your thumb, Data. Your finger. You can't put your *finger* on it."

The android's eyes opened just a little wider. "Ah. Of course. My *finger*—the generic term, rather than the specific. I shall endeavor to remember that." A moment later, he had switched back to his discourse mode. "In any case, the fact remains—there is information I cannot interpret."

"Then by all means," said Riker, "call up an example. Let me see what *I* can make of it."

Tap. Tap. Tap. Two figures in the foreground. One lying prone on a table, armored to the waist and naked above it, except for a heavily bandaged shoulder. The wounded one was large and muscular, with the bluish flesh tone of a Pandrilite.

The other foreground figure was a female—slender, with light brown skin and delicate, dark features. A *human.* Apparently, she was the one who had done the bandaging; she was just finishing as they looked on.

"The individual being administered to has been identified as Jorek Tovin—the helmsman of the *Gregor Mendel,*" said Data. "The other individual is Dani Orbutu, listed as zoologist and second medical . . ."

Riker stopped him. *"Orbutu?* Are you sure of that?"

The android confirmed it. "Why, sir?"

The first officer realized he was on the verge of betraying the captain's confidence. "It's nothing. Sorry to interrupt."

Data picked up as if he'd never left off. "Note that even though they occasionally glance at one another, they do not converse. They served on the same ship, yet they have nothing to say to each other."

Riker considered that. "Perhaps conversation is prohibited."

"A logical assumption," said Data. "Yet my studies have shown that this is not the case. The conscripts seem free to speak with one another almost whenever and wherever they please. And the medical facilities are no exception."

Riker leaned closer to get a better look. "Can you amplify the woman's face for me?" he asked.

The android complied. The projection flickered for the briefest instant, and then Dani Orbutu's attractive countenance filled it from edge to edge. Of course, the quality of the image suffered as a result—he could now see the individual lines of color that comprised it.

But it was clear enough to show him what he needed to see. Specifically, her eyes.

There was no recognition in them. Not even when she looked directly at her crew mate's face. Mostly, she seemed distant. Preoccupied.

Lost. As if she'd forgotten something—something important.

Like . . . *who she was.*

Riker squirmed a little at the thought. "Could it be," he asked, "that they no longer know each other? That they've been deprived somehow of those memories?"

Data's eyes grew larger than normal. Under other circumstances, Riker might have thought it comical.

"Of course," said the android. "If they did not *remember* serving on the *Mendel* together . . . they would hardly have a *reason* to converse. They would seem as strange to one another as any other two beings in the conflict zones." His brow creased again. "But then, the same would be true of our away team. Even if they met, they would not know each other. Not even on the field of battle."

Suddenly, the room was too cold for even Riker's liking.

Up close, the edifice seemed even more ominous, more foreboding than at a distance. The walls, constructed of large blocks of dun-colored stone, were taller than he had guessed. The only gates were made of a metal as dark as the stone; they were barely big enough, Picard estimated, to permit a wagon and its driver to pass through. That is, if the driver were not too tall, and if he didn't mind hunching over a bit.

The sky above the structure was dirty, the terrain around it dull and colorless. Altogether, not a cheerful picture.

He hadn't seen the figures on the wall for quite some time—not since their path had twisted down and then up again in their approach to the place. From the drivers' present perspective, someone would have had to poke their head over the edge of the barrier to be seen.

But the last glimpse he'd gotten of them had been curious indeed. For they had been dressed in hard, bulky garb—not at all like the plain homespun the drivers wore. And their faces were obscured by some sort of half-masked headgear.

Why? What for? Not against the weather, certainly; the drivers weren't freezing even in their simple tunics and cloaks. For protection, then? Against what?

Picard considered those questions in the light of last night's discussion with Ralak'kai. After most of the drivers had gone to sleep, huddled against their wagons or whatever better shelter they could find, he and the golden-eyed one had stirred the fire's embers and talked.

"But why, Picard? Why would anyone live in so isolated a place? There are no rivers to nurture it, no fertile fields, no forests full of game. It is as desolate a location as one can imagine. So I ask you again: why?"

Picard had shrugged. *"Perhaps whoever lives there has been isolated for a reason. Perhaps they are . . . diseased. Or deranged. Or in some other way dangerous to a larger population."* He'd grunted. *"Not a happy prospect for us, eh?"*

"No. Not a happy prospect at all." Ralak'kai had paused then, peering in the direction of their destination—though one couldn't see much under the overcast sky. *"And yet, my*

friend, I don't think it's here for any of those reasons. I have a feeling that there's another purpose to it entirely."

"Such as?"

"You saw those figures on the wall, didn't you? They seemed to be guarding something, did they not?"

"Yes. They did."

"They were looking outward—not inward. As if they were more concerned about someone coming in than someone going out."

"I noticed that—but I believed it was us they were looking for. In anticipation of the supplies we're carrying. Or just for the sake of something to do."

At the time, Ralak'kai had nodded and said no more. That explanation had appeared to make sense.

Now, Picard wasn't so sure.

He was less than a hundred meters from the gates, and still they remained closed. If there had been a sense of anticipation about the supply train's arrival, wouldn't someone have come out by now to hail them? At the very least, would the gates not have swung aside to give them access?

Unless Ralak'kai had been correct, and that which the sentinels were guarding against was *outside* the walls. Suddenly uneasy, Picard took a quick look around. But there was nothing dangerous to be found. No wild animals, no weather aberrations.

There weren't even any marshals in the vicinity.

Turning his attention to the edifice again, he noticed something else. The stones immediately around the gates were scarred—as if someone had struck them repeatedly with something hard and sharp and heavy. In fact, as he got closer, he saw that the gates themselves were marked with any number of dents and more than a couple of sizable depressions. Without question, someone had been trying to get into this place.

That would make it a fortress—wouldn't it? An installation designed to defend against hostile forces.

The more Picard thought about it, the more that sounded

right. After all, there could hardly be a site easier to safeguard against an enemy. Nothing but sheer slopes and precipices all about, and the only approach a narrow one—much to the drivers' chagrin.

But if all this were true, what was the fortress guarding? Surely, not territory. This was the far end of the valley, a cul-de-sac.

Something inside, then? A treasure of sorts, which could not be guarded as well in the midst of a more densely populated milieu?

And whatever it was the fortress guarded—*who* was it being guarded from? Who had inflicted those scars on the gates in their desire to win inside?

Even as Picard turned these matters over and over in his mind, he saw a small plate in one of the doors slide aside. He was no more than thirty meters from them now; those within could hardly have waited any longer.

"Stop there," came a voice, deep and brusque.

Picard complied, drawing in on the reins with a firm but gentle hand. Down the line, he knew, the other drivers were following suit.

A moment later, one of the gates creaked open and half a dozen figures slipped out. One was very tall, at least a head and a half bigger than Picard. The others fell somewhat short of their companion in height, but not in girth. They were all broad, powerful looking, intimidating.

And all of them were dressed in that strange, bulky garb. Picard could see now what it was—a kind of flexible armor. Their helmets, which allowed only slits for their eyes, were made of something else—some sort of metal. Nor was that the extent of their protection.

Each one also had a weapon strapped to his back—either a mace or an ax or a broadsword. As the tall one approached, he released his weapon and took it in his gauntleted hand.

But he made no threatening move, so Picard sat where he was. And suffered the giant's approach.

"We need to check your wagons," said the tall one. His voice was high-pitched and flutelike—a little unexpected in one so huge. Picard was almost inclined to chuckle at it, but he decided to practice discretion under the circumstances. "You will remove yourself and stand off to one side."

"As you wish," said the human. He hopped down from his seat and retreated a few paces—all the path would allow. At the next wagon, driven by Ralak'kai, the same procedure was taking place.

What was this about? Picard wondered. He caught Ralak'kai's eye, and the other driver shrugged. Apparently, he had no idea either.

Only the tall one had lingered at Picard's wagon. He took hold of one of the straps that held the cargo-protecting tarpaulin in place and, with an enormous wrench, snapped it in two. The tarp seemed to know it was free; it expanded like a living, breathing thing.

Weapon still in hand, the tall one moved to draw the covering off altogether. But before he could do so, something happened—something so quick and unanticipated that it was over before Picard knew what was going on.

A second later, the tall one was lying motionless on the ground, his helmet half-crushed. And the pair who had sprung from the back of Picard's wagon—also armored, also armed—were sprinting for the still-open gate.

At each of the foremost wagons, it was the same thing. Guards surprised and cut down, their assailants pelting hell-bent in the direction of the fortress walls. Farther down the trail, there were even more of them.

And all along, Picard realized, they had been hiding in the wagons. Hiding in *his* wagon. Since when? Late last night, after he and Ralak'kai had finally quit their discussions and dozed off? Or early morning, just before the drivers woke?

He could scarcely believe what he was seeing. It had a strange sense of unreality to it. Yet the guards must have known that something like this was possible—otherwise, why stop the wagons outside the walls? They just hadn't expected the raiders to be so numerous—or they would have sent out a larger contingent.

Picard watched, fascinated, as the invaders clashed at the gate with a knot of defenders who'd come out to meet them. At first, it was more or less an even fight. The raiders were unable to force their way in, and the defenders were unable to force them out. Axes and bludgeons rose and fell; there were screams of anguish and bodies flung to the ground, but the casualties were on both sides.

Then, as more and more of the newcomers clustered at the entrance, the situation changed. The battle started to go their way. And suddenly, like a river tearing apart a poorly made dam, they poured in through the open gate—leaving the dead and the dying and a couple of isolated combats in their wake.

It was gruesome, awful, stomach-sickening. And yet, he couldn't seem to tear his eyes away from the sheer savagery of the spectacle.

Feeling a pressure on his arm, Picard sought its source. He found himself looking into Ralak'kai's face—a study in urgency.

"Let's go," said the golden-eyed one. "While their attention is elsewhere."

The human shook off the spell of the battle and allowed Ralak'kai to drag him away. "Yes," he said, understanding that either side might be feeling antagonism for the drivers at this point. "By all means, let's get out of here."

They didn't have the luxury of a great many options. The only route open to them was to retreat down the trail they had ascended. Nor were they thinking beyond that, of what to do next. For now, it would be enough to put distance between themselves and the fortress.

Unfortunately for them, one of the raiders had other ideas. As they cut a path between the wagons and the dizzying brink at the path's edge, he placed himself squarely in their way.

"Where do you think *you're* going?" he growled.

"Look," cried Picard, pointing suddenly over the warrior's shoulder.

Fate was merciful. The armored one followed his gesture without thinking. And as he did, Picard turned the incline of the trail to his advantage. With all the force he could muster, he plowed into the warrior, knocked him off his feet—and kept on going.

He could hear Ralak'kai a few paces behind him—and up ahead, the path was clear. It appeared that they might make it after all. Perhaps, if the other drivers followed their lead, they might *all* make it.

Then, out of the corner of his eye, Picard caught a flurry of motion on the side where the wagons were. Too late, he tried to avoid the dark thing that came whistling at his head.

There was a moment of great and terrible pain. And afterward, oblivion.

Chapter Twelve

IT WAS ON his way home from work, two days after the incident in the tavern, that Dan'nor saw his father again. One moment, he was walking alone; the next, Trien'nor was walking beside him.

"Come," said the older man, looking straight ahead. "We'll walk down to the wharf. You know where it is?"

"Yes." Dan'nor watched his father's face, more accessible now even in the flat, sunset light than it had been in the tavern's back room. It had been a long time since he'd seen Trien'nor, but the man showed no signs of having aged. Pure First Caste blood had its advantages.

However, there *was* something different about him. Something that had been missing in the simple, unambitious factory clerk who had raised him—the man who'd spent so much time looking out the window with that sad little smile on his face.

He was almost . . . *Military*. Was that it? Yes. For the first time, Dan'nor could picture his father in a uniform—a young, proud First Caster with a shining future.

Was there a connection between this and Trien'nor's skulking in the shadows? Dan'nor shivered when he remembered the faces around that room, and the way his father's seemed to fit among them.

"You've changed," he said, the words coming out of their own volition.

Trien'nor smiled a thin smile but didn't respond otherwise. Their heels made a soft scraping sound on the pavement.

"What's happened to you?" he asked. "What were you doing with those men?"

Again, no answer.

Dan'nor decided to try another tack. "How did you find me?"

Trien'nor shrugged. "You can probably answer that for yourself." A pause. "I have ways of finding things out."

It was almost more evasive than no answer at all.

As they got closer to the river, the breeze picked up. It swept Trien'nor's hair back—the red hair of an aristocrat. Dan'nor had inherited the color of it but not its agelessness; his was just beginning to show threads of silver.

"So," said the older man, at last turning to his son. "It seems you are no longer in the Military." The words were gentle, unoffensive. However, his eyes—pale gold like those of his forebears—seemed to probe where the words could not.

"I was . . . *ousted,*" said Dan'nor. Even now, it wasn't easy to say the word. "My own fault, I'm afraid."

"Care to tell me about it?"

Dan'nor told him, leaving out only the most insignificant details. When he had finished, he somehow felt better about it. It still hurt, but the pain no longer had an edge to it.

"You were unlucky," said Trien'nor, "that's all. No less efficient, no less cautious than anyone else would have been in the same position. Just in the wrong place at the wrong time."

The Military had never been a topic of discussion between them. What little he knew of Trien'nor's aborted career he had learned from his mother.

And yet, here they were—discussing Military matters. It felt strange—but no stranger than the rest of this conversation.

They came to the bottom of the hill and the river narrowed to a dark blue violet band—a reflection of the deepening sky. The wharf was a few blocks down on their right; Dan'nor's flat was to the left, past the tavern and over the footbridge.

"Perhaps," he said, "we could go to my place instead. Or at least stop there first—to turn on the videoscreen."

Trien'nor shook his head. "Don't worry about it. Lots of people miss an evening at home to see the Conflicts in the taverns. As long as you don't do it too often, no one at the Viewership Service will think twice about it."

Dan'nor hesitated. Something inside him wondered if he could trust that advice.

And then he almost laughed. *This is my* father, he told himself. *A little different, maybe, but still my father. If I can't trust* him, *who can I trust?*

He stifled his doubts.

They turned to the right and walked along the water. On the other side, downriver and beyond the buildings, clouds were gathering. The dying sun, slipping out of sight, painted them in dusky reds and pinks. The river's version of the clouds made them look darker—like blood.

Trien'nor muttered something beneath his breath. Dan'nor couldn't make it out very well, but the Viewership Service seemed to be at the heart of the matter.

The older man shook his head. "Do you remember the Two Rules?" he asked.

Dan'nor dredged them out of memory. They came up easily—so easily it surprised him.

"Yes," he said. "I believe I do."

"Rule One," said Trien'nor. "That which is withheld is more greatly desired. Things are more precious in small quantities."

Dan'nor was about to recite the second rule, but suddenly he felt ridiculous. After all, he was no longer a child.

When he saw his son's reluctance, Trien'nor voiced the second rule as well. "That which costs nothing is worth nothing. Something of true value is always expensive."

It was a game they had played when Dan'nor was young. A cryptic sort of game, the meaning of which had always escaped him.

Now, at long last, he thought he'd figured it out. "Is *that* what the Rules were about?" he asked. *"Viewership?"*

Trien'nor shrugged a second time. "Certainly, viewership is a good example. If they let us watch the Conflicts all day and all night, we would quickly tire of them. But by doling them out only at certain times, they keep us hungry—eager for the next viewership period."

"And the second Rule," said Dan'nor, "would apply to the viewership fee."

"A fee," added his father, "which most of us can't afford. But if it were any less costly, we might not look on it as such a luxury—such a thing to look forward to."

Dan'nor nodded. It was twilight now. The clouds had lost their color; they were nearly as dark as the rest of the sky. In the east, there were faint stars.

The breeze had just shifted, and the stench of the river was all around them. It was thick with dead fish and garbage and factory waste.

"But you say viewership is only an *example,*" continued the younger man. "The Rules apply to something else as well?"

Trien'nor seemed to hesitate before speaking. And when he finally broke the silence, it was with a question of his own.

"Why did you join the Military?"

Dan'nor looked at him. It seemed that he should have been able to snap out an answer—but it wasn't quite that simple. Nor, when he finally came up with one, was it easy to voice it to the man beside him.

145

"I suppose," he said, "because I thought it was something I had lost—*we* had lost—when you chose to marry my mother. It was something I felt I had a right to."

Trien'nor nodded. "Fair enough," he said. He gave no indication that he had taken offense—to Dan'nor's relief. "And if I had not left the Military? If I had married a woman of my own Caste, become powerful enough to grant you a high-ranking position as soon as you came of age?"

Dan'nor had never thought about it.

"Would your drive to achieve have been as great?" pressed his father.

The younger man pondered the question. "I don't know," he said. "Perhaps not."

"Perhaps not," repeated Trien'nor. "But it was withheld from you—so you desired it. And once you had your first small taste of success . . . you desired it all the more."

The words sounded awfully familiar. "Rule One," said Dan'nor.

"Yes. Rule One. And now, another question: what did you pay for your success?"

Dan'nor didn't understand. It must have showed in his face.

"Payment may come in any number of forms," explained his father. "Money is but one. Anything one gives up to achieve something else may be considered payment. So the question becomes: what did you give up? What did you lose that you had before?"

Now Dan'nor saw the direction in which Trien'nor was headed. Or thought he did.

"My family," he answered. *"You."*

It was no less than the truth. An implicit condition of Dan'nor's acceptance into the Military had been his estrangement from his past—from his Lower Caste mother and—even more importantly—from his father. He had had to deny his heritage to show that he wouldn't do what his father had done.

Dan'nor had expected the older man to acknowledge his answer—and go on with his speech. He was unprepared for the sudden pain he saw in his father's face—the look of utter vulnerability.

It was an expression Dan'nor might have expected from that supremely contained man who'd spent so much time staring out the window. But not from the man he had just been talking to. The transformation was shocking and somehow comforting at the same time.

It took Trien'nor a moment to recover. And when he did, the lost look was gone. "Gods," he said. "I hadn't even thought of that." A beat. "I meant what was lost of *you*. The ability to look at things with your own eyes—and not those of the Military. To see beyond the prescribed goals and behaviors—to the truth."

Something stiffened inside Dan'nor. "What do you mean?" he asked. "That I don't look out for myself? Because I *do*."

Trien'nor shook his head. "No. You *think* you do. But while you pursue what you believe are your own purposes, your own ambitions—you're really pursuing *theirs*. You have innocently become just another cog in the Military machine." He sighed. "Just as I was."

Silence for a moment. The raucous cries of hungry birds wheeling over the river.

"You're bitter," said Dan'nor, "about Mother's death. That's why you're talking this way. That's why you've joined those men who sit whispering in the dark."

The wharf was just ahead. Past it, they could see the silhouettes of empty fishing vessels rocking gently in their slips.

"No," said Trien'nor. There was a tinge of anger in his voice, though his face did not betray it. "It is not bitterness. I felt this way *before* your mother's death—long before." He licked his patrician lips. "Your mother told you, no doubt, that I was aware of the penalty if I married her."

"Yes," said Dan'nor. "She told me."

"At the time," said Trien'nor, "I thought my sacrifice was based entirely on my love for her. And certainly, I loved her very much. But there was more to it than that. I had seen things I could not abide—in the Conflicts, in the world. And most of all, in myself. I could no longer be a part of those things. Yet I also could not fight them—or so I believed at the time. So I took the coward's way out. I married your mother, and forced the Military to separate me from the things I couldn't tolerate."

Dan'nor heard the words, and began to understand what that staring out the window had been about. A searching— not for lost opportunities, as he'd sometimes thought, but for courage.

Now, apparently, Trien'nor had found it. But where was it leading him?

"Of course, I did not realize any of this until after her death. But once I did, it opened my eyes. I saw that there were others around me who felt the same way I did. And who wished to *do* something about it."

The younger man didn't like the sound of that. He said so. "You can't defy the authorities. They'll crush you—no matter how many of you there are."

Trien'nor laughed. It was not a particularly pleasant sound. "You're wrong. The authorities are much more fragile than one might think. It's just that no one has ever challenged them."

Dan'nor regarded him. "And *you* plan to do that?"

His father shrugged. They came to the planked walkway that led down to the riverside. It was too narrow for them to walk shoulder to shoulder, so Trien'nor went first.

"You watch the Conflicts," he said, offering it to Dan'nor over his shoulder. It was more a statement of fact than a question.

"I put them on," amended Dan'nor. "But I don't always watch them."

"Do you see anything different about them?"

Dan'nor thought about it as he descended. A bird dove perilously close to the walkway and disappeared beneath it.

Come to think of it, he *had* noticed something. "The battles seem to be getting bigger. Bloodier. Is that what you mean?"

Trien'nor glanced back at him. "Exactly." He grunted. "You've seen it too, then. That's a good sign."

"Of what?" asked the younger man.

But his father seemed not to have heard. "Did you notice any unusual combatants?" he asked. Trien'nor reached the wharf level and turned. "Anyone out of the ordinary?"

Dan'nor wanted his question answered first. But this was his father's game. It had been since he first made his appearance.

"No. I mean, aren't they *all* out of the ordinary?" He joined Trien'nor on the wharf and they began to walk again. Beside them, the river murmured in its own slow, dark language.

"You'd have recognized this one," said the older man. "He's a Klah'kimmbri."

Dan'nor searched his father's face. But there was no sign of dissembling there. No sign of a joke either.

"What do you mean?" he asked. "How would a Klah'kimmbri have gotten into the Conflicts?"

Trien'nor's eyes narrowed. "Simple. They put him there. He's a political criminal and they have chosen this as his punishment."

Dan'nor shook his head. "Come on. The last Klah'kimmbri soldier came home sixty years ago. It's unthinkable that it could happen today."

"Why?" asked his father. "Because it would be barbaric? And yet, we don't hesitate to subject off-worlders to the same barbarism—do we? We call them criminals for having trespassed in the space around our planet, and then we take away their memories so that they do not know otherwise.

That's the kind of people we have become—ready to overlook slavery and wrongful death if it serves our ends. Or rather, our Council's ends. But there is something more offensive, you think, in all of this happening to a Klah'kimmbri?"

"Of course." The reason came to Dan'nor a moment later. "Because if it could happen to one of us, it could happen to all of us."

Trien'nor nodded. "You're right. And that's the reason it offends me, too. You see, there *is* a Klah'kimmbri among the combatants. I can even tell you his name: Ralak'kai. And the reason I can do this is because, just a few weeks ago, he was whispering in that dark room along with the rest of us."

Ralak'kai. Dan'nor had heard the name spoken by Trien'nor's friends before he'd been discovered outside the door.

"And they arrested him for *that?*"

His father shook his head. "Not just for that. There was a matter of sabotage as well. A factory—one owned by Councilor Fidel'lic. It was temporarily disabled."

"Gods!" blurted Dan'nor. "Is that the kind of thing in which you're involved?"

Trien'nor smiled his First Caste smile. "Yes. It is. So you see, Ralak'kai's fate has a special meaning for me."

Suddenly, Dan'nor had a feeling he was being watched. He darted a glance behind him—but there was nothing there. Only the birds, gliding on the foul air over the river.

"Don't worry," said his father. "We're safe here."

Dan'nor looked at him. "How do you know that? How can you be safe anywhere while you're part of . . ." He lowered his voice self-consciously. "Part of *that?*"

"Because," said Trien'nor, "we watch the watchers. And we know that they don't watch *here.*"

The younger man believed him. Was it something in his voice? In any case, it calmed him a little.

"You see?" said Trien'nor. "The authorities can be dealt

with. They're not all-powerful—and they know it. That's the reason they conscripted Ralak'kai. They want to make an example of him. So that *we* will fear *them* as much as *they* fear *us.*"

Dan'nor's knees were feeling weak. He found a seat on a weathered wooden bench.

"And there will be more like him. Those who've committed similar acts of rebellion over the years—worse acts, perhaps. They'll turn up in the Conflicts, one by one, until we all get the message."

Dan'nor felt as if his whole world were turning upside down. It was more serious than he'd thought—*much* more serious. And it wasn't a stranger speaking of his involvement. This was his *father.*

"At the same time, this solves another of the Council's problems. You know those bigger, bloodier battles you mentioned? They're the Council's way of fighting a decline in viewership. And it has always worked for them in the past. But now, it seems, they're having trouble bringing viewership back up. So the battles are getting even bigger, even bloodier. Also, a good deal more frequent. The result? The ranks of the combatants are being depleted at an alarming rate. The Council needs a new source of bodies— and they've found it in men like Ralak'kai."

Dan'nor shook his head, tried to think straight. His father's ideas seemed to expand in his brain, to crowd out any others.

"Did you ever wonder," asked Trien'nor, "why it is necessary for people to work in the factories? In a world where we can transform light into deadly force—or snatch aliens off their distant ships, atom by atom—why is it we can't create machines to make our shoes?" The water lapped at the wooden pylons that supported the wharf. "Because then the people would have time on their hands. Time to think, to consider. And to wonder why there must be such a thing as the Council."

It was the truth, of course. Dan'nor knew it. But it was a *dangerous* truth, razor-sharp and stained with other people's blood.

"The Conflicts," said his father, "are supposed to do the same thing—to distract us from our subjugation. To siphon off the energy of our minds as the factories leech the energy of our bodies. The Conflicts *enslave* us. And now, with the conscription of Ralak'kai, that enslavement has taken on a much more literal dimension."

The younger man looked up. It seemed to him that Trien'nor looked placid as he sat there. Almost serene. The councillors he'd seen were only a parody of stoicism compared to his father.

In the distance, a boat was approaching from downriver—a shadowy hulk with lights fore and aft, casting tiny brightnesses into the water. It had to be a cargo vessel; it was much too big to be a passenger ship.

"Why are you telling me this?" asked Dan'nor.

But then, he'd known the answer to that all along—hadn't he? From the first moment he'd recognized his father walking beside him.

"Because," said Trien'nor, "I need your help. We're planning something important—something difficult—and something much more dangerous than that for which Ralak'kai was jailed. But to do it, we'll need more hands and hearts than we currently have available. And experience in the Military certainly won't hurt."

Dan'nor muttered a curse. The madness of it all threatened to overpower him. The sheer insanity of a world where he could even be *asked* to do such a thing.

"Don't say any more," he told Trien'nor. "I'm not like you. I'm not a skulker—and I never will be."

His father fixed him with his gaze. "You're more like me than you can imagine. You're like I *was*. Proud, stubborn, ambitious—always looking for a way to improve your lot at the expense of someone else. And yet, deep down, you know that it's wrong. That your life, your ambition, is based on a terrible lie. And whether you believe it or not, this had as much to do with your ouster as the so-called facts that prompted it."

Dan'nor breathed in, breathed out. The river smell was sharp and pungent in his nostrils.

"No," was all he could get out. And then: "I can't."

"Two threads in the fabric of oppression," said the older man. "The thread of the Conflicts, the thread of our servitude. I offer you a chance to fray them both—to start the unraveling."

Dan'nor let his head drop between his shoulders. He stared at his shoes, as if he could find some wisdom there.

Trien'nor got up. He came over, put a hand on his son's shoulder. Dan'nor couldn't remember the last time he'd done that.

"It's all right," he said. "Courage was a long time coming to me, too. It's all right. Really."

The younger man looked up then and saw the strain around those perfect golden eyes. There was an emotion there that had nothing to do with justice or conspiracies or Councils.

"Listen," said Trien'nor. "I want you to be careful—*very* careful. The other night, in the tavern, the others wanted to kill you. They thought you were a spy; I knew you weren't, because no Military man would have gone in there unarmed. But if you *had* been a spy . . . if you had threatened our movement and the lives of those in it . . . I would not have intervened."

Dan'nor peered into that face, both familiar and unfamiliar and then familiar again, and understood. This was not a threat. It was the simple concern of a father for his son.

"Since then," Trien'nor continued, "you have been watched. If you had given any indication of going to the authorities, you would have been prevented. If you had only been a little indiscreet, and decided to share your experience with your coworkers . . . again, you would have been stopped. Do you follow what I'm saying?"

Dan'nor nodded.

"Good. Then we will speak no more of this. Maybe we'll see each other again. Who knows?"

With obvious reluctance, the older man took his hand away, and slowly departed, leaving Dan'nor with a heavier burden than he had known could exist.

He watched his father retreat up the walkway, attended by a chorus of screeching birds. And then he was gone.

Every couple of days during the building of the bridge, a runner had come to inspect their progress. The last one had shown up shortly after it was finished. Dressed in dark body-armor and a helmet that extended down over part of his face, he had tested the structure: walked from end to end and back again, pausing to inspect the critical junctures where the wood had been tied together with extra care.

Apparently, he had been satisfied with the quality of their work. Not that he had said anything to that effect. But if he had seen anything amiss, he would no doubt have pointed it out.

With the runner gone and the job done, there seemed to be nothing else for them to do. However, though the bridge was certainly functional, they all knew there was no such thing as a structure that could not be made more secure. So with the materials they had left, they devised ways to build in secondary supports against the unlikely failure of the primaries. Toward this end, they also dragged up the ruins of the earlier bridge and cannibalized it for parts.

When the structure's first real test arrived, Geordi was completing a flexible end-support system he'd anchored in crevices along the cliff face. He resisted the impulse to see what all the commotion was about until he'd tied off the last knot. Then he swung up onto the surface of the span, gratified by the solidity of the wooden planks under his feet.

"What is it?" he asked someone as they rushed by him for a better look.

"Wagons," came the response. "Up there."

Geordi followed the gesture and saw for himself. Sure enough, there *were* wagons—coming over a rise on the other side of the ravine. As he and the others watched, the train strung itself out. Before the rise was vacant again, they'd counted eight of the vehicles.

They were driven by dark, bulky figures, helmed and armored just as the runners were—but bigger than the runners, Geordi thought. He could hear the clatter of their wheels on the rocks now—even over the murmuring of his coworkers, the *shushrush* of the wind.

Would they, at long last, get a chance to see what all their hard work had been about? What purpose the bridge would serve? Geordi hoped so, he really did. It was nice to be able to look at the thing and know he'd had a hand in its construction. But he'd feel even better if he knew what ultimate good it might be supporting.

Before long, the first wagon had trundled out onto the span, and the crowd gradually gave way—either shuffling off to either side or retreating altogether. Geordi was one of those who stayed on the bridge to watch the passage.

Little by little, he got a better look at the first set of drivers. There were two of them, sitting side by side. One actually did the work; the other, apparently, was just along for the ride. As they went by, Geordi noticed that both of them had weapons strapped to their backs.

The runners had had weapons, too—but not quite as big or heavy. Geordi had assumed they were used to ward off wild animals, like the ones that had approached the construction site from time to time—especially at night. Even though the beasts had never actually attacked anyone, that didn't mean they weren't capable of it.

And these wagons might have traveled through places where the animals were more apt to be daring. Enclosed places, maybe, where they could strike from above.

Maybe.

But Geordi wasn't quite convinced. Something in the way the drivers stared at them through their narrow eye slits made him wonder if the weapons might not have another use.

Of course, there would be no point in the drivers' hurting *them*. The builders were there to *help*—they'd made it possible for the wagons to cross the ravine, hadn't they?

He had almost talked himself into a false sense of security when the third wagon passed by him. And he got a look at its cargo.

Whereas the first two vehicles had had their loads under wraps, the third did not. *Could* not. Because its burden was *alive*.

Geordi felt the wind on his face turn cold suddenly as he realized what was in the wagon: *people*. Two beings not unlike himself, each with a pair of arms and a pair of legs. Of course, they didn't wear seeing bands like the one *he* wore—but then, he seemed to be unique in that respect.

The beings were tied together, back to back, sitting upright. As they went by, they returned his gaze—regarded him, it occurred to Geordi, with the same mixture of curiosity and apprehension that *he* felt about *them*.

One of them had a wash of dark, dried blood from his temple to the point of his jaw—though the wound it came from must have been a shallow one because he seemed composed enough. Almost dignified, even in his sorry condition.

The following wagons brought more of the same. Not *every* one, but most of them. In a couple of cases, the prisoners' wounds were grievous ones—to the point where they moaned softly every time their vehicle jolted a little on the rough-hewn planking.

What did it mean? Who were they, that the drivers had trussed them up like this? Where were they going?

As he wondered these things, the *old* questions came back to plague him as well. Once again, he felt the pit yawning before him. Once again, he had to drag himself back from the brink of it—reach out for one of the bridge supports to convince himself that *something* was real.

This is wrong, he thought. These are *people*. They shouldn't be tied up and hauled around—they should be free to serve some purpose.

Then it came to him what *his* purpose had been—to smooth the way for the transportation of these pour souls. To aid and abet their enslavement.

How *wrong* he'd been—how *incredibly* wrong. And yet, when he'd first lent a hand, he'd been so certain that the bridge could be only a *good* thing—as certain as he was now that it was a *bad* thing.

It made him feel dirty—repugnant even to himself.

Geordi looked around. He could see that some of the other workers were discomfited by the sight of the prisoners. But not to the extent that he was. Maybe they'd seen this sort of thing before; maybe they were getting used to it.

As he pondered the question, he saw that the lead wagon had found a slope it could negotiate, and was stopping in an area of high ground. Its drivers got out to stretch their limbs as the next wagon pulled up alongside them.

Geordi peered up at the sky, noted the placement of the sun in it. It would be dark soon. And the terrain that lay ahead of the wagons might be even less accommodating than what they'd seen here.

When the third wagon came to rest beside the first two, with its living cargo, it became obvious that the drivers had decided to camp in this vicinity. To spend the night.

Geordi stayed on the bridge for some time, until the last of the wagons had made its way up the hill. He took pains to note the configuration created by the vehicles, especially the positioning of the ones that carried the prisoners—though at this point, he still wasn't sure what he would do with the knowledge.

"Mutated?" echoed Riker, gazing at Fredi and Vanderventer through the transparent quarantine barrier.

"That's right," said Burtin. "At some point, the organism spawned a strain that our antibiotic can't touch. And this strain, unlike the original bacterium, is contagious—as you can see for yourself."

The first officer grunted. *"How* contagious?"

Burtin sighed. "That's a good question. So far, only Vanderventer's managed to catch it. And he's been in close contact with Fredi for quite some time now. But that doesn't necessarily mean anything. Casual contact could be all that's needed—in which case anyone Vanderventer's seen over the last several days is a candidate to get the disease. Also, anyone *they* came in contact with."

Riker looked at him. "So what you're telling me," he said, "is that just about anybody on the ship could get it. In fact, could have it already."

"Exactly," said Burtin. "That's why I needed to talk to you in person—rather than over the intercom." He tapped on the barrier with a fingernail. "I can handle a dozen cases of this disease—maybe a couple more than that—without too much difficulty. As long as I continue to purge their blood, they'll at least survive. But if this thing really spreads before I can find a cure, I'm going to have problems. There are only so many blood-purification units on board—only so much space in sickbay that can be fit to quarantine standards."

He could see the muscles in Riker's jaw working beneath the surface of his beard. "I think I see what you're getting at," said the first officer. He frowned. "You're requesting that we proceed to the nearest starbase—where they have full-blown research facilities. And a larger supply of blood purifiers. Right?"

"Yes," said Burtin. "Even if we couldn't beam our patients down, for fear of infecting the starbase population, we could still draw on their resources."

Riker pondered that. "And yet, if I do what you're asking—if I leave our present position—I'll be abandoning

Captain Picard and the away team. Not to mention the people we set out to rescue in the first place." His nostrils flared. "You understand that?"

"I do," said the doctor. "Believe me, I do. Remember, Kate Pulaski is one of the missing. But I've got a duty to the population of this ship—the thousand or so people who are still with us. And in line with that duty, I'm making a formal request. Take us out of here, Commander. Before this thing gets too far out of hand."

Riker looked him in the eye. "You're not making matters easy for me," he said.

"I'm doing my job," returned Burtin. "That's what I'm here for."

Riker nodded. "Of course you are. But so far, there's no solid evidence that this could turn into an epidemic. You yourself suggested that prolonged contact may be necessary —in order for the bacterium to be communicated." His eyes narrowed as he mulled it all over. "While the danger to the away team is certain and immediate. If I leave them, there's a good chance they'll have been killed in one of those bloody battles before I can get back."

Burtin remained silent. He had said about all he could. Now it was up to the first officer.

"I think," Riker said finally, "that our best course is to stay put—at least for the time being." He glanced in the direction of Fredi and Vanderventer. "But I want you to keep me posted. Let me know if anyone else comes down with the disease—or if it mutates again. Agreed?"

"Agreed," said Burtin. "However, I'm going to have to file my request in the medical log. That's procedure."

The first officer's expression softened. "I have no problem with that. Do as you see fit, Doctor."

And he turned to go.

"Commander?" said Burtin.

Riker stopped, looked at him over his shoulder.

"Sorry to put you in this position," said the doctor. "I

know we don't know each other very well yet—but I'm not the kind of doctor who can't see the big picture. I know you've got your priorities."

The first officer smiled. "Don't worry about it. You've given me a new sense of urgency. I should thank you."

And with that, he strode out of sickbay—a man with a purpose. The double doors slid closed behind him.

Burtin felt a tightness in his neck; he massaged it.

He had known in advance what Riker's decision would be. He'd likely have made the same one if it had been *him* sitting in the command chair.

Probably, it had been a sign of panic on his part to make his request official. To include it in the log. Would Pulaski have done the same thing—or was he overreacting to something he should have been able to take in stride?

Hell, there was still a chance that he'd find the cure before too long. That is, if he got some work done instead of jawing with the first officer.

Sighing, Burtin headed back to the lab.

Days before, some of Worf's comrades had made an attempt to sneak into the fortress—concealed in the enemy's supply wagons. Apparently, that attempt had failed.

Now, they were using a more straightforward approach: a siege. Various raiding parties—including what was left of his own—had spilled out of the hills and coalesced on the road to this place. Before long, more than a hundred of them had come to hunker down outside the walls, eyeing the fortress as a hunting beast eyes its natural prey.

The ladders arrived not much later, transported in sections on mountain-worthy carts. The carts were driven by scrawny beings who wore no armor and carried no weapons but who put each ladder together before turning around and moving off again.

Worf wondered at the precision of it all, the sense of organization. Who had sent out the runners to gather the troops? Who had arranged for the delivery of the ladders? It was even rumored that a battering ram was on its way—a tale told by the most experienced in the camp, who claimed they'd had occasion to use such a tool in other sieges.

On the other hand, none of them had ever seen an assembly of warriors as large as this one. It was unprecedented, they claimed—unheard of.

"Things are changing," grunted the veteran in Worf's circle, as they dipped their naked hands in the common gruel pot. His name was Harr'h; his tiny pink eyes were barely visible beneath an immense mane of spiky, black hair. He sniffed the wind through the slit that served him as a nose. "If I didn't know it, I could smell it."

Someone leaned forward to scoop out another handful of the thin, tasteless porridge. "What do you mean? Changing *how?*"

Of all those the Klingon had encountered, Harr'h's memory was by far the longest. Certainly, there were veterans who were older than he was, and who looked it. But of everyone in camp, Harr'h had spent the most time *here*—as a warrior.

It garnered him a certain amount of respect.

"We fight more often now," he observed, meeting Worf's gaze for a moment over the gruel pot—another item that had arrived in the wagons. "Also, in bigger groups. There is more death, more blood."

"Is that bad?" asked another in their circle. He laughed a little as he slurped at his food.

Harr'h shrugged. "No, not so bad. Unless you are one of the dead—and you are not quite ready for paradise."

Worf thought he caught a note of disapproval in the veteran's tone. Perhaps even a veiled warning. But neither Harr'h nor anyone else could come out and speak of fear. Or concern for anyone else.

These were not the traits of a warrior. They were marks of weakness—and one did not stand beside the weak in battle.

Fortunately, no one remembered Worf's reticence to

fight, early on. Those who had witnessed it were all dead now, and his present companions would never credit the story anyway. After all, how could anyone so vicious in battle be a coward at heart? As far as his comrades were concerned, he was every bit the blood-maddened killer he seemed to be. And, of course, no one stopped in the middle of the battle to scrutinize him—or to count up his victims.

Nor had his attack on his own ally—not so long ago— earned him anyone's undying enmity. Not even that of the one he'd attacked. The mantle of *berserker* covered a host of deformities—and it was a reputation the Klingon had worked hard to earn. It was one thing to have to accept his own incompleteness—but to have *others* know about it . . .

Worf scanned the faces around the fire. Was it possible that any of them shared his incapacity? After all, he hadn't watched them any more closely than they watched him. Could they have been wearing mantles of deception as well?

Or was he truly unique—and therefore truly alone? He bared his teeth reflexively at the thought, drew wary glances from those about him.

Pah. Even the one who'd been of *his* race, *his* kind—even that one had had no inkling of what plagued Worf. If even his racial brother failed to understand him or his troubles . . .

In the sky, there was a rumbling. Worf looked up at the sound, peered at the full, purple-bellied clouds with mild interest.

The weather had been turning sour all day. Soon, there would be rain.

Chapter Thirteen

As RIKER APPROACHED the lounge's conference table, and those gathered around it, he instinctively headed for his customary seat. He had to stop himself, remember that his place was now at the head of the group—in the captain's chair.

Troi had noticed the glitch in his behavior. But, apparently, no one else had.

He claimed the position of authority as unobtrusively as possible. As he sat, he realized that Modiano was absent—though Merriwether, Geordi's second assistant, was in attendance.

"Where's Modiano?" he asked.

"Down with the disease, sir," responded Merriwether. Her voice was just a little higher-pitched than it should have been. She wasn't used to sitting in on executive-level conferences.

Down with the disease. That made four people altogether —and two of them in sections other than medical. Riker filed the information away, made a promise to himself to look in on Burtin again. After this meeting was over, of course.

"As you know," said Riker, "we've been scanning A'klah for quite some time, and we've yet to turn up a single familiar bio-profile. We need a different approach." He glanced from face to face, and he couldn't help but yearn for the expertise of his missing colleagues. "Data tells me that Mister Fong has some ideas which may help in this regard." He turned to Worf's temporary replacement. "Go ahead, Li."

The security officer took a moment to gather his thoughts. "My best guess, sir, is that these conflicts—which probably *are* a form of entertainment, as Mister Data posited—had their roots in the Klah'kimmbri experience with the Cantiliac armada."

Fong jerked a thumb over his shoulder, in the direction of A'klah—though, seen at this distance through the lounge window, it was indistinguishable from the rest of the celestial array.

"The Cantiliac, of course, hadn't set out to destroy A'klah's budding empire. They were departing the galaxy, for reasons which we can still only guess at. But Trilik'kon Mahk'ti lay in their way.

"We'll never know who fired the first salvo—the Cantiliac, impatient to sweep aside an obstacle in their path, or the Klah'kimmbri, who must have seen the armada as something directed at *them*.

"Judging by what we've observed, however, the Klah'kimmbri were nearly annihilated. Their colonies were destroyed, their outposts crushed. No doubt, A'klah itself sustained serious damage. Such a complete and utter defeat must have left its mark on the Klah'kimmbri—affected them as a culture." He cleared his throat. "While I could find no similar cases on an interplanetary scale, I *was* able to locate relevant *intra*planetary case studies. Instances of expanding, warlike civilizations suddenly beaten down by unexpected and vastly more powerful enemies. The Mutil, for instance, of pre-colonization Stanhague. The Lek of Fythrian'n Five. And others.

"In each case, the lesser culture was traumatized by the brush with extinction. Even given a new opportunity to engage in imperialism, it ignored that option—and turned its aggressive instincts inward, upon itself, in the form of factionalization, feuding and quite often self-destruction."

"Very interesting," said Riker. "Then the military encounters we recorded might originally have been *real* conflicts." He turned to Data. "Border wars—wasn't that your first thought when you saw the broadcasts?"

The android nodded. "It was, sir."

"That's certainly one possibility," Fong resumed. "In any case, if I'm right, there were *some* sort of battles going on—Klah'kimmbri against Klah'kimmbri. But it was far from irrational, I believe, or they probably would have finished the job that the Cantiliac started. As we know, wars are often fought for other reasons than those put forth to the general population; I think it was that way on A'klah. The military establishment—or establishments—must have recognized that the only way for them to remain in power was for there to be war. If not interplanetary, then *intra*planetary. So they created and maintained a series of token conflicts. Serious enough to hold the people's interest —but not so destructive that it would finally obliterate Klah'kimmbri society.

"Eventually, these clashes became televised—apparently, to rebuild the shattered morale of the various populations on the planet. The Klah'kimmbri saw once again that it was possible to emerge victorious—perhaps on a daily basis. It might have been a key force in the resurrection of this civilization."

"However," said Riker, "it's no longer the Klah'kimmbri carrying on these battles. They may be watching them—but they're being fought by off-worlders."

The security officer nodded. "I have a theory about that, too. You see, people—*any* people—will tolerate a war only for so long. In time, they get tired of dying—of giving up their loved ones. That's true even of so-called popular wars.

So as the Klah'kimmbri military redeveloped the planet's technological base, it put an emphasis on certain programs. For one, an advanced transporter capability—so crews could be snatched off passing ships. Particularly, when those ships are unable to defend themselves—either because they're damaged or for lack of armaments. Another technology that would have been critical is the one that produces the energy mantle. In that way, the Klah'kimmbri could prevent casual observers—or rescue missions, like ours—from discovering what they're up to with all those offworlders."

Merriwether leaned forward. "Do you think they made a mistake," she asked, "when they beamed down the captain and the others? I mean, if these people have gone to such lengths to keep their operation a secret—why steal our away team right from under our noses? Why arouse suspicion?"

Riker hadn't thought about it up until then. "You may be right," he told the engineering officer. "It *may* have been some kind of blunder. A failure of the right hand to know what the left hand was doing." He shrugged. "At any rate, they're not about to admit to it—or to anything else, for that matter."

"So where does all this leave us?" asked Troi. She'd been silent up until now, listening. After all, that was a large part of her job. But it was also her job to put matters into perspective from time to time. To keep them on the right track.

Riker realized that he'd been so enthralled by Fong's theoretical constructs—so absorbed in the historical forces that may have shaped the present-day Klah'kimmbri—that he'd lost sight of their goal momentarily.

On the other hand, time taken to better understand an adversary was time well spent.

"Well," said Fong, in answer to Troi's question, "if everything I've described so far is more than just speculation—and if Mister Data's right about these battles being prearranged—then there must be some pretty sophisticated facilities coordinating all this activity. Say, one in each geographical area where the battles take place." He laid his hands out on the table. "It's possible that each such facility would have information on the placement of off-worlders assigned to its zone. What kind of role they were given—warrior, wagon driver or whatever else—and their physical point of entry."

Merriwether was nodding. "If there were such places, we could probably isolate them on the basis of our existing scanner readings. By looking at concentrations of electronic activity in each battle zone, since the rest of the zone should be pretty much empty in that respect."

Fong picked up again as soon as Merriwether paused. "But the only way to get at that information, sir, is in person. Someone has to beam down and access their computer files."

Riker didn't accept that conclusion at face value. He didn't like the idea of placing additional personnel in jeopardy. But the more he thought about it, the more he thought Fong might be right. To win this pot, they might have to up the ante.

And he *did* have this disease breathing down his neck. Patience was no longer an applicable virtue.

"What did you have in mind?" he asked Fong.

"First," said the security officer, "we have to establish which part of A'klah's surface we were aligned with when the away team was spirited off. That will give us some idea of where to start looking. Then we locate the nearest battle zone and—maybe using Merriwether's idea—determine whether or not there *is* a control center. If there *is,* we send a small team of security people down to the surface."

"Along with a couple of engineers," Merriwether amended. "To figure out the Klah'kimmbri computers—they're bound to be different from ours."

Fong nodded in deference to the engineering officer. "With a couple of engineers, then." He turned to Riker. "And, sir—*I* volunteer to lead the team."

The first officer felt a little twinge. Yet *another* away team without him at the head of it. This time, there was no one to overrule him if he decided to go—but there were too many reasons for him to stay. With the captain gone, he was the only experienced executive officer left to the *Enterprise*. And with all that was going on, he didn't want to leave her in less than experienced hands.

Nor did the irony of the situation escape him. For once, it was Riker who was indispensable. More clearly than ever before, he understood how the captain felt as team after team beamed down without him. The word that seemed most appropriate was *stuck*.

On the other hand, there were a few problems to be resolved before an away mission could take place. Problems that were occurring to him only now.

"We seem to be putting the cart before the horse," he said. "What happens when the Klah'kimmbri realize that someone's tampering with one of their control centers? The first thing they're going to do is regenerate that mantle of theirs. Suddenly, even if you find what you're looking for, there's no way we can beam you back up—or anyone else, for that matter. You may be able to send the information through to us, but we won't be able to do anything about it."

"What if we got in and out before we were noticed?" suggested Merriwether.

Riker shook his head from side to side. "There are too many ways that you could be detected. Unless you were extremely lucky, you'd never be quick enough to . . ."

"Sir?"

It was Data who'd spoken. Riker swiveled in his direction, giving him implicit permission to go on.

"I believe," said the android, "that *I* would stand a better chance of obtaining the information quickly—*and* without being detected."

In a moment, Riker understood. He wondered why he hadn't thought of it immediately.

First off, Data could work much faster than any human,

thanks to his positronic brain. Second, he had a well-known affinity for computer dynamics.

Third—and just as important—he was a dead ringer for the Klah'kimmbri. Or at least for the only Klah'kimmbri they'd ever gotten a good look at—the members of the planetary council. They had the same pale skin, the same amber eyes. The only significant difference was the color of their hair; Data's was a dark brown while the councillors' was bright red. But that could easily be taken care of with some dye, which the ship's computer would be only too happy to whip up.

Before going any further with this, Riker offered his thoughts to the others. The reaction was mixed—perhaps because they recognized the drawback to Data's plan.

And there *was* a drawback. Riker was trying to think of a politic way to bring it out for discussion when the android himself saved him the trouble—much to the first officer's relief.

"Of course," said Data, "I *do* tend to be somewhat naive regarding certain aspects of social behavior. There is some doubt as to how well I would succeed in my pose."

There it was. Fong leaned back, nodded.

Apparently, however, Troi had another opinion. "Actually," she said, "you are considerably less naive than you think, Data. In most instances, your behavior is quite appropriate. If we didn't spend so much time with you—if we didn't know you as well as we do—we might not notice your little faux pas all that much."

"But we're talking about *human* behavior—a mode with which Mister Data is familiar," said Fong. "Klah'kimmbri behavior is, no doubt, something else entirely. In a strange environment, one must think on his feet—and that's an area in which an android would be at a decided disadvantage." He didn't appear comfortable talking about Data like this—especially in the android's presence. However, if he'd kept his misgivings to himself, it would have been a breach of his responsibility.

"On the other hand," said Riker, "he *does* look like them—and that's half the battle. Plus, the speed of which Data is capable would minimize his need to interact with the Klah'kimmbri."

The android took in the conversation with perfect equanimity. He didn't seem offended by it in the least.

The first officer looked at him, came to a decision. "I'm going to put my money on Data. Despite his shortcomings."

Fong's lips compressed, but to his credit he kept his reaction to himself. Merriwether seemed a little disappointed—yet it didn't keep her from wishing Data good luck.

"Thank you," said the android.

For two days and more, Dan'nor thought about what his father had said. He went to work, but his mind wasn't on making shoes—it was elsewhere. In the evenings, he ate his solitary meal in front of his videoscreen. The Conflicts raged on, but he took little notice of them. There were conflicts inside of him that were more compelling.

Dan'nor hated the idea of a conspiracy. It seemed loathsome to him—dark and unclean—as compared with the brightness and precision that characterized everything Military. And yet, he could find no fault with his father's arguments. As much as he wanted to be able to deny them, to discard them, he couldn't.

Could the truth be such a frail and dingy thing that it could only be whispered in the shadows? Could falsehood be so appealing?

His thoughts kept returning to the way Trien'nor had looked the other night. The strength that had been so evident in his bearing. The air of dignity that Dan'nor had never before associated with him. And beyond either of those things, a sense of calm—of being at peace with himself.

Dan'nor envied him all of that—most of all, the sense of peace. In the end, it was that which gave form to his decision. More than the logic of his father's words, more than the terrible rightness of his sentiments—because those alone did not reach down deep enough inside him.

But an inner tranquillity that could find a *man* even in mild-mannered Trien'nor . . . *that* was something he had to know more about. *Despite* the danger.

After work on the third day, Dan'nor made his way back to the tavern. Somehow, it seemed larger this time, easier to distinguish from the shops around it. The wooden door seemed larger, too—heavier, more portentous.

This night, there were just as many people as that other night, but they were distributed around the place differently. The crowd about the videoscreen was smaller; more people clustered around the bar.

Dan'nor took a table not far from the screen, simply because it was available. He pretended to watch the Conflicts, but his real attention was focused on the corridor that led to the back room.

His plan—one he hadn't realized he'd had until just a few moments ago—was to sit here and wait for his father. Of course, he couldn't be certain that Trien'nor was back there—but he had a feeling. And if he was wrong, he could always return another night.

He wouldn't break in on the conspirators' meeting. And fear wasn't the reason, he told himself. It was because setting foot in that room again would mean he'd joined them—and he wasn't ready to do that. Not by a long shot.

He just wanted to talk to Trien'nor. *Needed* to talk to Trien'nor. For now, that would be enough.

Before long, he saw one of the serving women take a tray into the back. At least, he noted, *some* of the conspirators were here. It was a good sign.

Nor did anyone approach him to ask if he wanted a drink. He caught sight of the serving maid who had taken his order the first time he was here; but she was working behind the bar, too busy to wait on tables. Dan'nor wondered what had made the customers so thirsty all of a sudden.

Then a mug of foamy, dark liquid slammed down on his table, startling him. He looked up into the face of someone he'd never seen before. Someone who had drunk more than he should have.

"There," said the man, as Lower Caste a specimen as Dan'nor had ever seen. "No one goes without a drink the day the video works blew up."

Dan'nor took a moment to make sense of that. "The video works?" he repeated dumbly.

The man nodded, leaning a little closer. His eyes were bleary, his chin wet and shiny in the glare from the screen. And his breath smelled worse than the river.

"That's right," he said. "You mean you haven't heard?" He barked out a laugh. "They blew the thing up into little pieces—just before morning." Straightening, he lifted his drink in a clumsy salute. "Here's *to* them. No work for *me* today, Brother, and I thank them heartily for it."

Dan'nor didn't have to ask who *they* were.

The man couldn't have known that the saboteurs to whom he drank were quite likely in this very tavern—but that didn't seem to dampen the kinship he felt with them. For the first time, Dan'nor realized that his father's movement was more than just a small group of activists. Somewhere along the line, it had captured the imagination of the people—or at least some of them.

It somehow put matters in a different light. Gave the conspirators' efforts a kind of legitimacy.

He recalled what he'd heard on his last visit here: the argument between the ones called Ma'alor and Zanc'cov, about the capacity of the masses to rise up against the authorities. Perhaps that capacity was starting to assert itself after all.

Dan'nor himself had yet to see the captured saboteur—Ralak'kai, wasn't it?—on the videoscreen. But that didn't mean that Ralak'kai hadn't appeared at one time or another; Dan'nor hardly watched the Conflicts as much—or as closely—as he had before.

Had Ralak'kai's presence on the battlefields roused the anger of the people, as Zanc'cov had expected? Or did the incidents of sabotage have more to do with it?

No matter. In either case, something was *happening*. Something huge, something frightening.

The man was still looming over him, holding his mug aloft—as if he wanted some kind of response from Dan'nor. Dan'nor gave him one.

"To *them*," he said. He raised the mug the man had given him.

That seemed to suffice. Grinning, the man withdrew into the crowd that surrounded the bar.

It was only a moment later that he saw his father. Apparently, the conspirators' meeting had broken up for the night.

Trien'nor had been the first to emerge from the hallway. Behind him was Ma'alor—Dan'nor would never forget the dark hair, the unrelenting scowl behind the knife.

The younger Tir'dainia rose to catch his father's eye. He felt a faint apprehension that the others in the group might disapprove of his being there. But if Trien'nor had invited him to join their movement, it had surely been with the group's approval. They would not condemn him out of hand.

And in any case, this was a public place. The conspirators couldn't risk a show of violence here, not even before a largely sympathetic crowd. It would only draw attention to them.

Sure enough, Trien'nor and Ma'alor noticed him at the same time. And neither of them looked all that surprised to see him there.

Still and all, Dan'nor did not leave his place. He sat down again and waited for his father to join him.

The elder Tir'dainia exchanged a couple of words with Ma'alor. Then he started to thread his way among the tables, as his compatriots headed for the door or the crowd at the bar

Before Trien'nor had gotten halfway to Dan'nor, however, the tavern door burst open. And a flood of blue uniforms came pouring in.

The Civil Service, he realized. *Here.* To get Trien'nor and the others—for what they'd done. Somehow, they had been identified. Traced here.

Dan'nor was transfixed for a long, painful moment. But his father was not. Without hesitation, Trien'nor flipped a table out of his way and met the rush of Civil Service agents head on—entangling himself with them, slowing down their progress into the tavern.

There was a blow to the older man's head, another to his stomach. Dan'nor felt his insides clench. He moved to help, to come to his father's rescue—but someone grabbed him from behind.

He managed to twist around a bit, to see who was holding him. He knew the face—it was one of the men in the back room circle, one whose name he had never learned. Dan'nor struggled to free himself, but the man was immensely strong. And his eyes carried a message—which, after a frantic second or two, began to sink in.

I'm not to intervene, Dan'nor interpreted. *I'm to stand by and let my father be dealt with as the Civil Service sees fit.*

He was not unfamiliar with the tactic; he'd learned about it in the course of his Military training. Cut your losses— live to fight another day.

But it wasn't so easy when it was one's father. Dan'nor twisted around again, saw that Trien'nor had gone down. He was doubled over, firmly in the grasp of a half dozen agents. But his efforts hadn't been for nothing, it seemed.

Ma'alor and some of the others were streaming back down the corridor, headed in the direction of the back room. The crowd, galvanized by Trien'nor's act of courage —and even more sympathetic than Dan'nor had guessed— was doing its best to get in the way of the uniformed invaders. There were shouts of defiance, bottles smashed.

For every citizen who got a blaster-butt in the face, another managed to fill the breach.

As the confusion mounted—and the promise of a full-blown riot became more and more a reality—some agents stepped aside and Dan'nor's father was revealed to him. Trien'nor's face was mottled and bruised; there was a thin trickle of blood oozing from the corner of his mouth. Their eyes met across the room, and Dan'nor felt something he hadn't felt since he was very small. There was a thickness in his throat that he couldn't swallow away.

Suddenly, there was a greater commotion coming from the back of the tavern—the place to which Trien'nor's comrades had retreated. More blue uniforms came shooting out from the corridor, pushing a couple of the conspirators before it. One of them was Zanc'cov—Dan'nor knew him by his smallish stature, his sharp-featured face.

But Ma'alor wasn't with him. Nor were many of the others. Somehow, they had escaped.

With the influx of reinforcements, the crowd was intimidated into backing off. After all, these people weren't part of the movement; they had been only momentarily inspired by the destruction of the video works. More than likely, they'd be as docile as ever once this day was forgotten.

Unless, Dan'nor couldn't help but add, there were *other* days like this one. Other incidents of sabotage, other Civil Service raids on suspected conspirator gathering places.

As this occurred to him, the mob was contained and moved away from the bar. The man behind him let go of his arms, knowing he couldn't penetrate the wall of citizens that had formed between him and his father. Before long, they were forced all the way to the wall.

Dan'nor himself had his back to the screen. The man beside him—the one who had restrained him from helping Trien'nor—was bathed in the lurid light of the Conflicts. Some battle or other crawled behind them, a fitting backdrop to the more immediate violence before them.

Minutes later, the crowd had more or less subsided. It was still surly, but it had no heart left. The Civil Service agents had skillfully carved out the ringleaders, those most inclined to rebellion.

Dan'nor couldn't see very much—not with all the bodies that pressed against him. But as the citizens' noises diminished, a voice rose above them. An even voice, a trained voice. Obviously, one of the Civil Service officers.

"Tonight," he said, "you were spared the presence of criminals in your midst. Apparently, you were unaware of them, and of their crimes—or you would never have attempted to defend them as you did. In the future, all law-abiding citizens will provide more cooperation—or they will be considered criminals themselves—and treated as such."

The door opened and there were scuffling sounds—as of prisoners being dragged out against their will. Then the blue uniforms must have filed out after them, because those he could see dwindled in number. Finally, they were gone altogether.

This night, Geordi's fellow workers had built their fire on the other end of the bridge. Normally, they would have slept on the side where the armored ones had decided to settle— but as if at an unspoken signal, understood best by those who had been here the longest, they'd placed the ravine between themselves and the newcomers.

The switch didn't seem to bother anyone, however. Everybody drowsed off before true darkness fell—everyone except Geordi himself. He waited just long enough to establish that all the others had closed their eyes.

And then he made his move.

He stole away from the dying fire. Slunk out onto the bridge as silently as he could. Crossed it, hugging the fiber guides and supports on one side, so as to minimize his chances of being seen. He felt the thrumming of the wind in the planks, the subtle swaying of the entire structure as it displayed its meticulously crafted resiliency. Caught glimpses of the ravine, deep and black and hungering beneath him.

Finally, as he neared the far terminus, Geordi slipped down from the wooden surface and took to the jumbled face of the cliff. Making good use of all the hand- and footholds provided, he moved sideways for ten meters or so before pulling himself up onto a ledge.

The drivers' fire was now almost directly above him, marked by a trail of spitting embers and thin, whitish smoke. The wind, noisier up here than usual, carried the sparks past him into the updraft from the ravine, where they became lost among the plentitude of stars. He could hear the snapping of the wood as it burned, the rough-edged ebb and flow of voices.

Unlike the workers, it seemed, the armored ones were still awake. He'd prepared himself for this possibility—it would just mean additional care on his part.

Holding his breath, he climbed a little higher, pressing himself into the gravelly incline—hoping fervently that he wouldn't dislodge a sizable rock and send it crashing down onto the ledge. Fortunately, he was familiar with this particular slope, though he'd never given it such close attention as he was giving it now.

At last, he'd hauled himself up enough. Nestled under a strangely situated outcropping, he craned his head up and around the side of it. At a glance, he learned all he needed to know for the moment.

The drivers had made a campfire of scattered wood splints apart from the clustered wagons. They appeared to find the company of their prisoners distasteful—even more so than the company of their burden-beasts, who stood full-bellied and content, tethered nearby to individual formations of rock.

Geordi didn't have to concentrate on the wagons for very

long. Their relative positions seemed to correspond with the mental picture he'd made of them; his earlier scrutiny had come in handy.

Rather, he focused on the armored ones themselves. And saw that although some were still aware enough to engage in conversation, others were beginning to doze. Unfortunately, the dozers were still in the minority.

Geordi ducked down again. *Damn.* He could wait, sure. But it only increased the chances of someone taking a stroll and spotting him.

Should I slip farther down the slope? he asked himself. *Maybe go back to the bridge and hide underneath it for a while?*

The craziness of what he was doing began, for the first time since he'd conceived it, to sink in. *This is suicide,* he mused. *Insane. If I had a rational bone in my body, I'd go back to the other side and forget the whole thing.*

Maybe he *was* a criminal, as Beff't—the oily-looking one—had suggested when he first woke up in this place. If he was capable of what he was doing *now,* he was probably capable of *anything.*

And yet, even all his self-flagellations weren't prying him off the incline. Not after what he'd seen on the bridge.

The stone was cold beneath him. It began to eat through his homespun garb, to excite tiny shivers in him.

And here I am without a cloak. Of course, he couldn't have brought it. It would only have slowed him down.

Geordi was just preparing himself for a long wait when he heard the voices above him become clamorous. For a moment, he froze, wondering if his presence had been detected after all. Then, when there were no approaching footfalls, he dared to poke his head up a second time.

What he saw almost made him want to smile. Two of the wagon drivers had stood up and begun to strip off their armor, while the others—those still awake, anyway— moved to arrange themselves in a circle. From the way the standing ones were eyeing each other, from the way the onlookers hooted and jeered and roared, Geordi was able to get a pretty good idea of what was going on.

The two on their feet were going to engage in a physical confrontation. As an entertainment, apparently, for the rest of them. But not a fight to the death; they were making too big a show of tossing their weapons away. Then what? A wrestling match?

Geordi didn't wait to find out. He'd gotten just what he needed—a distraction. Something to hold the armored ones' attention while he did what he'd set out to do.

As the din became even louder, he traveled sideways again, gingerly edging his way closer to the wagons, but not without a certain sense of urgency. There was no telling how long the confrontation might last.

When he'd milked his concealment for all it was worth, he crawled up off the slope and onto the flat. Half creeping, half wriggling, Geordi closed the gap between him and the nearest wagon. As luck would have it, it was one of the vehicles filled strictly with supplies. But it provided some cover for him, allowed him to breathe a little easier.

It was good that the beasts had been tethered elsewhere, apart from the wagons. Otherwise, it would have been nearly impossible to pull this off. As likely as not, he'd have been trampled before he got very far.

Geordi negotiated the forest of wooden, metal-bound wheels and came up on the far side of the second wagon. This one contained a couple of the prisoners, still sitting back to back because their bonds prevented them from shifting to another position.

One was bird-faced and dark, darker even than Geordi himself. The other was pale, so much so that one could see the blood vessels beneath his skin. Neither of them was sleeping. What's more, they must have seen his approach because they didn't look startled in the least—nor did they make a sound. Not even when he took out the sharpened rock he'd tucked into his tunic and leaned toward them with it.

The fiber that bound them was the same kind that held the bridge together. It didn't yield easily, not to so rudimentary a cutting tool. But in time, the rock had its way with it.

A quick look of gratitude, some rubbing of tortured limbs to get the circulation back. Then the two of them were clambering silently out of the wagon, headed in the direction of the incline and, ultimately, the bridge.

By the time they were out of sight, Geordi was working on the next pair. Like the others, they appeared to be ready for him, to divine his intentions. Again, the liberation process went without a hitch.

The same with the third pair.

When he reached the fourth wagon, however, Geordi had a sense that the noise surrounding the drivers' combat was diminishing. Dying down, like their fire.

His heart seemed to enlarge in his chest. It banged against his ribs so hard it hurt.

But he couldn't stop now. Not yet. There was still time to free this last pair, wasn't there? How damned long could it take?

Thrusting his edged rock between them, he sawed furiously. And as he did so, he glanced at their faces.

He saw the caked skin of blood from the temple down to the jaw, recognized the man who had impressed him with his dignified demeanor. These, then, were the first prisoners who had come over the bridge. The ones who'd given him his first inkling of the deception under which he'd labored.

It renewed his sense of anger—of having been violated. And because of that, he gritted his teeth and worked even harder.

Finally, the fiber gave way. The pair should have been free now to unravel the rest of it themselves.

But they weren't. For some reason, these two had been bound more surely than the others. Each was tied hand and foot with his own fiber, in addition to the one that had held them together.

Geordi glanced in the direction of the fire. Most of the

armored ones were standing now, bodies bulked against the night. The confrontation seemed to be over, or almost over.

There was no time, he told himself, to cut both of them loose. So he tugged at the bonds of the nearest one, the wounded man, and worked on those.

Sweat trickled down the side of his face, cold and clammy, the product of his exertions. He could hear his breath rasping a little in his throat and he tried to control it.

It took longer than he'd expected, but at last the still-living strands of the fiber began to fray. To break and peel back. Finally, the whole fiber just snapped.

Quickly, efficiently for one whose arms and legs had to be awakening with pain, the prisoner turned around and applied himself to his companion's restraints. With his fingers alone, he clawed at the knots.

"No," said Geordi, leaning closer in—his voice barely a whisper, yet crystal clear in its insistence. "We've got to move—*now.*"

He saw the muscles work in the wounded one's jaw. "I have no choice," came the response, hissed over the man's shoulder. "He saved my life."

Geordi had done all he could. If he waited any longer, they'd *all* get caught. But even so, he couldn't pull himself away. He couldn't abandon them.

Cursing himself for a half dozen kinds of a fool, he put his rock to work again.

The wounded one looked at him. "Thank you," he whispered.

Geordi just grunted and concentrated on his sawing. That is, until he heard the sudden uproar among the drivers—and saw a number of them lumbering toward the wagons, weapons in hand.

There wasn't a second to waste. If he bolted now, he might still make it over the bridge ahead of them. Maybe lose them in the shadowy terrain on the other side. At least, he had a *chance.*

But the wounded one might make it too—if he tried. And

having gone to the trouble of freeing him, Geordi was reluctant to see him bound again. Particularly when there might be reprisals for trying to escape.

"C'mon," he said, grabbing the man by the shoulder. "It's too late—let him be!"

The wounded man resisted. "No—*you* go. Just give me the rock."

The drivers were getting closer. There were five or six of them—and though they moved cautiously, they were definitely headed this way.

Geordi pressed the rock into the other one's hand.

But he didn't retreat toward the bridge. Instead, he scurried under a wagon and came out in the open—where the drivers could see him.

Geordi waited just long enough for one of the armored ones to note his presence—to point and alert the others. Then he took off, determined to make the best possible use of the jagged formations that punctuated this high ground.

He had no illusions that he could elude these drivers forever. After all, the only reasonably sure escape route was in the direction of the bridge, and he had already forsaken that option.

But if he led them on a wild enough chase, the prisoners would have a better chance to get away. Not just the wounded one and his companion, but the ones who'd already made it over the bridge.

He would be trading *their* freedom for *his*. It didn't make much sense from the point of view of self-preservation. But *damn*—it sure *felt* right.

At the first sizable upthrust, Geordi stopped and peered back at his pursuers. So far, they were right on his trail. And progressing pretty efficiently, despite their armor.

From hereon in, he would have to make it more difficult. Confuse them a little.

He dropped down again, trying to keep to the shadows, and scuttled straight back. There was a sheer drop no more than thirty meters away. He would have to turn before that—maybe veer off to his left, where there were a couple of squat formations he could take advantage of.

Geordi was halfway to the cliff when the terrain turned against him. The rocky surface that had appeared so solid just gave way beneath his right foot. And though he tried to take the slip in stride, he found he couldn't.

His foot was stuck, wedged into a crevice he could barely see. When he pressed his hands against the ground and attempted to pull free, all he got for his efforts was a shoot of agony through his ankle.

Geordi set his teeth, tried to twist in another direction. This time, it hurt so much that he almost cried out.

Not that it would have mattered. The drivers were bearing down on him, their bulk blotting out the stars on the craggy horizon.

Geordi's mouth went dry as he saw the way they held their weapons. As if they meant to *use* them . . .

No, he told himself. They would calm down once they saw what they'd been chasing: one man, unarmed and helpless.

But as the armored ones loomed above him, he could read the fury in them. The *murderous* fury. For no good reason, except that maybe that wrestling match had worked them up to a frenzy.

Suddenly, Geordi realized that his good deed might have cost him more than his freedom.

It might have cost him his *life*.

Chapter Fourteen

IT HAD BEEN A RISK, O'Brien told himself—but an unavoidable one.

After all, the transporters couldn't work at quite the same distance as the ship's sensors—not even under the best of circumstances.

And of course, present circumstances were far from the best. All the debris in the area made the teleportation process somewhat trickier than normal; O'Brien had had to compute an ungodly number of path-density changes. It was one thing to beam someone down through atmosphere and then, say, a known depth of bedrock. But to direct a set of molecules through metal and vacuum, metal and vacuum, a hundred times or more—before even *entering* the planet's atmosphere—now that was a horse of a different color.

What's more, their information on A'klahn surface details was fairly sketchy. Oh, sure, they had programmed in all the topographical macrocontours captured by the sensors. And they had chosen as open a place as possible. But what if the ground rose suddenly in a particular spot? Or fell? What if there was some sort of building they hadn't detected? An animal, a tree?

They had a little more margin for error with an android than with a human being. Data was durable, extraordinarily strong and agile. However, if he materialized inside some Klah'kimmbri's favorite monument, he'd be in as much trouble as anyone else.

All of this meant that they'd had to close the distance between themselves and A'klah in order to ensure Data's safe passage—a mandate that hadn't exactly thrilled Will Riker. "If we get too close," he'd said, "we'll be noticed. Then they'll regenerate that damned energy shield and we'll be back up the creek without a paddle. With no possibility of beaming down, no one to gather information for us planetside—and more than likely, no second chance at sensor reconnaissance."

In the end, Lady Luck had turned up on their side. They had established the position O'Brien needed—and so far, the Klah'kimmbri showed no signs of having detected them.

But it was foolish to tempt fate any longer than they had to. O'Brien's fingers flew deftly and surely over the few controls he hadn't been able to preset. Within moments of their having breached the maximum-distance bubble, he glanced at Riker.

"Ready to transport," he said.

The first officer turned to Data, who stood front and center on the transporter platform. The android nodded once—smartly, O'Brien thought.

"All right," said Riker. "Energize."

In the next second, Data was surrounded by a cylinder of shimmering light. It seemed to absorb him, to suck all the substance out of him. Finally, the cylinder vanished—and the android along with it.

O'Brien consulted his instruments. "Transport complete," he announced. And hoped that it had been accomplished with a minimum of discomfort to Data. There was no way of knowing, unfortunately, until the android established a communicator link—and that wasn't supposed to happen until he'd completed his mission.

"Good," said Riker. He spoke to the ship's computer. "Conn."

"Ensign Crusher here," came the response over the intercom.

"Take us back to our previous position, Ensign Crusher. As quickly as possible."

"Aye-aye, sir."

Up on the bridge, Wesley had already programmed the course change—in accordance with Riker's orders. O'Brien thought he could feel the engines engage by way of a slight vibration in the deck.

The first officer turned back to him. He still looked pretty grim.

"Cheer up, sir," said the transporter chief. "It couldn't have gone any better."

Riker grunted. "It's not that. I have every confidence that he arrived in one piece." He sighed, shook his head. "I just can't help but feel it should have been *me* down there instead of poor Data."

Nor was he speaking as a first officer—O'Brien recognized that right away. Riker was speaking as a man worried about his friend.

Worf waited for Harr'h's signal, battle senses taut and alert. The sky, which had been darkening steadily, looked impatient for the assault to get under way—as impatient, almost, as the warriors themselves.

Of all of them, only the Klingon was not looking forward to the combat. For him alone, the taste of imminent violence was a bitter brew, mulled by the awful knowledge that he would falter at the prospect of a kill.

He peered at the defenders on the walls, the marshals who swung high in the bruised and purpling heavens, weaving circles around the flying-eye machines. His comrades had only one set of enemies to look out for—Worf had two.

Then Harr'h called out the attack—a long, ululating cry

that bound the siege-makers to the battle and the battle to the siege-makers, until both were one and the one was a thing of fierce, feverish beauty.

Everyone bounded forward at once. Worf had been chosen as one of the squad leaders. In his right hand, he carried his mace. In his left, he bore the foremost part of a tall, sturdy siege ladder. Behind him, nine other warriors shared the ladder's burden.

There were ten squads altogether, all similarly equipped. Each had been assigned a point of attack.

Up on the battlements, some of the defenders brought forth heavy stones and chunks of masonry—missiles with which to bombard the invaders, to pare their numbers and slow them down. Others hefted spears, designed for more long-range use.

Unfortunately, encumbered as the siege-makers were, it was impossible to close with the fortress as quickly as they would have liked. Their ladders were too heavy, too unwieldy. What's more, not all of them were made for speed, and each squad could move only as fast as its slowest members.

It made them easy targets.

Before they had come within twenty meters of the barrier, they paid the price for their plodding pace. There was a sudden rain of shafts, and a *thudd*, and the warrior behind Worf cried out. The Klingon allowed himself only a quick look back—and was sorry he had. The spear had gone right through its victim and stuck in the ground—leaving him twisted but erect, like some grim scarecrow.

He put the sight behind him. Not the best way to die, Worf told himself. But at least it was a death in battle.

There was a second volley of arrows, and a third. Miraculously, no one else in Worf's squad was cut down. But in the squads on either side of them, the casualties had been heavy. There were barely enough warriors left to carry those two ladders.

It was a bad sign. When Worf's ladder went up, it would attract that much more attention.

Cursing beneath his breath, the Klingon pounded toward the wall. His heart beat like a caged beast. His blood throbbed in his temples.

He knew they were almost there when the rocks started to fall. There was a bellow of pain behind him, and suddenly the ladder grew a little heavier. For a moment, his squad faltered. Then they got going again, amid a hail of plummeting debris.

One piece of it seemed to zero in on his head. He ducked to one side but couldn't avoid it entirely. It came down hard on his shoulder, sending shots of pain through his bad arm.

But he didn't drop his weapon. Nor did he drop the ladder. Teeth grinding, he lurched for the wall.

And then, abruptly, the fortress seemed to embrace them. To shelter them; it would be difficult for one of their enemies to hit someone directly below. The bombardment continued, but most of the missiles caught the jutting stones that comprised the barrier—and bounced away. Or carried too far by virtue of their momentum.

On the other hand, they were hardly safe here. Haste was still critical if they were to avoid being crushed one by one.

As they turned and hefted their ladder, Worf had the sense that the other teams were doing the same. But he didn't pause to make sure. He could only hope that enough of them had reached their goal to keep any one squad from being isolated and destroyed.

Just as they managed to plant their ladder against the wall, to wedge it in tight, Worf felt another rock strike him. It was smaller than the first one, and not nearly so heavy. But it hit him in his bad shoulder, just like its predecessor, and he didn't appreciate that.

Rage boiled up inside him and he roared a challenge to the defenders up above. They answered with more rocks, and the Klingon had to hug the barrier to avoid them.

Careful, he told himself, forcing the words through the red haze of his anger. *Save it for when you get up top.*

In the next moments, his vision cleared. Two of his comrades had already begun climbing; he started up after them. The remaining members of their squad stayed below, to anchor the ladder—to keep the defenders from dislodging it too easily.

A *chinking* on his armor. Were they throwing down pebbles now? Worf glanced up past the bulk of the warrior just above him—saw the droplets slanting by, lashed by the wind.

Rain. *Finally.* It was getting hot inside his armor.

But soon, it became more than just a spattering of drops. The rain fell harder, heavier. The stones began to darken, to grow slippery with it.

Up above, something cracked like a whip in the sky. The rain began to hiss, to strike a mantle of mist off the wall.

It dampened the sound of the ram striking the gates, the war cries as the first of the invaders reached the battlements.

Worf's ladder jerked—once, again—as the defenders tried to repel it. But the warriors at the base held it in place, and soon the enemy stopped testing them. Apparently, they had their hands too full up *there.*

Suddenly, something fell past Worf. Only after it was lying limp on the ground did he recognize it—as the pierced and lifeless form of one of his comrades. The one who'd been topmost on the ladder.

His lips pulled back in an involuntary snarl. At the smell of death, the din of arms clashing, the blood-passion was surging in him—as it should. Even as he climbed, as he tightened his grasp on his weapon, he nurtured it. He fed the fire in his heart, hoping that *this* time it would not fail him.

Out of the corner of his eye, he saw a marshal hovering. Watching. Strangely, though, the sky rider was looking up—at the sky, where it was growing as dark as night. As if he was worried about something. The winds seemed to toss him about, the sheeting rains to discomfit him.

But the Klingon couldn't attend to the marshal for long. Before he knew it, the warrior above him had made his way up onto the battlements—and plunged into a knot of defenders.

Then it was *his* turn.

Just as Worf dragged himself up over the wall, an adversary came forward to fill the breach. Almost too late, he rolled, his legs flopping over on the wrong side of the parapet. His enemy's broadsword encountered nothing but stone, raising a swarm of orange sparks.

Wind whistled through the chinks in his helmet. The rain pressed down upon him—a torrent that choked and blinded, making it difficult to get up. He had never known a storm this bad—at least not in his brief span of remembrance.

Just in time, the wind shifted direction. Worf squinted through his dripping visor at his opponent's sword—slicing the air as it headed straight for him.

Klanngg!

His mace took the blow, turned it aside. But his enemy had put too much of his weight into it. He slipped on the rain-slick stones, dropped on Worf with the force of a falling burden-beast.

Too close now for weaponplay, they grappled. The Klingon tried to obtain some advantage, but the other warrior was just as strong—just as determined. And Worf was still draped half over the parapet, his feet scrabbling for purchase on the vertical surface of the wall.

Finally, the Klingon wrestled one hand free and struck his opponent a damaging blow across the visor. Before the warrior could quite recover, Worf brought a leg up— wedged a booted foot between them and pushed for all he was worth.

His enemy went sprawling backward, lifted nearly to his full height.

And in that same moment, the world split apart.

Even afterward, Worf wasn't sure what had happened.

There had been a flash of light, reflected in the cavernous sky and the figure of his adversary. And immediately afterward, a deafening clap that shook the very stones beneath them.

The Klingon hadn't seen the source of the light; it had come from somewhere behind him. But apparently, his adversary *had*. He was holding his head in his gauntleted hands, his weapon dropped and forgotten.

Had the warrior been blinded by the sudden brilliance in the sky?

And what the *hell* had caused that all-consuming brilliance?

Worf's second question was answered first. Way off in the distance, among the clouds on the other side of the valley, there was a darting of light down to the hills. A second or two later, it was followed by a cascade of sound—something like boulders clashing.

Then he got the answer to his first question as well—when his enemy removed his helm to reveal the being within. A blockish head, broad features, three rubylike eyes set beneath an overhanging brow. But none of those eyes seemed blind.

On the contrary. The warrior was using all of them to look right at him.

Worf didn't know what to make of this behavior. And as he scanned the battlements—out of an instinct for self-preservation—he saw that his opponent wasn't the only one who had appeared to lose his mind.

All up and down the line, warriors had taken off their helmets. They were staring at each other, at the sky—even at their own garb.

Only a handful still stood helmeted and armed, ready to fight. But like the Klingon, they were watching the helmless ones.

Worf's adversary took a step toward him. Not a belligerent step; it seemed tentative, uncertain. "Where am I?" he asked, rain spilling down the sides of his face. "What am I doing here?" Another step—and now there was a flare of anger in those ruby red orbs. "Where is this place?"

These were questions that Worf himself had asked—but only in the beginning. As he listened, he heard them repeated over and over again, all along the battlements.

And not just *there.* Over the sizzle and spatter of the rain, Worf could hear cries of bafflement in the ranks of his comrades down below—the ones who had been scaling the ladders. The same sounds came from within the fortress walls. And from even farther away, among the squads of invaders that had been held back for a second rush.

Had the flash caused them all to lose their memories again? The idea made the Klingon shudder. After all, they remembered so *little* as it was. Losing even that would be unbearable.

Or had something else happened to them? Indeed, they did not look so much bereft as . . .

Before Worf could complete his thought, he caught sight of a sky rider swooping toward them—angling out of the maelstrom of churning, black sky. Instinctively, he crouched, prepared himself to accept the blast of agony.

But it never came. Instead, the marshal's beam hit the one whom Worf had been fighting—the one who stood so innocent and weaponless on the battlements.

There were no screams, no convulsions. The warrior just collapsed—and lay there, a target for the rain.

Nor did the sky rider stop there. He strafed the parapets, blasting nearly everyone. By the time he had nosed his sled up again, the only ones still standing were those like Worf. The ones who still wore their helms, who still grasped their weapons.

Everyone else lay still. As Worf watched, one limp form slipped from the wall and fell into the courtyard below.

The Klingon crept closer to his fallen adversary, touched the warrior's neck just below his jutting jaw. There was no pulse.

Dead. And not honorably, in battle—but at the hands of that misbegotten dog on the sled!

It was happening all over. Everywhere the madness had made a warrior cast off his helm, a sky rider followed—bringing not torture but instantaneous death.

A sense of loss came over Worf, lodged in his throat. He felt shame—for those who had perished without glory. Remorse—for it seemed to him that he should have touched these lives as they fled, heralded their passing somehow. And savage, unendurable hatred—for those who could kill with such cowardice.

Something took hold of him. It was more than a scream. It was an outpouring of his soul, a release of his great and terrible pain into the bawling heavens. Somewhere off to his side, there was a slender quick-stitch of distant light, and the heavens roared back at him.

A second time, one of the sleds came his way. This time, it came too close. Without thinking, fired purely by instinct, Worf launched himself from the parapet.

And caught hold of the marshal's leg.

Earth and sky reeled as the sled swung about, thrown off by the sudden and unexpected weight. The sky rider tried to shake off his newfound burden, to break Worf's grip by pounding at his hands with the blaster's pommel.

But Worf wasn't letting go. In fact, spurred by the emotions that roiled inside him, he was climbing higher—improving his grip on marshal and machine.

"Go ahead," he growled, glaring up into the pale, narrow countenance, beyond which the sky was a spinning chaos. He was almost close enough to strike it, to crush it. "Use your stinking weapon. Slay *me* as you slew *them!*"

But the marshal held back. Perhaps, at this range, he could not fire for fear of being caught in the backlash. Perhaps he had other reasons.

In any case, he did not bring his death beam to bear. And though his mouth gradually stretched in a rictus of mounting fear, though his eyes darted wildly, he gave up his pummeling as well.

Slowly, fighting the centrifugal force that threatened to tear him loose, the Klingon dragged himself closer to his goal—closer to the object of his revulsion.

And then, suddenly, he saw something dark and massive looming up before him. The wall—*they were going to crash into the wall!*

A spark of reason welled up in the darkness of his fury. He leapt from the sled, unsure of where the ground was—but certain he would rather fall a long way than strike the stone barrier at that speed.

As it turned out, Worf did not have far to fall at all. He hit the ground hard, but not *that* hard—rolled and sought his bearings.

If the marshal was going to be destroyed, he wanted to savor the moment. His aching hatred demanded it.

But in saving himself, he had rescued the sky rider as well. One moment, the sled seemed doomed to hit the top of the wall; the next, it rose just high enough to skim past it. With Worf aboard, it never could have done that.

Nor did the marshal deign to look back at his tormentor. He merely continued ascending, past the keep and into the storm.

The Klingon burned with his failure. *Again* he had proven he was no true warrior—he had fallen short of the kill.

However, he was too spent to roar at his squandered chance for revenge. Too drained to bellow anymore at the sky.

In the lee of the walls, all was confusion. Those still standing milled about the bodies, lost and without purpose. Somehow, the siege no longer seemed so urgent.

Worf spat out blood from beneath his visor, picked up an ax lying on the ground—to replace the weapon he seemed to have left behind.

He would try to understand all of this later on. Right now, he just wanted a dry place to lick his wounds.

Data had materialized not fifty yards from the Klah'kimmbri control facility—a large, gray box of a building that stood by itself on a high, windswept plateau.

There was no door in either of the walls visible to him, so he circumnavigated and stuck his head around a corner.

Sure enough, the entranceway was now in sight. And it was guarded by two armed Klah'kimmbri.

Data was armed also—though his weapon was not functional. Ignorant of the technology that went into Klah'kimmbri firearms, the *Enterprise*'s computer had been able to fashion only a hollow duplicate—to go along with the rest of his disguise.

In any case, the android wasn't depending on force to get him what he wanted. Rather, he was hopeful that he could accomplish that through subterfuge.

On that note, and without further reflection, Data left his hiding place and made his approach. He attempted to simulate an air of confidence.

The guards didn't seem to notice him at first. Perhaps they did not expect anyone to approach from this direction. Or, for that matter, to approach at all.

When they *did* notice him, however, they instinctively drew their weapons. He did not think it prudent to respond in kind; rather, he continued his inexorable but unhurried advance.

Within a few seconds, they must have recognized him as one of their own, for they restored their weapons to their belts. Rather quickly, in fact.

The disguise, it seemed, had worked. So far, so good.

Now, however, came what Commander Riker had dubbed "the tough part." Once engaged in conversation, Data knew, he might have to produce any number of details concerning his supposed life and career on A'klah. Indeed, thanks to his research, the time he had spent learning the Klah'kimmbri language and the extensive briefing he'd had with the first officer, the android could recite a long though somewhat sketchy personal history—from his earliest beginnings to his current need for information on certain conscripts.

"Greetings," he said, stopping before the guards. "Perhaps you can help me."

One of them answered immediately—almost before Data had completed his sentence.

"Certainly, Revered One. Would you like to see the Coordinator?"

Revered One? Data noticed now that the guard stood rather rigidly—with his hands at his sides and his eyes averted. Likewise, his companion.

Had they mistaken the android for someone else? If so, for whom?

And would the mix-up enhance his chances for success here—or render his mission more difficult?

"Yes," said Data—too abruptly, he feared. "I would like to see the Coordinator."

"Very well," said the guard. And while his comrade stepped aside, he pressed a pressure-sensitive plate beside the entranceway. A moment later, the door slid aside; there was a vaulted lobby within, with corridors leading off it.

Revered One?

As Data followed the guard inside, he wondered how a Klah'kimmbri might come to merit reverence. It occurred to him that the knowledge might prove useful.

Chapter Fifteen

MA'ALOR HAD NOT ESCAPED without injury. His jaw was a deep, painful-looking purple blotch, and there were cuts above both his eyes. He had sustained the bruise at the hands of a Civil Service agent, the cuts as he crashed through the window high on the wall of the tavern rest room—launched through it by his compatriots.

The dark man's scowl hadn't left him, Dan'nor noticed. If anything, it had deepened.

"So," said Ma'alor. "You want to become one of us."

Dan'nor nodded. "That's right."

They sat on wooden chairs in a small, furnished room. It wasn't obvious whether anyone had lived here or not before Ma'alor came to use it as a hideout. There were two others in the room with them. One was the man who had brought Dan'nor here—the same one who'd held his arms in the tavern.

Ma'alor grunted. "Trien'nor was right about you, it seems. I confess I doubted that you would ever see things our way." A searching pause. "What made you change your mind?"

Dan'nor shrugged. "A number of things. Let's just say I'm wiser now than when we first met."

"You grew wise in a hurry," said Ma'alor. "Some men take a lifetime to do that."

"And others never grow wise at all," said Dan'nor. "But then, we're not really talking about wisdom—*are* we?"

Ma'alor's eyes narrowed almost imperceptibly. "No," he agreed. "We're not. So I ask you again: what made you decide to join us?"

Dan'nor thought about it for a moment. "I saw what they did to my father. I can't just do nothing in return."

Ma'alor nodded. "Good. I have no use for intellectuals—Zanc'cov was the only good one I ever met. I'll take a man with a reason to hate over an intellectual any day."

He leaned forward and held out his hand. Dan'nor took it.

Ma'alor sat back. "Now, then. What did your father tell you about our activities?"

The younger man tried to remember. "He mentioned a factory owned by Councillor Fidel'lic. One you had sabotaged. And a plan—something important and very dangerous. He said that my Military experience might have played a valuable part in it."

A beat. "That's all?" asked Ma'alor.

Dan'nor thought some more. "I believe so."

"Did the name *Ralak'kai* ever come up?"

"Yes. It did. My father said Ralak'kai was one of you—and he'd been captured. Placed among the combatants—in the Conflicts."

Ma'alor's eyes were still trying to see into him. Dan'nor realized that the dark man didn't quite trust him yet.

"It's true," Ma'alor said finally. "Ralak'kai has been seen on the videoscreen. He's there. And so, I expect, is your father. Or if he's not, he will be soon. Along with Zanc'cov and the others who were taken prisoner the other night."

"That," said Dan'nor, "is what I thought. What I feared." He returned Ma'alor's gaze. "But—unless I miss my guess —you are going to do something about them. Are you not?"

A board creaked where Dan'nor's escort was standing.

"You figured that out all by yourself?" asked Ma'alor.

"Yes. Is it true?"

Ma'alor nodded. "But it need concern you no further."

Dan'nor was caught off guard. "And why is that?"

"Simple," said the dark man. "You have never worked with us before. And we can't afford to make any mistakes."

"But my father . . ."

Ma'alor held up his hands—a peremptory gesture. "Your father was wrong. We can use you, all right—but not for *this*. For other things." He stood. "Go now. We'll get in touch with you when we need you."

Dan'nor didn't go. He didn't even get up.

"You're lying," he said. "It's not my inexperience that troubles you. It's that you still don't trust me."

Ma'alor regarded him. "Would *you*, if our positions were reversed?"

"No. I suppose not. But I want to help my father. And I trust his judgment. If *he* thought my Military experience could help you—who are *you* to say otherwise?"

Ma'alor obviously hadn't expected that. Anger smoldered in his eyes.

"Is there anyone else among you who knows anything about the Military?" asked Dan'nor. "Who has been trained by the Military? Lived his life in the Military?"

The dark man continued to glare at him. But when he answered, his voice was under control. "No," he said. "You are the only one—other than Trien'nor, of course." The anger in his eyes died. "And he, unfortunately, is of little use to us now."

Silence. As Dan'nor sat before Ma'alor, he was reminded of the Council's scrutiny on the day he went before it.

Except this time, he had no fear. And because of that, this time, he knew he would win.

"Very well," said Ma'alor at last. "You will be part of it, Tir'dainia. Part of our big event." He laughed—a surprising sound, coming from *him*. "But you may wish you had not been so eager to get involved."

And in the hours that followed, Ma'alor outlined their plan.

Worf huddled in the keep with the other invaders, glad for the shelter from the cold, driving rain. They sat in a high-raftered hall, listening to the echo of helmets and weapons as they dropped against the smooth, stone floor. Worf's comrades seemed too tired to lay their gear down carefully. And more than tired—they seemed almost not to care.

Inside, it was dark, the corners of the place softened with deep shadows. Outside, it was darker still. Except for the infrequent stroke of light, which illuminated in quick, staccato bursts the piece of courtyard framed by the open doorway.

It was in these flashes that Worf saw the bodies—*many* bodies, and most of them had not died at the hands of other warriors. Still, he did not need to see the helmless corpses to remember what the marshals had done. It was branded on the backside of his eyes, carved there like a blood eagle, so that even shutting them was no relief.

The defenders—or what was left of them—had all departed by now, gone up into the hills and vanished. Nor had anyone bothered to stop them. It was as if a truce had been called—one without words, understood by both sides.

And now what? Would they wait until the rain stopped— and then pursue their enemies as before? Or stay here and defend the place as if it were theirs now?

When Harr'h got up and stood before them, Worf thought

he would find out. But that was not the veteran's purpose in addressing them.

"You know me," he said. "I am no stranger to you." He looked about. "Nor am I one of those linked to the sled riders, who guide us in our forays."

A few of the other veterans shifted uncomfortably; the Klingon tried to mark them in the darkness. He began to understand better how the warriors' orders came down, and from whom.

"So when I speak," Harr'h went on, "I have nothing to gain. And what I say is *this:* forget what you have seen this day. Forget it as quickly as you can. Warriors who think too much become weak; they fall to the first quick blade that comes along. Believe me. I have seen this before—the flash of light, and the madness, and the way the marshals strike down the maddened ones. Because I put it from my mind that earlier time, I still stand before you now. Those who could not do that are long dead." He shrugged. "That is all I have to say."

Having finished, Harr'h returned to his place. But not before casting a look in the Klingon's direction. Nor was it a random glance—he knew exactly whom he was looking at.

And what he said with his eyes was not what he had said with his mouth. For Worf, he seemed to have a different message.

You are not like the rest, Harr'h appeared to say. You *cannot* forget. For you, the burden will be much greater.

And the advice proferred in that secret glance was unmistakable: to *endure.* To fight on as if the fight were honorable, knowing all the time that it is not. To strike a bargain with himself, trading dignity for a chance at survival—just as Harr'h himself had done, battle after battle after battle.

But as well as the veteran seemed to know him, he didn't know him well *enough*. Such a bargain was unacceptable to the Klingon.

His cowardice was bad. It was a terrible, shameful thing.

Yet to participate in a combat empty of honor was worse. He would not fight for those who could do what the marshals had done.

Somewhere out there, past the courtyard and the walls, there had to be an alternative. Perhaps even an escape.

Despite the difficulty of surviving alone in the wilderness, despite the likelihood that a sky rider would find him and destroy him . . . he had to risk it.

At his first opportunity, he would desert.

"Will that be all?"

Data nodded. "Yes. Thank you. You may go now."

The Klah'kimmbri left, shutting the door behind him. The android found himself alone, at a somewhat primitive keyboard-and-monitor setup, with access to the installation's entire array of data.

"Well," he told himself, "this *is* a pleasant development —if an unexpected one."

From the beginning, no one had questioned his identity. What was more, as soon as he had voiced his purpose in being here, the ranking functionary—the Coordinator— had personally ushered him to this private workstation. He had even been offered assistance with the workings of the computer system—which he, of course, declined.

In the meantime, he had gotten an inkling of the reason for his preferred status. It was not that he had been mistaken for an individual, as he had first believed—but rather, that he had been associated with this world's ruling *class*.

The crucial factor in all this was his hair—that gaudy shade of red that had characterized the locks of the Council members. Since the councillors were the only examples they had seen of Klah'kimmbri up close—and since none of them had had anything *but* red hair—the ship's xenologists had assumed that it was a common trait.

He saw now that they had been wrong. Everyone at this installation had *dark* hair—more like Data's natural color.

He couldn't help but smile at the thought. *Natural* indeed. Could anything be natural in an artificial being like himself?

In any case, his hair color had set him apart as some sort of dignitary—perhaps even a member of the Council itself. Without question, a stroke of luck.

Still smiling, he set to work.

The Klah'kimmbri computer system was not all that difficult to decipher. It took the android but a few moments to familiarize himself with the ways in which it diverged from the Federation approach to information technology. Mostly, he decided, the Klah'kimmbri model was just less sophisticated.

He punched in a request: INFORMATION ON CONSCRIPT JEAN-LUC PICARD.

NO SUCH REFERENT.

Data hadn't believed that there would be—but it had been worth a try.

All right, then. A different approach: GENERAL INFORMATION ON CONSCRIPTS.

A menu came up on the screen. It offered Data a breakdown of available information according to ARRIVAL TIME, GEOGRAPHIC DISTRIBUTION, SKILL CATEGORY and something called CURRENT STATUS.

Out of curiosity more than anything else, the android called up CURRENT STATUS. It turned out to be a separation of the living and the dead. Each conscript was described by an eight-digit code; the last digit, apparently, indicated whether the conscript still survived.

The larger subfile, by far, was the one that listed the dead. Data recognized that some of his comrades might be included there. However, CURRENT STATUS would not be the logical place to begin his search.

Returning to the menu, he opted for ARRIVAL TIME.

There were three of them in the wagon now, each bound to a part of the vehicle. And a good deal more securely than before.

"For a moment there," said the dark man, "I thought I was a goner."

Picard managed a chuckle. "I know the feeling. The first time I woke in this wagon, I was glad of it—believe it or not. Even all trussed up, I was delighted just to be alive." He scanned the lifeless, forbidding slopes of the valley through which they were traveling. "Of course, I am no longer quite so pleased with the situation."

"You should have escaped while you had the chance," said Ralak'kai. "Both of you."

Picard shook his head, though his friend couldn't see it. "No. I couldn't just leave you here—not after what you'd done for me."

Ralak'kai grunted. "And look at the results."

"I didn't hear you protesting at the time," said Picard. "In any case, I really thought we would make it. If you're looking for a brave fool, it's our friend here."

"Geordi," said the dark man.

"Geordi," repeated Ralak'kai, by way of a greeting.

"Pleased to meet you. My name is Picard. And my traveling companion is called Ralak'kai."

"And we thank you for helping us," added the golden-eyed one. "Or rather, for *trying* to help us."

Geordi shrugged. "I *had* to, I guess. It didn't seem right—your being prisoners and all."

"Don't downplay it," said Ralak'kai. "It was heroic."

"Yes," said Picard. "You're a hero, Geordi. We are *all* heroes, each having risked his life for one of the others. And now that we have established that, can we find something more practical to talk about?"

Geordi laughed. It was a rich, full laugh—out of place in such stark environs.

"Neither of you seem too broken up about your imprisonment," he noted. "If I'd known you were so content, I might not have been tempted to rescue you."

"Don't mistake our banter for jubilation," said Ralak'kai. "We would still rather be free—like the others."

"Agreed," said Picard. He sighed. "Although it is good to know that at least *some* of us made it over the bridge."

He looked back at the train of wagons behind them. Of course, his remark was an understatement—they were the only prisoners left.

It had been a good night's work.

But there weren't likely to be any other nights like it. Having been burned once, their guards weren't going to be so lax a second time.

"Incidentally," said Geordi, "does anyone have any idea of where we're going?"

"Unfortunately," answered Ralak'kai, "no."

"Nor," said Picard, "do we know what is intended for us when we get there."

The dark man nodded. "I see."

Picard still hadn't decided if that metallic-looking band around the upper half of Geordi's face was part of him or not. At first glance, with only the stars to see by, he had assumed that the thing was some sort of sensory appendage.

In the daylight, however, it was apparent that the band was something Geordi *wore*. Though for the life of him, Picard couldn't guess the purpose of it—or, for that matter, how he could see with that thing covering his eyes.

"Obviously," Ralak'kai told the newcomer, "your people have excellent manners—wherever it is you come from."

Geordi looked at him. "Why do you say that?"

Ralak'kai smiled a little. "You haven't asked me about my resemblance to the marshals." He indicated Picard with a tilt of his head. "My friend here had hardly introduced himself when he inquired about that."

Picard harumphed, getting into the spirit of the exchange. Anything to keep from thinking about what would happen to them at their journey's end. "How impolite of me."

"Actually," said Geordi, "I *had* wondered about it. Did you . . . I mean, do you . . . ?"

"Have any idea why it should be?" Ralak'kai shook his

head. "Not the least clue. Perhaps *you* can guess—we seem to have exhausted all *our* theories."

Geordi settled back to think about it.

They passed the better part of the day chewing the subject to the bone before they let it drop. By then, they had emerged from the far end of the valley, and spotted the distant fortress that made that other one seem tiny by comparison.

It was late. Dan'nor was surprised by the knock on the door.

Ice water trickled the length of his spine. *We've been found out. The Civil Service has come to get me.*

He composed himself, opened the door—and breathed a sigh of relief. It was Ma'alor.

He came in without being invited, made his way to a chair. Dan'nor closed the door, noted the look in Ma'alor's eyes. There was no mistaking it, even in the dim light.

"What's wrong?" he asked. Something about his father?

The dark one told him—but it was a moment before Dan'nor could grasp the import of what Ma'alor was saying.

"How can that be?" he said, as it finally sank in. "Ralak'kai is a *Klah'kimmbri*. And anyway, that sort of thing has never been part of the Conflicts."

Ma'alor grunted. "It is *now*. As I say, they must be desperate. Maybe there's been a drastic decline in viewership. Or who *knows* why. The point is that they're *doing* it."

Dan'nor shook his head. "So now what?"

"A change of schedule," said Ma'alor. "We move sooner than we had planned." He leaned forward. "I must tell you, it's going to be tougher than it would have been before. *Much* tougher." He let the late evening silence elaborate on his behalf. It did so, eloquently. "Are you still with us?"

Dan'nor nodded.

* * *

"Commander?"

"Data—*damn,* but it's good to hear your voice."

"I apologize for my tardiness. There were circumstances here which prevented my communicating earlier."

"That's all right," said Riker, leaning back in his command chair. "Just hang on and we'll beam you right up."

The first officer was just about to contact O'Brien in the transporter room when Data stopped him. "Request permission," said the android, "to remain planetside."

Riker chided himself. He had just assumed that Data had completed his work down there. "You need more time to locate our people?" he asked.

"I *have* located them," said the android, "in a *general* way. However, precise coordinates are unavailable. Therefore . . ."

By now, Riker had a pretty good idea of how Data's mind worked. "You think the quickest way to find them," he expedited, "is to go after them yourself. Correct?"

"Correct, sir."

The first officer was all too aware of the need to keep this conversation short—to pack up and retreat to a safe distance again, before the Klah'kimmbri noticed an extra blip in the sky.

But he didn't want to rush this decision. It was too important—not only to Data, but also to the whole of the conscripted away team.

"You have the means to accomplish this?" he asked.

"I do, sir," said the android.

"I can't give you much time. That disease that Fredi had—it's spreading. Before long, I'm going to have to leave this sector—get us to a starbase. You understand, Data?"

"Perfectly, Commander. Allow me two A'klahn days. I believe that is all I will need."

The first officer could feel his molars grinding together. "All right," he said finally. "You've got two days—exactly. Riker out."

He looked to Wesley. The ensign was turned around in his seat, waiting for instructions.

"Take us back to our previous position," said Riker. "We're going to stick it out a little longer."

"Aye, sir." Wesley tapped in what had by now become familiar coordinates. "Ready."

"Engage."

Silently, Riker cheered Data on. If anybody could find the away team in that mess, *he* could. But in two days?

What the hell did Data have in mind?

Chapter Sixteen

IT WAS COLD up in the hills. The wind raised goose bumps wherever it touched Pulaski's bare skin.

The day before, shortly after the last of their patients had been taken from them, a horde of silent wagoneers had come and packed up the med enclosure. There had been no warning. But the other meds seemed to accept it, so Pulaski didn't try to stop it either.

She had been educated by experience. One did not stand in the way of things—unless one was ready to get knocked down. And although the fight hadn't quite gone out of her, she had determined that she would pick her spots.

No doubt, it was intended that they should set up their installation somewhere else. But where? And for whom?

She didn't know. Then again, she didn't know a lot of things—still. In some cases, she had answers—those supplied by the other meds, or even by the warriors—but they were unsatisfactory. Or insufficient.

For instance—what was all the fighting about? And if it was something important enough to risk lives for, why did the lordly ones—the marshals—decline to participate? What was their function, after all—other than to wrench her patients from her before they'd had a chance to heal correctly?

As for the theory that they were here because they were criminals—it was certainly possible, if that referred to political crimes. Certainly, *she* could have been capable of such activity, if the marshals were any indication of what the authorities were like *outside*.

Pulaski doubted, however, that any of the meds could have been guilty of baser crimes. She had seen them in action. They were dedicated, concerned—if a little too afraid of the marshals. Definitely not the throat-cutting type.

The wind picked up and she pulled her cloak closer about her. The soles of her feet were starting to hurt. Her boots weren't made for this terrain. It seemed she could feel every pebble, every bit of gravel that littered their trail.

And as far as she could tell, it was only going to get worse. For some time, they had been able to see a path amid the high ground to their right. As they progressed, the path had descended—as if it would ultimately meet the one they traveled now. Pulaski had a pretty good idea that they would be on that higher trail before very long.

Great, she told herself. *That means it'll get even colder. And in time, my boots will peel off altogether.*

She scanned the descending path more closely than before, resolved to check the equipment wrappings again before they started up. The way was narrower up there— there wouldn't be any room to slip around the sides of the vehicles and make adjustments if something began to come loose. And there were too many items in short supply already for them to . . .

Pulaski stopped in mid-thought, gasped. She couldn't help it. What she had seen had caught her completely off guard.

There was a watcher on that trail up above them. He had concealed himself as best he could, but the place didn't offer much cover. It was amazing, in fact, that he had managed to escape their notice for so long—to blend in with the hillside, despite his size.

In that first shocked instant, Pulaski's eyes had locked with his. And there was an intensity in that gaze that had shaken her to her roots.

Nor, as time resumed its passage, was she able to tear her eyes away from the watcher's. Not until after he conceded her discovery of him and clambered to his feet.

There were cries of surprise from the other meds, sounds of fear from the wagon drivers. For they had no one to defend them—and this watcher posed a threat. It was obvious in the way he held his weapon—some sort of broadax—and in the way he scrutinized the carts full of medical supplies.

Pulaski could see now that he was a warrior. But for reasons she couldn't fathom, he had discarded his helmet and part of his armor. His black hair blew in the swirling winds; his savage eyes narrowed against the flying grit.

Why was he alone? Was he the last survivor of an ambush? Or was there some other reason?

No matter. Regardless of how he'd arrived at this pass, he certainly wasn't a bearer of good tidings. He had been stalking them like a predator for who knew how long, waiting to pounce.

Apparently, there was something he wanted from them.

As frightened as they were, med and driver alike, no one ran. Everyone seemed to prefer the anonymity of the group.

So when the watcher made his way down from his perch—a difficult task, and one that he accomplished with animal ease—they were all at his mercy.

He approached the wagon train warily, his eyes darting here and there. He shifted the ax from one hand to the other, as if waiting for someone to challenge him.

Pulaski thought about how much damage that ax could do to the contents of the wagons. How many lives might be lost if the intruder were allowed to proceed unchecked.

If she had had more time to consider it, she probably

wouldn't have intervened. But she didn't have that much time.

As Pulaski slipped between the warrior and the cart nearest to him, she drew his scrutiny again. Up close, his gaze was even more fascinating—more frightening.

"What do you want?" she heard herself ask.

Cruel eyes widened beneath that dark and massive brow. For a second or two, Pulaski thought he would strike her—just as the marshal had, but with killing force.

Then his strangely expressive lips shaped a single word: "Food." His voice was a rumble, but the meaning was clear enough.

Pulaski relaxed a little. *Food?* Well, that was something they could surely stand to part with. After all, big as he was, the warrior could hardly take it *all* with him.

"Kopaa'kar," she called to the med nearest the end of the train—never taking her eyes off the intruder, as if she could hold him with her gaze as surely as he held her. "Uncover the food. Let him take what he wants."

As Kopaa'kar hurried to comply, the warrior's attention was turned in that direction. Pulaski felt grateful as he moved away, drawn toward the last wagon.

She was shaking, she realized as she watched him go. But that was all right. He'd take some food and soon he'd be gone.

Just as she thought that, she felt another kind of scrutiny—a more familiar kind. By now, she had developed a sixth sense about it.

The flying machine, like the intruder, seemed to come out of nowhere. And as if it were a kindred spirit, it headed right for him.

The warrior noticed it before it had come within half a dozen meters of him. For some reason, he seemed to feel threatened by it. And with alarming quickness, he tried to squash it with his ax.

The flying machine jerked out of harm's way—and the ax

struck a covered mound of wagon cargo instead. There was a *craak*—the sound of equipment breaking beneath the tarpaulin.

Then, with a snarl, the warrior ripped his weapon free and went after the flying device again.

Pulaski couldn't believe it. She had come *this close* to avoiding any damage at all. And now every one of their precious instruments were in danger.

How could she just stand there and watch? She had to *do* something.

The flying machine was staying just a step ahead of the warrior—all the time keeping him before its lens.

An idea came to her—a way to end the destruction—and she lunged for the nearest wagon. With any luck, there would be some metal support-pole components among the cargo—*hah*. Wrestling with the tarp, pushing aside other pieces of equipment, she got a grip on one of the long pieces of metal. Fortunately, it didn't offer much resistance—it just slipped free.

By now, the machine was retreating in her direction—pursued by the flailing warrior. It was facing the other way—still oblivious to her presence.

Just before it came within striking distance, Pulaski realized that she was smiling—in anticipation of what she was about to do. It was like finishing the job she'd started back in the enclosure.

Then the machine retreated a little more, and Pulaski swung with all her might. She felt the impact as the metal strut connected solidly with her target.

And a moment later, her eyes were scraped raw as the damned thing exploded in her face.

She recoiled, staggered, fell against something hard. Tried to squeeze out the pain along with the tears.

My god, she thought, *I'm blind. I'm blind . . .*

But she wasn't. When she opened her eyes, they hurt—like the rest of her face. But she could see fine.

That wasn't the problem at all. The problem was that she didn't have the slightest idea of where she was—or how she'd gotten there.

When she looked around, she saw a host of strange faces gathered around a long line of wagons—the entire tableau framed by a severe, mountainous landscape. At her feet, there was a smoking, sparking machine of some sort.

None of it looked familiar. None of it.

Her mind reeled with the immensity of her loss. Something had happened to her memory . . .

Someone walked past her—someone big, with an ax in his hand. He kicked at the sizzling hunk of debris on the ground—and looked at her over his shoulder.

He was dangerous looking—not the kind she'd want to get too close to. But the sight of him kindled a spark inside her. A spark of recognition. Did she . . . know him? Yes—she *did*.

The name escaped her for the moment. But she knew exactly who this one was. A scene flashed in front of her—the inside of a cabin, and a group of people standing around a gaming board . . .

It was all coming back now. She just needed a few minutes to sort it out.

The one with the ax didn't linger, however. He went to one of the wagons, the one farthest from her, and ripped off the tarpaulin that still half covered it.

One of the strangers came over to her and put his arm about her shoulders. "Pulaski, are you all right?"

Pulaski. That was her name, wasn't it? And she was a *doctor*—a medical officer on . . . on a ship of some kind. The . . . *damn,* it was on the tip of her tongue . . .

Someone else came over and applied something cool and wet to her face. It stung for a moment, then it felt good. She leaned back against the wagon behind her, letting the pain of her burned skin leech away.

Abruptly, there was a name in her head. *Enterprise.* Of course—that was the name of the ship. And that other place she'd recalled, the cabin—that was on another ship, the *Gregor Mendel.*

Faces and events spilled over one another as the dam inside her broke. Picard, Geordi, Riker . . . she'd called Riker after Badnajian disappeared. Worf . . .

Worf!

Tearing away the dressing that covered her face, Pulaski looked around for the Klingon. But he was nowhere to be seen. At the last wagon, there were people working to put the tarpaulin back into place.

"Where did he go?" she asked.

"Who?" asked one of those tending to her. "The warrior?"

"Yes," she insisted, "the warrior. Where did he go?"

The stranger pointed to the path above them. "That way," she said. And then, misinterpreting the reason for Pulaski's question, "You need not worry about him. He spared us."

Pulaski frowned. There was no evidence of Worf on the trail either. Being a Klingon, he could move quickly on treacherous terrain.

What had happened to him, that he didn't know her—that he could leave her here like this, as if she were just another stranger in a crowd of strangers? Indeed, what had happened to *her* that she hadn't recognized *him?*

Had all of them who'd been on the *Mendel* had their memories tampered with this way? But why—for what purpose?

And how was it that she'd gotten *hers* back?

More to the point, now that she was starting to remember, what was she going to do about it? Stay with the line of wagons and bide her time—or follow Worf, knowing all the time that she might not be able to help him once she found him? *If* she found him.

Pulaski made her decision, moved past those who had been helping her. They watched her skirt the wagon, then head for the steep slope that separated them from the upper trail.

"Pulaski? What are you doing?"

"I'm going after him," she called back.

"You can't," someone said. "He's a warrior. He'll *kill* you."

Certainly, there was a chance of that. She didn't discount the seriousness of the warning.

But she didn't turn back either.

"Sorry, sir," said Radzic. "It was just a false alarm."

Riker looked at him and nodded. "Of course. Keep at it, crewman."

On his way past the science stations, he had an urge to strike something. He curbed it.

Damn. For a moment, he thought that they'd actually gotten somewhere. That they'd located one of the crew on the *Mendel*—a Tetracite named Seedirk. No question—it was a Tetracite all right. Two of them, in fact. Only, upon closer inspection, neither one had turned out to be the *right* Tetracite.

The first officer was beginning to see why Data had opted to find their people on his own. Even after they had discovered the Tetracites, it had taken hours to check their physical particulars against Seedirk's profile.

At a closer distance, they'd have accomplished it in much less time. But they didn't dare linger at a closer distance—a fact that twisted in him more and more with each passing minute.

It was increasingly clear that their hopes rested with the android. Though Riker still didn't know what Data's plan was—and nearly half of his allotted time had come and gone.

Riker had barely reached the command center when the turbo doors opened and Burtin strode onto the bridge. The first officer saw him out of the corner of his eye, bit his lip and met the doctor halfway.

He should have checked in with sickbay some time ago.

He knew that. But with this Tetracite affair and his trying to figure out what Data was up to, it had completely slipped his mind.

Burtin looked a hell of a lot more determined than Riker had ever seen him. His words were clipped, insistent: "We've got to talk, Commander."

"Certainly," said Riker. He indicated the observation lounge and they both stepped inside.

Burtin didn't bother to take a seat, so Riker didn't either. They stood beside the conference table, and even the gentleness of the lighting didn't soften the lines in Burtin's face.

"You know," said the doctor, "for a long time, I was in awe of this assignment. Kate Pulaski, Captain Jean-Luc Picard, the *Enterprise*—these are names you *hear* about. *Read* about. You don't get to see them up close—especially if you're only a bone-splicer out on the frontier.

"Out there, Commander, we take every little sickness seriously—and I mean *seriously*. I know that's not the case here. You've got the latest technology—the latest equipment, the latest medicines. *And* you've got the best-trained personnel. So when a little old disease comes along, you don't panic. You just take care of it.

"I figured that that's what *I* would do. I mean, Doctor Pulaski wasn't all that frantic about Fredi's ailment. *Concerned*, yes, but far from frantic. So I tried to take it in stride—as I thought *she* would have. Even when the godforsaken thing mutated. I tried to act as I thought the assistant chief medical officer of this ship *should* act. I got to work on the problem—and I didn't make an uproar about it.

"Then it got worse. It started spreading. But did I rock the boat? No. I calmly apprised the ranking officer of the situation. I calmly recommended a course of action. I only gave in to my instincts in one regard—I recorded my misgivings for the record, despite the fact that I thought I'd ultimately be laughed at. 'Hey, look at this—some crazy quack dragged the *Enterprise* to a starbase because two people on the ship got sick. Amazing. Didn't he know he wasn't on the frontier anymore?'

"Now I see that I didn't go too far at all. If I made a mistake, it was in not going far *enough*. We've got seventeen patients now. Every available blood-purification unit is in constant use. Critical care is completely engaged—we're spilling over into the less secure areas, having rigged up portable field generators to maintain the quarantine.

"It's gone too far, Commander. I can't state that strongly enough. Twenty-four hours from now, we'll see twice as many cases—and twice as many again twenty-four hours after that. By then, of course, you and I will probably be among the afflicted." Burtin paused. "The nearest starbase is six days away at warp nine. I checked. In six days, half the population of the *Enterprise* could be writhing in the corridors, gasping for breath."

He took a deep breath, let it out. "Strangely enough, I still feel as though I shouldn't panic. But I *am* panicking, Commander. I want this ship headed for Starbase Ninety-One—*now*. And I don't *care* if we leave behind that away team or not."

Riker frowned. Was that what he was doing? Sacrificing the many for the few? Or was he keeping a cool head—knowing that medical officers always painted the worst picture possible, and that things seldom turned out as badly as they predicted?

Finally, he shook his head. "I gave Data two full days. I can't leave before then. I'm not discounting what you're saying, Doctor—believe me, I'm not. But I can't just abandon our people down there without giving them a chance."

Burtin's eyes narrowed, and he nodded. "It's your choice, Commander. That is, until you come down with the disease yourself—at which time I have every intention of relieving you of your command." And with that, he headed for the exit.

As the lounge doors opened, Burtin turned again—as if he had thought of something else to say. But he was interrupted by the commotion outside, on the bridge.

Both men were spurred to action. The first officer, a little quicker, was only a step behind the doctor as they emerged . . .

And saw Wesley Crusher sprawled on the deck beside his conn station. Troi was kneeling beside him, clasping his shoulder.

"What happened?" asked Riker—though he already knew the answer.

"He collapsed," said Troi, her face taut with Wesley's pain and fear. "Not more than a few seconds ago."

"It's all right, sir," said Wesley. "I think the symptoms are just beginning." He tried to get up under his own power, failed and slumped against the deck again. "But I'm going to need a gurney to get to sickbay."

Burtin was kneeling beside the ensign too, now. He looked up at Riker, said nothing. But his silence was thick with accusation.

With the return of full circulation to his stiff, rope-scored limbs, Picard was beginning to feel the pain he'd been spared since his failed escape attempt. It had already gotten so bad that he winced with every halting step.

"Get a move on," called the marshal behind him. "Or I'll give you a taste of what *real* agony is like."

The courtyard echoed with his threat. Other marshals heard and turned their heads. When nothing happened, they turned away again.

Ralak'kai and Geordi walked on either side of Picard, similarly hobbled by their physical discomforts. They exchanged glances.

"A taste," suggested Ralak'kai, "of the hospitality we have to look forward to?"

Picard grunted. "No doubt."

The marshals might have been less testy, the human

observed, if the full complement of prisoners had arrived. They had been quite vocal in their anger when they saw all the empty wagons.

Unlike that other fortress, there had been no careful guards to greet them here. Nor could Picard, now that he was inside, see more than a few casual watchers up on the walls.

Obviously, there was no fear of invasion in this place. And indeed, what need was there for guards when the fortress was crawling with sky riders—and nothing *but* sky riders? The only warriors he saw were those who had brought them in the wagons.

Was this some sort of headquarters for the marshals, then? A dispatch point?

And if that were the case, why had Picard and the others been transported here? Not for punishment alone, he thought. After all, *that* could have been meted out a while ago, and with a lot less effort.

Then why? As some sort of work force? He looked around. There didn't seem to be a lot of work that needed doing. Or . . .

"Move it, I said!"

Picard felt a blow in the middle of his back, and his legs were too inflexible to absorb the impact. He pitched forward, caught himself on hands and knees as a cloud of dust rose around him.

He didn't quite see the action that ensued, but he gathered that Geordi had come to his defense. Perhaps even shoved the marshal as the marshal had shoved Picard.

What he *did* see was a second sky rider striking Geordi down from behind. As the dark man fell, the metal band he wore on his face went flying.

In that moment, Picard understood that the band was not part of Geordi. And he understood more than that —for without it, the dark man seemed confused—disoriented.

The band is some sort of *seeing* device, he realized. Geordi is *blind*.

To his credit, the dark man didn't whimper or cry out at his loss. But then, even after knowing him only this short time, Picard hadn't expected him to.

Instead, Geordi calmly and methodically searched the ground around him with probing fingers. And when after a few seconds he hadn't found anything, he resolutely got to his feet.

There was no point in begging, he knew. It would not get him anywhere.

Picard saw where the metal band had landed. So did Ralak'kai. But the marshals weren't about to let them recover it for their companion.

"Come on," said one of the sky riders. Picard felt another jolt, though this time he managed to stay on his feet. "Are you deaf or something?"

"My friend dropped something," he said, confronting the marshal. "Let him have it back." It grated on him to say the next word: "Please."

The sky rider's mouth spread slowly into a leering grin.

"What happens to *him,*" he said, "is no business of *yours.*"

He removed his blaster from his holster.

"Unless you insist on making it so."

"It's all right," said Geordi, taking a step in the other human's direction. Apparently, he'd heard the sound of the weapon being withdrawn. "Don't push him—I can live without it."

Nonetheless, Picard was about to press his suit—when one of the warriors stooped to pick up the metal band. Without hesitating, he went over to the dark man and placed it in his hands. Then, still silent, he went back to his place by the wagons.

Nor did the marshals make him pay for his benevolence. There was a large number of warriors in the courtyard right now—perhaps the sky riders thought it unwise to antagonize them.

In any case, they waited long enough for Geordi to slip his device back into place. But no longer.

A third time, Picard felt a prod from behind. Except that this time, it was with the barrel of a blaster.

"Go on," said the marshal who wielded it. "Give me an excuse."

But the human didn't give it to him. He no longer had a reason to. He walked as best he could across the remainder of the courtyard, until he was swallowed by the stone-cold maw of the keep.

Chapter Seventeen

PAY DIRT!

Riker himself directed the security force that ushered the *Mendel* survivors off the transporter platform. Troi was there, too, to help assure them that they were in a safe place—a friendly place.

It had been apparent from the second the survivors materialized that Riker's hypothesis had been accurate: they had absolutely no idea of where they were. Their memories were gone—though with some rehab therapy, they would probably get most of them back.

To compound their confusion, they had been beamed up without any warning—another quick-as-blazes, get-in-and-get-out maneuver, which brought the ship within transporter range for just the few moments they needed. Fortunately, though they were pushing their luck pretty hard, there was still no sign that the Klah'kimmbri had spotted them.

As Riker scanned the survivors' faces, he felt a little rush of vindication. Sure, they looked scared and uncertain. But they were *alive*. And if he'd listened to Burtin, they would probably have died by the time another rescue vessel showed up.

Not that it made the doctor's warning any less valid. But it was a victory—and Riker felt he'd earned the right to revel in it. Victories of any sort had been exceedingly rare since they'd arrived in the vicinity of A'klah.

It was also good to know that Data's plan—whatever it was—was working. There was no way that these eight survivors could have come together by coincidence. Somehow, Data had rounded them up and kept them in one place—though stumbling on them without instructions from the android had been a stroke of luck.

Seeing that the *Mendel*'s people were in good hands, Riker turned to Chief O'Brien.

"Good job," he said.

"Thank you, sir. I do my best." A fleeting smile, and then O'Brien was intent again on his board—reducing energy levels by careful stages.

"Commander Riker," intoned an ambient voice. The survivors looked around warily for its origin.

The first officer, however, recognized that it was Fong calling him from the bridge.

"Riker here."

"Sir—I think we've got *another* group—believe it or not. Seven more—and Palazzo is one of them."

The first officer felt himself grinning.

"Oh well," said O'Brien. "At least they didn't wait until I'd powered down completely."

"Excellent news, Mister Fong," said Riker. "Make the necessary course adjustments and proceed at optimum speed."

"Receiving coordinates now," said O'Brien. "They're not too far away from where we found *this* bunch."

If Data had been with them in the transporter room, Riker might have hugged him. The android was working some kind of miracle down there.

His jubilation was tempered only by one factor—the names that were still among the missing. *Picard. Pulaski. Geordi. Worf.*

Of course, it was possible that they'd be discovered in yet another group. Or that Data was busy gathering them up *now*.

But the android was running out of time. His deadline was less than a day away.

Data had already done more than anyone had expected of him. How much more could he do?

And then, no matter *how* efficient the android was, there was one obstacle even *he* couldn't surmount: the fact that some of the *Mendel*'s crew—and perhaps some of their own people as well—were already dead. Already beyond rescue.

Riker hoped with all his heart that his friends weren't in that number.

It hadn't been easy for Pulaski. Her feet were killing her, she was cold and the wind had rasped away patiently at her facial burns until they stung like the devil. Also, she wished that she'd taken some of that food herself.

But she had managed to find the Klingon, and then to keep him in sight without being spotted. That made all her smaller problems seem a good deal more tolerable.

What's more, her memory had come back—*all* of it. Not just up to the moment when she vanished off the *Mendel*, but also all the events that had transpired *since* then—first in the Klah'kimmbri installation where they'd apparently blocked out parts of her memory, and then, later, her experiences as a med.

She remembered how the flash of light from the destruction of the flying monitor had brought everything to the surface again—after a brief period in which she couldn't seem to remember *anything*.

And she recalled, as well, the straits in which she'd left the *Enterprise*—at the mercy of a disease that had the potential to be devastating. She wished she had her communicator, or that she could somehow get word to the ship—for *she believed she had a cure*.

She couldn't be certain, of course. But in all the time she'd spent here—wherever *here* was—the disease hadn't touched her. And if she was right about the bacterium's capacity for mutation into something contagious, she should have felt the symptoms by now. In fact, the disease should have killed her. Hell—it should have killed anyone that she'd come in contact with after her initial exposure to Fredi; without knowing it, she would have been a carrier.

Yet she was alive, unafflicted. And so, apparently, was Worf.

Something in this environment had to be protecting her. Something that she and the Klingon had in common.

Pulaski thought she had a handle on what that something might be. Unfortunately, the *Enterprise* could become a plague ship before she got a chance to test her theory.

Which only made the pursuit of Worf that much more critical. In the three or four hours since she'd left the transport train behind, she had been thinking up ways to approach the Klingon—and discarding them. She knew it wouldn't be enough to just tell him she was a friend. Or to try to explain the situation and ask him to help. At best, he'd take off, leaving her to fend for herself in this ungodly wilderness. At worst, he'd silence her for the danger she represented—as someone who could draw attention to him.

Recently, however, she'd come to see another possibility. Based on her observations of his progress, it seemed to her that Worf had a destination in mind. He was far from lost.

More than that, she had a feeling, he was not on his way to link up with other warriors. In the enclosure, her patients had kept their armor at their bedsides, and they always put it on before they left.

The Klingon, on the other hand, was missing parts of his protective garb—most notably, his helmet. No enemy would have taken that from him. The only other conclusion was that he had thrown it away himself—as an act of rebellion.

Knowing Worf as she did, and knowing his force of

character, she wouldn't have been surprised if he'd decided that these battles were somehow beneath him—somehow contemptible. After all, even *without* his memory, he was a Klingon—and Klingons, he'd said often enough, placed honor above everything. How honorable could these combats be, if the behavior of the marshals was any indication?

Was it possible, then, that he was deserting—and that he knew a way out of here? That if she just hung on a little longer, he would lead her to some sort of civilization— where she had a chance of contacting the ship?

There was no guarantee—but she hoped so. And until she had a viable plan for defusing a confrontation with Worf, she decided to try and ride that hope.

Even as she pondered these things, Worf dropped out of sight over the brink of a long, stone escarpment. Pulaski was scared to death to lose him—especially now, so deep into the wilderness—but she also couldn't go after him right away. First, she had to make sure that he was well beyond the escarpment—that he'd had enough time to descend farther, and wouldn't hear her scrabbling around behind him.

At times like these, Pulaski wished she had the Klingon's hunting instincts—not to mention his surefootedness. A single wrong step and she'd be one sore physician.

When she had waited as long as she possibly could, she emerged from her most recent hiding place—some rocks beside a gentle incline that twisted into the steep one—and started down. Of course, there was no way to know if her timing was true until she reached the bottom.

Staying low, using her hands as well as her feet in crablike fashion, the doctor got down the escarpment without any slips—or, for that matter, any noise that would have alerted her quarry. Her arms and legs were charley-horsed by the time she was done, and there was a sharp pain in her left knee from her unaccustomed exertion—but it could have gone a lot worse. Not for the first time that day she was grateful for her good fortune.

As she neared the edge over which Worf had disappeared, Pulaski could see the kind of terrain that prevailed below. It was a broad, meandering valley between two ridges, with a white river frothing at the center of it. One of the ridges was what she and Worf had just climbed out of. Just below her was a drop of another few meters, and then a slope as steep as the escarpment—although this one was grassy, nurtured by the flood.

It was open territory, affording few places where one could conceal oneself. The Klingon should have been plainly visible from the doctor's vantage point.

But he wasn't. She couldn't find him anywhere. Pushing herself up a little off the incline, Pulaski tried to get a slightly better view.

It didn't change anything. Somehow, Worf had eluded her.

The doctor staved off the panic she felt rising inside her. It doesn't make sense, she told herself. He's got to be down there. She looked about the sheer cliffs that defined the slope, seeming to stand guard over it. He couldn't have scaled *those* things—nor would he have had any reason to.

There was a thin trickle of ice water down her back. *Unless he suspected that he was being followed.*

Pulaski scanned the cliffs again, then the slope. Could he have made it all the way down to the river? It didn't seem possible—he hadn't had enough time.

Still, it was the least impossible possibility. And that was the one she'd been taught to pursue back in med school.

Allowing herself to slide forward, she dangled her legs over the edge of the naked-stone slope. Then, with a gentle thrust of her arms, she slid the rest of the way over the brink.

Her landing wasn't dignified, but it was effective. She found herself sitting at the top of the grassy incline, her rear end having taken the brunt of the impact.

That's when she heard the crunch of gravel behind her,

and whirled—just in time to see Worf come out of his crouch at the base of the escarpment. His ax was poised at shoulder height, and there was a killing lust in his eyes.

Without thinking, Pulaski launched herself forward. She tumbled end over end down the slope, certain that the Klingon would bury his axhead in her back at any moment.

When she somehow twisted sideways, and started to skid rather than somersault, she had a fraction of a second to see that Worf wasn't on her heels after all. She'd left him well up the incline—though he *had* started after her.

The doctor's body ached from her tumble, from the nightmarish rigors she'd put it through. As she tried to arrest her descent, to get her feet beneath her again, she began to think: *what should I do? Where can I go that he can't follow?*

Or was it best to stop and wait for him—to try to confront him now with his past, before the blood fever could rise to a crescendo in his Klingon brain?

She was still deciding when she noticed the *other* figures on the slope. They were past Worf and off to the side, though her frantic scrambling made it difficult to discern any more about them.

Worf didn't seem to notice the newcomers. He was too intent on catching up with Pulaski.

But that didn't last long, because a couple of seconds after Pulaski sighted them, one of the strangers opened fire on the Klingon.

It was a soft, almost indiscernible beam—more of a rippling effect than any visible sort of light. However, it hit Worf like a ton of bricks.

The Klingon toppled, rolled and finally slid to a halt, sprawled on the verdant slope. His ax ended up a couple of meters from his open hand.

As she gained her balance, and the strangers began to descend, Pulaski felt her heart sink. For she saw now how much they resembled the marshals.

Nor was there any way she could outrun them. Not as long as they had weapons like *that* one.

Vaguely, she wondered what the penalty might be for desertion.

While the others slid and scuttled down the slope to help the warrior's intended victim, Dan'nor approached the warrior himself.

Curiously, the still form was missing some of its armor. Dan'nor wondered how that could have come about—even as he stopped by its side and knelt, blaster at the ready.

It turned out, however, that there was no need for caution. The warrior was truly unconscious.

Replacing his weapon in his belt, Dan'nor turned the combatant over to get a better look at him—to see if he needed any immediate medical attention. After all, he could have injured himself when he fell.

The Klah'kimmbri was surprised to see a face that he recognized. He almost smiled. Wasn't this the one he'd seen on the screen that time? The one who had seemed so *efficient* to him?

He couldn't be *sure* it was the same warrior. After all, he'd had a helm on then, and it had concealed part of his face. But Dan'nor was *almost* sure.

What was he doing here, so far from the fighting? Dan'nor looked down slope, saw that the other rebels had caught up with the fleeing female. Perhaps *she* could shed some light on this.

As Ma'alor and the others trudged back up the incline, it seemed that the female was almost *eager* to reach the warrior. She was climbing faster than any of them. Strange behavior, thought Dan'nor, for one who was so recently striving to get away from him.

At the last, the female knelt on the unconscious one's other side. She pulled his eyelid up—to expose his staring eyeball—harumphed, and let it down again. Then she put a finger to his neck, just below the line of his jaw.

"He's not hurt," Dan'nor offered. "Not really. It was just a small jolt."

"He should be up in half an hour," said Ma'alor, standing over them—not an easy trick on this steep a hill. "Maybe less, judging by the size of him."

The female nodded. "I agree." She looked up at Ma'alor. "And since you didn't lie to me about *this*, I'm more inclined to believe the rest of it—that you *aren't* a pack of marshals bent on bringing us back for punishment." She surveyed the other faces around her. "But then, what *are* you? What are you doing here?"

Ma'alor shook his head. "First, I want some more information from *you*. How you came to find your memory, for instance. And what your link is to this one *here*." He indicated the warrior.

The female told them—appearing to hold nothing back. As she spoke, Dan'nor got an entirely new perspective on the error he'd made as Fulfillment Facilitator—the mistake that plunged this Pulaski and her crew mates into the Conflicts.

He also found that he liked something about the female. There was a strength in her, a *resolve*—not unlike the quality he had come to admire in Trien'nor.

"Remarkable," said Ma'alor, when she had finished. "You're saying that a simple, bright flash was enough to restore all your memories."

"That's right," said Pulaski. "Now it's *your* turn. If you're not marshals, what's your business here?"

Ma'alor didn't tell her everything, but he told her enough. More, in fact, than Dan'nor had expected he would. He spoke of Ralak'kai's initial imprisonment; of the innovation the Conflict Masters had so recently devised for him—a public execution, justified by his supposed attempts to escape from this Conflict zone. And, of course, of the concurrent executions of all those who'd aided him in his efforts—lending the event the proportions of a spectacle.

"We are here," Ma'alor explained, "to make sure that the

spectacle does not take place. To show the Council—and our people as well—that we will no longer stand for the Military's depravities."

Pulaski took a moment to digest it all. "So you're heading for that fortress now? The one where your friend is being held?"

Ma'alor nodded. "Yes."

She half smiled. "Then I wish you all the luck in the world."

Ma'alor eyed her. "You don't seem very optimistic for us."

She shook her head. "Forgive me—it's not that. I was just trying to think of a way you could help me, and I can't. I still have no way of getting out of here. No way of contacting my ship—and that disease could be running wild by now." She paused. "I know that sounds a little selfish, with all you're trying to do here—but I guess I've got my own problems as well."

"I see," said Ma'alor. "But tell me—would you be more interested in our venture if it were one of your crew mates that was to be executed?"

Pulaski's brows met above the bridge of her nose. "What do you mean?" she asked.

Dan'nor interrupted. There was something about the way Ma'alor was conducting this conversation that irked him. "We have sources," he said. "They've determined, as best they can, the identities of those who will die alongside Ralak'kai—and at least one came from the *Enterprise*. Possibly, more than one."

Ma'alor looked at him, but he did not berate him. Perhaps he would do that later. "It's the truth," he confirmed. "And we have actually seen someone of your race at Ralak'kai's side in the Conflicts. So my guess is that our information is accurate."

Pulaski looked more than just interested. Her eyes had become hard, unyielding.

"Take me to them," she said, "and I'll help in any way I can."

Ma'alor considered it. "All right," he said finally. "We can always use an extra pair of hands." He looked around, eyes narrowed like those of a hunting bird. "But you must keep up with us. Otherwise, we'll be forced to leave you behind."

Pulaski nodded. "I understand." She regarded the unconscious warrior. "But I'll need some help carrying *him*—at least, until he wakes up from that blast you hit him with."

Ma'alor looked at her. His mouth twisted as if he were about to laugh. "You don't understand after all. I meant that *you* could come along—not your friend here." Abruptly, his eyes became as hard as hers. "He would slow us down—we can't afford that. Not on open terrain like this, where we run too great a risk of being spotted. And not with Ralak'kai's execution approaching so quickly."

Pulaski didn't give in—not an inch. "Getting there is one thing," she said. "But once you're there, you're going to need help to free your friend." She placed a hand on the warrior's unfeeling shoulder. "No one fights like he can. No one is as skilled at moving quickly and quietly. He could be the difference for you between success and failure."

"Can he handle a blaster?" asked Rin'noc.

Pulaski turned to face him. "Better than anyone I've ever seen."

Dan'nor inspected the still, cruel features in a new light. Certainly, they could use the skills of a trained fighter. None of them were experts at this sort of thing—not even Dan'nor himself, with his Military background.

"That's all well and good," said Ma'alor. "But he doesn't know us. He doesn't even know *you*—not anymore. Why should he fight for us? Why not just tear our throats out and run at the first opportunity?"

Pulaski shook her head from side to side. "He won't hurt us. Not after I've had a chance to talk with him." She

233

paused. "I must admit, I'm not a hundred percent sure that he'll *help* us. But I know he won't *hurt* us."

Ma'alor spat. "How can you say that? Without question, he would have hurt *you*—if we hadn't arrived in time to stop him."

"I know," she said. "But it'll be different after I've had a chance to reassure him. He'll listen to reason—he always has."

Ma'alor made no attempt to mask his skepticism. "No," he said. "I won't allow it."

"However," said Dan'nor, "you don't necessarily have the final decision in this matter."

For the second time in the last few minutes, Dan'nor was subjected to Ma'alor's stare. But he went on anyway.

"I say we take the warrior with us," he told the others. "And I volunteer to carry him first."

There was a long silence. They could hear the rush of the river, the sighing of the wind on the open slope.

At last, someone spoke. "I'm with Dan'nor," said Rin'noc. "And I'll take my turn at carrying too, if I have to."

"I agree," said Ka'asot. "It won't hurt to have a warrior with us when we reach that fortress."

Nurel'lid had yet to voice his opinion. He seemed torn.

Until Pulaski fixed him with her gaze. "He'll die," she said, "if we leave him here like this. The only question is who'll get to him first—the marshals or the wild animals."

That tipped the scales. "All right," said Nurel'lid, though he couldn't face Ma'alor as he said it. "We'll take him."

Pulaski nodded, a smile tugging at the corners of her mouth. "Thank you. All of you."

Ma'alor scowled. "Very well then. We've prided ourselves on observing democratic principles. I bow to the will of the majority—though not without reservations."

He reached inside his pack, drew out his climbing rope— and tossed it to Dan'nor.

"If we're going to bring him along," said Ma'alor, "he

should be bound. So that he doesn't wake up and make short work of us."

Dan'nor didn't question the wisdom in that. Uncoiling the rope, he set to binding the warrior's arms and legs.

They were in three separate cells—Geordi nearest the narrow aperture that served as a window, then Ralak'kai, then Picard. And the flying eye device seemed to prefer Ralak'kai's company to that of his friends.

"I wonder why," said Geordi.

"Perhaps," suggested Picard, "it has something to do with your resemblance to the marshals."

Ralak'kai made a sound that was equivalent to a shrug. "Who knows? Like most of what we have encountered here, it is a mystery to me."

A clatter of footfalls came to them from down the dimly lit corridor. The maker of the footfalls had come quite close before they realized it was not their usual jailer—nor was he bringing them another round of that foul-smelling porridge.

This was one of the marshals. If anything, he seemed even haughtier in his bearing than the ones they had met so far. Geordi wasn't sure, but he thought that their visitor also wore more regalia than the average sky rider.

Like the flying eye, he stopped in front of Ralak'kai's cell; in fact, the machine appeared almost to perch on his shoulder. But he addressed all three of them, his golden eyes flitting from one to the other.

"You seem calm," he said.

A strange way to begin a conversation, Geordi thought.

"We would be *more* calm," noted Ralak'kai, "if we knew what we were doing here."

At that, the marshal's eyes lit up. "Ah," he said. "Now I understand. No one has told you."

Geordi didn't like the sound of that. "What do you mean?" he asked. "Told us what?"

The sky rider turned to face him. "It's very simple," he

said. "Just before day's end, someone will come for you. You will be escorted down to the courtyard. Then, with the sunset serving as a most dramatic backdrop, you will be executed—slowly, and painfully."

The words didn't sound real. It took some time before Geordi could come to grips with them.

"Executed?" he repeated. "But why? What for?"

The marshal appeared to grow slightly more serious. "For attempting to desert your companies," he said. "For trying to thwart the intent of the Conflicts. For compounding your crimes on the *outside* with aberrant behavior on the *inside.*" Suddenly, he smiled. "Do you think that's enough? Or should I heap on additional charges?"

"You are mad," said Picard. All Geordi could see of him was his accusing finger, thrust in their visitor's direction. "We aren't criminals and you know it. The only aberrant behavior *I've* seen has been on the parts of your blaster-happy cohorts." His voice gained in intensity as he went on. "As for thwarting the intent of your bloodbaths—I have no regrets about that. I'd do it again in a minute."

"Well said," offered Ralak'kai.

The marshal nodded. "Good. A little emotion—that's more like it."

"Wait a minute," said Geordi, catching on. "This is part of the show—isn't it? That machine is supposed to record our pre-execution hysteria."

"Of course," said Ralak'kai, as it dawned on him too. "Our tearful good-byes, our pleas for mercy."

Picard muttered a curse. "You can take your machine and go straight to hell—which, from what I've seen, can't be very far from here." He laughed—actually *laughed.* "We're through providing entertainment for you."

"That's correct," said Ralak'kai. "You can kill us if you want to. But it won't be the spectacle you're obviously looking for. Eh, Geordi?"

Geordi still felt numb at the prospect of being executed—

especially at the hands of this pompous ass. However, he played along with the others.

"Right," he said, noticing how the flying eye turned toward him now when he spoke. With less effort than he might have thought, he was able to fashion a grin. "You'd have more fun executing this flying pile of nuts and bolts."

The marshal looked at them. "Perhaps," he said. "We will see." He glanced at the window, as if to gauge the amount of daylight left in it. "I will be surprised if you still feel this way a few hours from now."

With that chilling remark still hanging in the air, he took his leave of them. The flying eye, however, remained.

"All right," said Ralak'kai, when the sounds of the marshal's departure had died. "Let's be true to those brave words now." He swatted at the machine, though he couldn't reach out far enough to actually have a hope of hitting it. "We may die—but we can do it with dignity."

Geordi grunted in assent. But he didn't *feel* as brave as his words. He found that he was trembling; his knees were unsteady. He had to sit down on his cell's only chair before he suffered the embarrassment of falling down.

My God, he told himself. *If you're like this now, what will you be like at the end?*

Chapter Eighteen

WORF WAS NO SOONER AWAKE than he was aware of the bonds that held him fast. He tried to break them, but they were too strong.

Where was he? What had happened to him? The last thing he remembered was turning the tables on that female who had pursued him.

Then he glimpsed movement over his shoulder—craned his neck to get a better view of it. What he saw made his stomach muscles tighten reflexively.

Marshals. Five of them. And another—the female!

Had she been some sort of bait? he wondered. Or a distraction, so that he would not pay attention to his real pursuers?

But no—that did not make any sense. Marshals needed no subterfuge. Not with their flying sleds and their blasters.

Perhaps she had merely drawn attention to him—his fear all along. Perhaps they had been tracking her, and then spotted him only when he emerged from concealment.

But why had she followed him in the first place? To recoup the food he had stolen? He did not think so. Nor did he believe she was a deserter—like him. A deserter would not be conversing so companionably with the marshals now.

If there were only some way he could free himself. Now, before they realized he was . . . *Damn*. Too late.

"Looks like your friend is awake," said one of them. The rest turned to regard Worf—and he wished he could shove their smug expressions down their throats, one at a time.

The female separated herself from the group and came over to him. Knelt beside him.

Her expression, at least, was not smug. In fact, she almost seemed frightened.

"Worf," she said. "Where do I begin?"

How did she know his name? He rumbled deep in his throat, not sure he liked the idea.

"Please," she said. "Don't shut me out. I know you're angry, afraid—but it's important that you listen to me."

There was something in her voice, in her choice of words, that caught him off balance. He was not certain what he had expected of her, but it was not entreaty.

"Why should I?" he asked.

"Because," she said, "I know who you are—who you *really* are. I know where you come from and why you're here. And the reason I know these things is because I come from the same place."

He inspected her individual features for a sign of insincerity—gazed deep into her eyes. "You look nothing like me," he spat.

"That's true," she conceded. "I don't. But that doesn't change anything. We come from a ship called the *Enterprise*. Does that sound familiar?"

He rolled it over his tongue. *"Enterprise."* It came more easily to him than he would have thought. On the other hand, it brought forth no images—no recollections.

"That's right—*Enterprise*. And we were transported here against our will—you and I and a handful of others. We were placed on these battlefields—but not before they took our memories away from us."

Worf grunted his skepticism—indicated her companions with a toss of his head. "If you were like me," he told her, "you would not be in the company of marshals."

She shook her head. "They're *not* marshals. Take a good look at them. They are of the same race as the marshals—but they are opposed to them."

He thought about that, sifted through it—uncertain of how much truth there could be in it. And yet, he was reluctant to reject it *all* out of hand.

"Give me a reason to believe you," the Klingon demanded.

"Why should I lie?" she asked. "Make no mistake—I *do* want something from you. I want help. But we can do without it. My friends here would probably prefer to abandon you—leave you to fend for yourself. Damnation—they've been carrying you half the day, and you're no lightweight."

Worf glanced again at the marshals, then at his surroundings. It was true that they had moved him from the last place he remembered. And there were neither sleds nor other conveyances in sight.

If they were trying to trick him, they had gone to great lengths. And as the female had said—what reason could they have to deceive him? Why not just kill him, or torture him, or bring him back to serve again as a warrior?

Worf eyed the female. "How is it that you have regained your memory—while mine is still a blank?"

"By accident. Purely by accident. Remember that flying-eye machine I swatted? And how it blew up in my face? Somehow the flash destroyed whatever block was placed in my brain—though at first, I remembered even less than before." She paused. "I would do the same for you, if I had a means of making the same kind of flash—and if I felt sure I wouldn't be damaging your eyes at the same time."

He thought back to the fortress, and how the sudden light from the sky had driven those warriors mad. Was *that* what had happened to them? If they had been allowed to live, would their memories have been restored?

And was that why they were murdered by the marshals—to prevent the existence of a band of warriors who could *remember?* And, remembering, who could stir up the others into some sort of rebellion?

That cinched it for the Klingon. Possibly, the female was not telling him the *whole* truth. But too many pieces fit together for her to be lying through her teeth.

"What kind of help do you want from me?" he asked. "What can *I* do that you cannot do yourselves?"

"We're going to try to free some of our people," explained the female. "Some of those who were taken from the *Enterprise* along with us. It means getting into a fortress that's crawling with marshals—and we thought that your experience as a warrior might come in handy."

He scowled. That piece fit into place as well. Too neatly? he wondered.

On the other hand, what did he have to lose? He could hardly help but improve his situation.

"All right," he said.

Her brow wrinkled for a moment, and she shook her head. "No. You still have your doubts—don't you?" She sighed. "What proof can I give you that I'm telling the truth? What can I say that will convince you?"

And then her eyes lit up.

"I know," she said. "When you were very little, you sustained a wound—some sort of hunting accident. And since Klingons don't believe in cosmetic surgery, you carry the scar to this day. In fact, it's just below your . . ."

He growled dangerously. "Enough," said Worf. "I believe you." He lowered his voice, so that the others could not hear. "But how did you know?" he asked.

The female shrugged. "I'm your doctor, Worf. I know everything there is to know about you—at least, from a medical standpoint."

That did not please him—nor did he disguise the fact. "You know so much about *me*—and I know so little about *you*. Not even your name."

She chuckled. "Pulaski," she told him. "Kate Pulaski." And under the watchful eyes of her companions, she began untying the ropes that held him.

"Puh-laskee," he repeated. He had heard some strange names in his time among the warriors, but that was one of the strangest.

Ensconced in the command center, Will Riker stared at the computer-enhanced image of A'klah on the viewscreen. He didn't need the computer to remind him of the seconds ticking away.

All around him, ship's personnel went about their duties. Like him, they were painfully aware of the time—though they didn't show it. There was a tension in the air—a sense of expectation that was almost tangible.

Troi emerged from the turbolift and took her usual path across the bridge. Gracefully, she settled into her seat.

"You're early," said Riker.

"I know," she answered. "But the *Mendel*'s people were all right for the time being. They've come to trust us, to feel secure." A pause. "And I felt that I should be *here* right now."

He tapped his fingers on his armrest. "Truth be told, Deanna, I'm glad you made that decision. It's starting to feel a bit lonely at the top."

A moment passed, during which he knew she was scanning his emotional ebb and flow. "Are you having a change of heart?" she asked.

He shook his head. "No—not really. How can I? There are twenty-six people down with that bloody disease now—not as many as Burtin predicted, but enough to scare the hell out of me." He shifted in his seat. Suddenly, it seemed too small for him. "I don't dare wait any longer. As soon as we make contact with Data, we'll beam him up—along with whomever else he's managed to round up. And that's *it*. There's no time for another extension on his deadline."

Troi didn't offer an opinion. That wasn't her function. But she *did* probe to determine the full extent of his feelings.

"Can you live with yourself," she asked, "if you have to leave the others behind? Or worse yet, if you have to abandon Data into the bargain?"

Riker thought about that, and not for the first time. "Good question," he told her. "I wish I had an answer."

Dov'rellir had been chosen as the marshals' field headquarters because of its uselessness as a true fortress. Whoever built it had—remarkably enough—failed to reckon with the eminently negotiable trails that led down the mountainside into which it was built. Any invader could descend along those trails and plunk himself down into the fortress, as long as he took some care not to be spotted.

The assumption that no one would be crazy enough to attack a keep full of marshals only made Dov'rellir that much more vulnerable. It was a situation for which Dan'nor found himself grateful as he picked his way down the mountainside, darting from cover to cover.

Of course, once they got down into the fortress proper, it would be a different set of affairs. There was no way around the sheer numbers of the marshals—nor was there any telling how long he and Rin'noc and Ka'asot would be able to distract them while Ma'alor and the others carried out their real purpose here.

As Dan'nor reached a spot within a few meters of the battlements, he stopped and considered the courtyard below. The gallows at the center of it was easy to see—it dominated the open area. What's more, there were two aerial monitors transmitting pictures of it from two different angles.

For a moment, he saw the tableau through the eyes of

someone still in the Military. Appreciated its drama, which would no doubt hold the masses enthralled in front of their videoscreens.

But the thought vanished in the midst of more immediate concerns. Strange, wasn't it? He had always hoped to make it to the Conflict zones—to be in the thick of the action. And now he *was*—though not the way he'd originally intended.

Rin'noc joined him, then Ka'asot. On the far side of the mountain, near the point where the wall curved around and met the slope, Ma'alor's party was ready also. They were waiting for him to make his move.

Taking a deep breath, Dan'nor slithered down from the trail, blaster in hand. Fortunately, the battlements were all but unguarded—a measure of the marshals' confidence. A single figure leaned against the stones of the wall, watching the proceedings in the courtyard.

Dan'nor's aim was perfect—the marshal never knew what hit him. Nor did any of the other sky riders notice as he crumpled.

Slowly, with great care, Dan'nor led the way along the battlements. He took up the point farthest away from the mountain, waited for Rin'noc and Ka'asot to establish themselves. Then, when he was sure that they were as secure as they *could* be, he opened fire on the uniformed figures below.

It was the signal for Ma'alor's group to come down off the mountain.

The plan was working. With Dan'nor and the others attracting all the attention, it had been simplicity itself to slip into the fortress and find an open entrance to the keep.

Ma'alor had seemed nervous when he armed the Klingon with an extra blaster—even if it *was* permanently set on stun. Even now, he kept glancing over his shoulder—to make sure that Worf was still on *their* side.

But the Klingon no longer had any doubts as to where his

loyalties belonged. Anyone who wanted to thwart the intentions of the marshals was worth helping, as far as he was concerned.

And if he really *was* liberating someone he had known on a ship somewhere . . . all the better.

The first corridor they came to was empty—as was the second, which ran at an angle to it. Blind luck? Or a trap?

When they turned into their third passageway, and there was still no sign of a defender, Ma'alor was becoming suspicious as well.

"Something's wrong," he said. "Where *is* everyone?"

Nurel'lid shook his head, baffled.

"I don't know either," said Pulaski. "But I'll feel better if we keep moving." She had declined a blaster—a good idea, Worf told himself. The doctor did not look at all comfortable in this endeavor.

As Pulaski suggested, however, they kept moving. A fourth corridor proved to be as empty of resistance as the first three.

And then, on the verge of yet another turning, they heard voices.

". . . do not understand. I thought you had been alerted to my mission here."

"I was *not* alerted to your mission. And without word from the Conflicts Commander himself, I cannot allow the prisoners to be removed."

The first voice seemed cold, dispassionate; the second was controlled but seething with emotion underneath.

"A laudable sentiment—laudable indeed. However, I have my orders as well. And they call for the prisoners to be removed to a more secure location."

"What? Are you telling me that Dov'rellir is less than secure?"

"I would not presume to disparage your efforts here. Nonetheless, there are places less vulnerable to the expected rescue attempt."

"Rescue attempt?" The voice had climbed an octave. Its control was failing.

"You have not been warned about the rescue attempt? Someone has not been doing his job." A pause. "After the transport of the prisoners is completed, I will have to investigate this matter . . ."

Pulaski turned to Worf. Her face was a study in apprehension. Her lips formed two words: "They know."

Worf nodded. It seemed that their mission had been anticipated.

Yet their plan had thus far gone without a hitch. They had gotten this far—expected or not, they had to forge ahead.

Ma'alor, the closest to the turning, glanced over his shoulder at the rest of them. He still *appeared* determined. Or was that a glimmer of doubt in his eyes? A sign that he was having second thoughts about their ability to free the prisoners?

No matter, Worf told himself. If the rest of them wish to retreat, *let* them.

The Klingon would not go back. Not now, when his chance to avenge himself on the honorless ones was just around the corner.

"Worf," whispered Pulaski, wide-eyed. "Where are you going?"

He shrugged her off as gently as he could, approached the turning of the corridor.

Ma'alor whirled, trained his blaster on him. The Klingon wondered what setting it was adjusted to.

For a moment, the two of them eyed one another—Ma'alor insisting on his right to lead, Worf challenging him to do what he had come here to do. And all the while, the voices of the marshals were ringing in the stone passageway beyond them.

Finally, Ma'alor let the nose of his blaster drop. Reaching out with his free hand, he clasped the Klingon's shoulder—a gesture of respect? Of gratitude for reminding him of his mission? Worf suffered it, knowing it brought him a little closer to that which he hungered for.

Crouching, they proceeded to the brink of the turning—all except Pulaski. Worf could see the muscles in Ma'alor's neck tense as he prepared to spring.

Then they were rolling and blasting in a corridor full of marshals, and there were screams of surprise and the *wssk* of weapons being drawn and the sound of bodies hitting the floor.

It was difficult to anticipate the blaster beams, as invisible as they were but for their eerie rippling effect. Nonetheless, Worf's battle-honed reflexes served him well. He bounced from wall to wall, dropping marshals with unerring accuracy.

Impressive, he told himself, considering he had never handled a blaster before. At least not that he could remember.

But it did not fill his aching need for revenge. It was too simple—too detached. He needed to take one of the slugs in his hands—to crush him, to feel his bones splinter.

For the shame and the suffering they had inflicted. For their leering laughter.

And for what his kind had done to Worf's kind back at the fortress.

Unfortunately, there were just a few of the marshals left standing. And as Worf looked on, Ma'alor and Nurel'lid dropped two of them.

That left but one. Apparently unarmed, he was hiding behind the prisoners.

Worf was oblivious to the half dozen or more figures that sprawled across the corridor. He had forgotten about the trio he had come in with, the comrades they had left outside.

Even the prisoners—one of them Klah'kimmbri—seemed to melt away. He had eyes for but one face, one despised form.

In the back of his mind, he wondered why the marshal did

not run away. Or pick up a weapon and fire at him. Or at least threaten him with reprisals.

But he did not wonder so much that it cooled his blood-fury. Never breaking his stride, he reached out and took the marshal by the throat.

Raised him off the floor with the strength of one arm. And with great satisfaction, began to squeeze the breath out of him.

But there was something wrong here. The flesh of the marshal's neck did not yield. Nor did his grasp seem to have any effect on the cursed one's breathing.

In fact, he was able to smile. And *speak*.

"It is a pleasure," he said evenly, "to see you again, Worf. I had feared I would not find you in time."

The Klingon's eyes narrowed as he squeezed harder. His arm trembled with the effort.

Yet it gained him nothing. The marshal still seemed unaffected.

"I would take this for a show of affection," said the honorless one, "but for the fact that you are incapable of recognizing me. Therefore, I must conclude that it is something else. Perhaps a display of aggression?"

"Worf!" The cry came ringing the length of the corridor. The Klingon looked back over his shoulder and snarled. Who dared?

It was Pulaski. And she was approaching with an obvious sense of urgency.

"Put him down," she insisted. "That's Data. Don't you— oh, that's right. You don't."

The Klingon turned back again, saw the affable expression on his victim's face. He did not quite understand, but one thing was obvious. This seeming marshal was another ally.

And a durable one at that.

In disgust, he thrust his burden from him. The pale one landed almost effortlessly on his feet.

"Gods!" roared Worf. His cry echoed unmercifully. "What must one do to find revenge in this place?"

Chapter Nineteen

AFTER THEIR INITIAL, attention-getting salvo, Dan'nor and his comrades had not had an easy time of it. Early on, Ka'asot had absorbed a beam, and he hadn't moved since.

Immediately afterward, an attempt had been made to storm their position on the catwalk. He and Rin'noc had been hard-pressed, and more than once a blast had splattered on the stones just behind Dan'nor. But in the end, they had turned their enemies back.

Now, it seemed, the marshals had decided that the price of dragging them down was too steep. They were playing a waiting game—until help could arrive from the field in the form of some flying sleds.

Of course, the plan had been to be out of here long before that time. To be up the mountain again and gone before the sky riders could arrive. Nor were the earthbound marshals likely to pursue—for once the rebels were above them on the slope, they would enjoy too great an advantage.

But Ma'alor was taking longer than expected. What was keeping him? Had the prisoners proved harder to find than they'd anticipated? Or had the marshals found them first and taken them out of the game?

Just when Dan'nor concluded that their gambit was a failure, he saw a figure emerge from the opening by which his comrades had entered the keep. No one in the courtyard seemed to notice as Nurel'lid headed for the wall, followed by Ma'alor and someone in rough-spun garb—someone who had to be Ralak'kai.

But that was it. No one else trailed after them.

Dan'nor swallowed. Worf. *Pulaski*. And the others who were supposed to have been imprisoned with Ralak'kai . . .

All gone? *All* of them—just like Ka'asot?

It was a lot to pay for one man's freedom. An awful lot. But if they could show the Council that they would not tolerate such things . . . then perhaps they had purchased more than they would leave Dov'rellir with.

To keep the others safe and unseen, Dan'nor opened fire again. A fraction of a second later, Rin'noc followed suit. In the courtyard, marshals scattered, some taking cover behind the gallows.

Dan'nor took some satisfaction in knowing that that ugly thing would never be used. That the aerial monitors would never have a chance to transmit their spectacle.

The marshals returned their fire. But they never saw Ma'alor, Nurel'lid or Ralak'kai climbing the wall—not until it was too late.

Nor did they offer more than token pursuit as the rebels escaped up the mountainside.

When the time came, it was even tougher to give the order than Riker had expected. But then, he wasn't just leaving an away team to face danger and the likelihood of death. He was leaving five of the people he loved best in all the universe.

Nor did he feel inclined to distinguish between *real* people and artificial ones. He felt as bad about Data as he did about the others. In a way, perhaps, worse—because the android had *volunteered* for this, had gone in with the hope that he could save his crew mates.

And now, the first officer was forced to choke off that hope. Maybe forever.

Doctor Burtin had chosen to be on the bridge as Data's deadline became imminent. Obviously, he had exercised his prerogative to keep Riker honest—though that was hardly necessary.

Duty came first. It was a viewpoint to which Picard would certainly have subscribed.

"All right," said Riker. "We've waited long enough." He turned to Sharif at the conn station. "Log in coordinates for Starbase Ninety-one."

Sharif did as he was told. "Logged, sir."

"Warp nine, Mister Sharif. En—"

"Commander?"

Riker shot to his feet. He knew that voice!

"Data!"

"That is correct, sir. I have five to beam up."

"Transporter room," cried the first officer, barely able to contain his exuberance. "Mister O'Brien . . ."

"Aye, sir. I'm locking in on them now. *Got* them."

"Energize," commanded Riker.

There was a long pause—or maybe it just *seemed* long. The first officer had time to look around the bridge—at Troi, at Fong. And at Burtin.

"They're here, sir," said O'Brien finally. "All five of them. Captain Picard, Doctor Pulaski, Lieutenants Worf and La Forge. And Lieutenant Commander Data, of course."

Riker nodded, feeling as if a great weight had been lifted from his shoulders. "I'm on my way."

One moment, he had been standing in a dank, stone corridor. The next, he found himself somewhere else entirely—on a strange sort of illuminated platform in a pleasant if austere-looking room.

The others were there with him. The warrior and Geordi and the woman and the marshal who had come to relocate them. Or had they determined that he was *not* a marshal, but rather one of Ralak'kai's people in disguise?

Picard was very confused.

"You can come down from there now," said the only other person in the room—a fellow half-concealed behind what appeared to be a machine. He was still tinkering with it as he spoke.

"Of course," said the one who resembled Ralak'kai. "As soon as Doctor Pulaski gets her bearings."

The woman appeared a trifle unsteady. She was clutching the pallid one's arm for support.

"Thanks for the help," she told him. "I guess androids are built to withstand the rigors of teleportation better than humans."

Androids? Teleportation?

Picard wondered what he had gotten himself into—though, no matter what it was, it had to be better than awaiting execution.

He turned to Geordi, and the dark man shrugged. "Don't look at me," he said. "I'm new here myself."

Grrr . . .

"Simmer down, Worf," said the female. What was her name? Pulaski? "This is the place I told you about—the *Enterprise.*"

Picard glanced back at the warrior, saw the wild and wary look in his eyes, and decided to give him as wide a berth as possible. Geordi must have had a similar thought because he followed Picard off the platform without a moment's hesitation.

At the same time, an opening appeared in the wall —in the *wall?*—and three people stepped through. One was tall and bearded; another, a female, was darkly beautiful. The third, another man, was unremarkable looking.

"Ah," said Pulaski, "just the people I want to see." Suddenly recovered, she made her way past the others.

"Data told me about the spread of the disease. We've got to move quickly."

The bearded man stared at her. *"Doctor*—you have your memory, don't you?"

"Yes. That's another thing we have to discuss."

"I too have something to discuss," said the pallid one, raising a slender finger for attention. He came down off the platform, leaving the warrior there alone. "I was able to bring together two other groups of Federation personnel. What's more, I have their coordinates, and . . ."

The bearded man stopped him with a clap on the shoulder. "It's all right, Data. We've got them already. We stumbled onto them while you were gone."

The one called Data seemed to brighten at the news. "Ah," he said. "Well done, sir."

"There aren't any *other* groups?" asked the bearded man. "Are there?"

The pallid one's expression changed again. "No, sir. There were no other survivors."

A somber silence swept the room. Finally, the bearded man dispelled it with a command—though he appeared to be speaking to no one in particular. It was almost as if he were addressing an invisible helper, hovering somewhere near the ceiling.

"Riker to bridge. Let's get out of here, Mister Sharif—any heading that appeals to you. Before we run out of luck with the Klah'kimmbri."

"I'm afraid we already have, sir. The energy mantle is materializing again."

The voice seemed to come out of nowhere. Picard looked around, but he couldn't catch anyone speaking.

The bearded man frowned. "All right, then. Maintain present position for the time being."

He turned toward Picard, nodded. "Welcome back, Captain."

Picard returned the nod. "Thank you," he said.

Captain?

Then the bearded man was exiting through that same hole in the wall—and taking half the people in the room with him.

The dark-haired female with the lovely black eyes seemed to be the one in charge now. She smiled at each of them in turn—first Picard, then Geordi, then the warrior.

"Relax," she said. "You are all safe here. In a little while, all your questions will be answered."

There was something about her that made Picard want to *trust.* He could feel some of the tension going out of him.

"But first," she said, "we must see that you are made comfortable. Won't you come with me?"

Picard was the first to comply. And why not? He was curious to see what was out there.

As the sickbay doors opened, and the four of them stepped through, Burtin was still bringing Pulaski up-to-date. Until *now,* he had restricted his monologue to medical information.

"And so," he said finally, "I advised Commander Riker to take off for Starbase Ninety-one—where we could have enhanced our ability to keep our people alive. We were on the verge of doing that when Mister Data here called up for a teleport."

Pulaski glanced at him. "You mean you were going to sacrifice me and the others so you could get to Starbase Ninety-one a little sooner?"

Burtin inspected her profile, taut with purpose. "Yes," he said. "That seemed to me to be the best course of action."

Pulaski nodded. "And you were absolutely correct, Doctor." Another glance in his direction, this time accompanied by a conspiratorial smile. "Though if my theory stands up, we can take care of this little epidemic without any help from Starbase Ninety-one."

Sickbay's diagnostic area was littered with field generators, most of them in use. There were biobeds everywhere, including more than twice the usual number in critical care. And every blood purifier they owned was hard at work, with a nurse to oversee it.

"How many?" asked the chief medical officer.

"At last count," said Burtin, "thirty. Less than I expected," he admitted.

Pulaski grunted. "It could have been worse." Reaching into her rough-spun garment, she removed a square of the same material that had been gathered into a makeshift pouch.

"Here," she said, handing the package to her colleague.

Burtin took it, looked at it. "What's this?"

"Gruel," said Pulaski. "Or the antidote, depending on your point of view. I snatched it from the captain's cell before we left."

Riker seemed puzzled, but not Data. He voiced the explanation even as Burtin was putting it together in his own head.

"Interesting," said the android. "Since none of the away team has come down with the disease, you have isolated a common denominator: an element in your diets."

"Exactly," said Pulaski. "And since all any of us ate was *this* foul-smelling stuff"—she indicated the contents of the half-open pouch in Burtin's hand—"it's not unreasonable to assume that it contains a natural antibiotic. Coincidentally, the one we're looking for."

Burtin regarded his superior with redoubled admiration. "Have you got a good feeling about this one too?" he asked.

"*Pretty* good," she told him. "But there's only one way to find out for sure. I want the gruel fed whole to Fredi and Vanderventer. And at the same time, we'll analyze it—so when it works, we'll have a fair idea why."

"What about the memory-restoration procedure?" asked Riker.

"That will have to wait," said Pulaski. "A few hours, anyway. It'll take time to set things up. And until I dose Fredi and Vanderventer, and get the analysis process under way, memory-restoration is on the back burner anyway—the epidemic is my main concern."

Now it was Data's turn to look puzzled. "Back burner?" he echoed.

"Come on," said Riker, turning him around. "I'll explain on the way to the bridge."

Chapter Twenty

PICARD LEANED BACK in his seat at the conference table. "You are to be commended, Data. If I were here, I must admit, I would have expressed the same reservations as Mister Fong. Yet you carried off your masquerade quite well. With—shall we say—a certain amount of *flair.*"

The android smiled, obviously pleased with himself. "It is good of you to say so, Captain. But I was fortunate in that my red-dyed hair and my uniform put me in a position of implied authority. Once I realized that I enjoyed certain advantages, I merely played along."

"You're too modest," remarked Riker. "Using marshals to gather the *Mendel* survivors into two groups—and to stand guard over them, so they'd each be in a predetermined place when we went to beam them up . . . that was nothing short of brilliant, Data."

For once, the android was speechless. Picard almost thought he could see Data blush—though it might have been a trick of the light and his officer's hair, which was still bright red.

The captain decided that it would be merciful to change

the subject. He turned to Pulaski. "I trust your efforts are continuing to meet with success?"

The doctor nodded. "That gruel really packs a wallop. Less than eight hours after ingestion, Fredi and Vanderventer were not only feeling better—they were completely free of the bacterium. And of course, now that we've isolated the antibiotic, we've been able to cut that time in half by injecting it directly into the bloodstream. It won't be long before the last of our patients is on his or her feet."

"What about the memory restorations?" asked Geordi. Naturally, that was a subject of some immediacy to him.

"No problems there either," said Pulaski. "We're just going slowly so as not to make any mistakes. The optic nerve is a delicate thing—since we're stimulating it directly, we have to exercise caution."

"Also," said Troi, "we cannot merely hook everyone up to machines and tell them to hold still. These are people who have been traumatized over and over again in a short period of time—as much by their sudden appearance on the *Enterprise* as by anything else. They must be emotionally prepared for the restoration of their memories and the brief period of confusion that precedes it." She glanced at Worf with a little half smile. "Or else they're liable to try to destroy the very apparatus that helped them."

The Klingon scowled and looked around, daring anyone else to comment on the incident. No one did.

"Actually," Pulaski continued, "the more troublesome procedure will be the removal of the language-translation implants that the Klah'kimmbri were thoughtful enough to lend us. But there's no harm in leaving them in until we've taken care of our other problems."

Picard grunted. "Not the least of which is what to do about the numerous representatives of Federation worlds that still toil under the A'klahn mantle."

"Completely unaware of who they are and where they come from," said Geordi.

"We can't just leave them here," maintained Riker. "It's our responsibility to set them free. To give them back what the Klah'kimmbri took from them."

"I agree," said Picard. "But how?"

Worf placed his elbows on the table. Apparently, he had been waiting for someone to pose that question.

"I say we *attack*," the Klingon advised. "Quickly—before the Klah'kimmbri can formulate a strategy of their own. We have enough sensor information now to determine where their planetary defense installations are. We do not need to see them in order to hit them. And once the Klah'kimmbri are defenseless, they will have no choice but to release the conscripts to us."

Riker shook his head. "We can't just go in there shooting. It would be an act of war. And as much provocation as the Klah'kimmbri have given us, war is to be avoided at all costs."

Provocation indeed, thought Picard. But of course, his first officer was right.

"Violence is not an option here," he confirmed. "Nor, I am afraid, is negotiation. The Klah'kimmbri High Council has demonstrated its reluctance in that regard."

"If only we could restore the conscripts' memories," said Pulaski. "Imagine what kind of chaos it would cause; the marshals would be swamped by a rebellion of that magnitude. The Council would almost *have* to deal with us—to have us remove our people before they posed a threat to the general peace."

"There *is* a way to do that," said Worf. His suggestion was simply put: "Fire the phasers."

Picard was about to rebuke him for repeating his earlier suggestion when the Klingon's meaning dawned on him.

"Of course," said Data, straightening. "A barrage calculated to light up the sky over each Conflict zone—without actually effecting any damage. The flashes of illumination would enable the participants to regain their memories."

"In *most* cases," amended Pulaski. "Not everyone's nervous system is set up like a human's or a Klingon's. But it sounds like a good idea to me."

Picard mulled it over. It *was* a good idea, he decided—but it had a major shortcoming.

"From our point of view," he said, "this would be a nonviolent effort. No question about it. But from the Klah'kimmbri point of view, it would be no different from an actual attack. And, unfortunately, we cannot ignore their point of view." He noted the disappointment around the table, sighed. "The use of weapons is out of the question. Period."

Suddenly, Geordi snapped his fingers. "Wait a minute. We don't *need* weapons to create a light display." He spread his hands. "All we have to do is take the debris that's floating in space, orbiting A'klah, and use our tractor beams to give it a nudge. Create a sort of meteor shower—except, instead of meteors, it'll be the Klah'kimmbri's own creations coming home to roost."

"Their own empire-building devices," noted Troi.

"Poetic justice," remarked Riker.

"And the flashes of light as the stuff burns up in the atmosphere . . . just *might* do the trick," said Pulaski. She shrugged. "It's worth a try, anyway."

They all looked to the captain. He took their scrutiny in stride, turned the idea around in his mind so as to inspect it from all sides.

"Yes," he said finally. "Perhaps it *is* worth a try." He addressed Geordi. "Of course, I don't want anyone hurt by falling debris. It has all got to burn up before it reaches the planet's surface."

The engineer nodded. "Absolutely, sir."

"Captain?"

Picard acknowledged the android. "What is it, Data?"

"I do not mean to . . . what is the expression? Gum up the works?"

"That's it, all right," said Riker.

"I do not mean to do that, but what about the non-Federation conscripts? Do we have the right to restore *their* memories as well?"

Again, the scrutiny. After a moment, the captain nodded.

"I think we do," he said. "We are not tampering with them. We are undoing the tampering that the Klah'kimmbri have already been guilty of. And the conscripts could hardly have been primitive beings to begin with, if they were snatched off spacegoing vessels."

The android seemed satisfied with that.

Picard was satisfied too—with the entire plan, and on all levels. As captain of the *Enterprise,* he had taken care of the Federation's concerns—the Prime Directive not the least of them. As someone who had been caught in the Klah'kimmbri web of tyranny and subjugation, he was grateful for the opportunity to turn the tables on his captors. Most important, as an ethical being, he was glad to be able to bring their ghastly Conflict machine to a grinding halt.

He included everyone present in his gaze. "Thank you," he said. "All of you."

"I guess," said Geordi, "I'll get us geared up to start moving all that space-junk around."

The captain couldn't suppress a grin—not entirely. Geordi was a good man to have around—with or without his memory.

"By all means," agreed Picard. "Make it so, Mister La Forge."

Weary. He was *so* weary.

Harr'h had thought he could put the incident of madness and slaughter behind him—just as he had counseled the others to do.

But it was harder this time. At night, he lay half-awake, wrestling with demons he had thought he'd conquered.

Is life that precious? they asked. Is survival worth the sacrifice of your pride, your very soul?

Maybe the brooding one, Worf, had been wiser than any

261

of them. Maybe desertion was the only real answer—the only escape from one's demons.

More and more, he had come to think so.

Now, however, he needed to put his doubts aside. Half a dozen meters below them, the enemy's raiding party was negotiating a narrow ledge. As soon as he gave the signal, they would pounce—and the battle would begin.

Somewhere, a flying-eye machine was waiting just as they were. Perhaps a marshal as well.

All eyes were on Harr'h. He raised his arm, prepared to drop it.

And then the sky began to rain fire.

"That's the last of it," said Geordi, from his position at the engineering station. "Except for the pieces that are too small to do any good."

"Excellent," said Picard.

"Should I attempt to establish contact?" asked Worf.

"No," said the captain. "This time, we will wait for *them* to make the first move."

Nor did they have long to wait. Within minutes, the Klingon received a transmission.

"Put it up on the screen, please, Lieutenant."

It was the first time Picard had seen the High Council of A'klah. But they were very much as Riker had described them.

Haughty. Self-confident, self-possessed.

Except that now there were subtle cracks in that confidence. Even signs of agitation.

"Councillors," said Picard. "To what do we owe the honor of this communication?"

The one who seemed the eldest spoke for all of them. "You have disturbed the ages-old serenity of our world. For what reason?"

"We have learned that you are in possession of our comrades. We want them back."

"We told you before—we know nothing of your comrades. And if we did, we would not be moved to release them by the mere inconvenience you have perpetrated upon us. To speak plainly, we thought you capable of greater force."

"We *are* capable," returned the captain. "But we opted not to destroy. As I said before, our only objective is to recover our people."

"And as *I* said before, we do not *have* your . . ."

"Enough," said Picard, rising to his feet. "The charade is over, Councillor. I know all about you—your Conflicts and your methods of propagating them. What is more, I know you have conscripted our people. And the reason I know is because—until recently—*I* was one of your conscripts."

The Councillor did not register the shock he must have been feeling. On the other hand, he did not seem to have a rebuttal.

"Soon," said the captain, "you will discover the *true* purpose of our maneuver—though I suspect you may have an inkling of it already. At that point, you will not only *admit* that there are conscripts—you will *beg* us to take them from you."

"Have a care, *Enterprise,"* said the councillor. He had finally found his tongue, and was trying to give the appearance of a strong position. "We too are capable of bringing force . . ."

But Picard saw no need to hear the rest. "Terminate contact," he told Worf.

A moment later, the image of the Council was replaced by that of the planet, swaddled in its golden veil.

Riker stood up beside him. "Good job, sir. I think they'll come around, now that they know where we stand."

Picard harumphed. "After their broadcasts are terminated, their marshals toppled, their cities threatened by an outpouring of angry off-worlders? Yes, Number One. I think they'll come around."

Chapter Twenty-one

PULASKI POINTED to the far side of the cargo deck.

"Over there," she told the crewman. "Where that big, blond fellow is standing. His name's Vanderventer—he'll know what to do with it."

The crewman grunted as he shifted the heavy storage module from one shoulder to the other. "Over *there*, Doctor?"

"That's right," said Pulaski. "Sorry to make you work so hard, but it's important we get those dermaplasts to where they're needed. Nobody's going to sport an open wound on *my* ship."

"Yes, ma'am," said the crewman, though not with the utmost enthusiasm. As Pulaski watched, he wound his way among the knots of Rythrians and Merethua and Tant'lithi that stood between him and the makeshift medical station manned by Vanderventer.

It would have been nice if they had had the room to use transport vehicles to carry supplies, instead of crewmen borrowed from every section on the ship. But with nearly eighteen thousand refugees crowding all available living quarters and cargo space, they were lucky to be able to get anything anywhere.

It certainly hadn't taken long for the Council to cave in and admit to the Conflicts. The captain had been right on target in that regard.

With their memories back, the participants posed a real—if primitive—threat to all manner of facilities and personnel in and around the Conflict zones. What's more, it would have been only a matter of time before some of the participants went marauding farther afield.

Of course, even after the Council had agreed to drop the mantle and release the conscripts, it had taken a while for all of them to be beamed up. A *long* while.

On the other hand, the limitations imposed by transporter capacities had been a blessing for those in medical and security sections—since it had fallen to them to allocate space and supplies to the refugees. If all 18,000 had beamed aboard at once, it would have been an impossible task.

Not that other sections of the ship's crew hadn't been busy. The command staff and xenology had had the difficult assignment of establishing contact with and screening the conscripts.

After all, to fulfill their agreement with the Council, they had only to remove *Federation* personnel. Among the non-Federation participants, they could not beam up anyone who failed to express a willingness.

Not unexpectedly, *everyone* had expressed that willingness. And so the captain had offered to take them as far as Starbase 91, where they could make arrangements to contact their respective home systems.

Underlying this offer, needless to say, had been the idea that all those rescued might serve as goodwill ambassadors, spreading a positive image of the Federation to cultures not entirely familiar with it.

"Doctor?"

Pulaski emerged from her reverie and saw Burtin approaching. He looked a little weary, but he was smiling through his weariness.

"A lot like the frontier?" she asked.

He surveyed the crowded cargo deck. "I guess it is." Burtin's smile faded, and he turned to her. "Which brings up something I wanted to discuss with you."

"I know," said Pulaski. "You're considering a transfer back to the frontier."

He nodded. "It's that obvious, huh?"

"To someone who knows you, yes."

Burtin shrugged. "What can I say? I just haven't been able to get comfortable on this big ship. I mean, I always thought it would be the best thing in the galaxy to serve aboard the *Enterprise*. I guess some of us are meant for less exotic assignments."

She met his gaze, held it. "It has nothing to do with the disease and the way you handled it? Because, for all your self-doubts, I couldn't have done any better myself."

He smiled again. "I don't believe that. And even so, that's not the issue. Here, I'm just a technician, overshadowed by a bunch of fancy equipment. If one is a genius at pathology —as I believe *you* are—then it's different. But when you're an old-fashioned sawbones like I am, your talents are wasted in a place like this."

He looked around. "Besides, there are lots of good, young doctors that would kill for a berth on the *Enterprise*. It's rare when you find one willing to bleed a gut on the frontier."

"Then I can't talk you out of it?" asked Pulaski.

"I'm afraid not," he told her.

She placed a hand on his arm, squeezed. "I'm going to miss you, Sam Burtin."

It took a moment for Burtin to respond. "Same here," he said finally. Then he was off to see to the distribution of some foodstuffs that had just come down on the turbolift.

"Eight years," said Strak. "Eight years since we were stolen off the bridge of the *Le-Matya*." As the Vulcan articulated the words, he endowed them with a certain wistfulness—like a dry wind in a barren desert. Quite a trick in the temperature-controlled environs of Ten-Forward, where some of the Federation officers among the conscripts had gathered to celebrate their freedom. "And yet," he went on, "it could have been worse. I might have perished on that planet—and never known I was good for anything but driving wagons."

Picard nodded. "I know the feeling—though I was subjected to it for only a short time." He paused. "And *I* am not a telepath. I had only my own pain to cope with."

"Fortunately," explained Strak, "I found ways to construct telepathic blocks. Or I could never have remained sane."

"In any case," said Picard, "your ordeal is over now. Once we arrive at Starbase Ninety-one, you will be able to secure passage to Vulcan—or to resume your career with Starfleet, whichever you choose."

"Yes," agreed Strak. "Though I will always remember A'klah." He paused to reflect. "And that is the way it should be. All experiences are pathways to wisdom. Even the distasteful ones."

"Indeed," said the captain.

The Vulcan looked around at the crowd, then at the exit. "I trust you will not be offended if I take my leave of you. I find that I am not in the proper state of mind for a large gathering."

"No need for apologies," Picard told him. "I understand."

With a simple nod, Strak departed.

But Picard wasn't alone for very long. He felt a slender hand on his elbow and turned.

"I thought that that depressing Vulcan would monopolize you forever," said Dani. She looked at him, perfectly deadpan. "Do you think it would be out of line to hug you in front of all these people?"

Picard could feel the color rising in his face. He cleared his throat.

"Perhaps," he said, "it could wait for a more private moment."

"I don't know," she said. "When I get the urge to hug you, you know I can't help myself."

He frowned. "Your father loved to embarrass me, too. Must you be such a chip off the old block?"

She laughed softly—but decided not to make good on her threat. Picard was grateful—particularly when he saw his first officer approaching.

"Captain," said Riker, inclining his head just a bit, out of respect. He turned to Dani. "Miss Orbutu."

The captain was a little surprised. He had been preparing an introduction in his head. "I didn't know that you two knew each other," he said.

"Actually," said Dani, "we don't." She smiled pleasantly at Riker. "I'm afraid you're one up on me, Commander."

The first officer returned the smile—but a little ruefully. "We intercepted some of the Conflict broadcasts, and you were in one of them. We were able to identify you based on the likeness in your computer file."

"I see," said Dani. Was that a bit of wanting-to-forget in her voice? "But I'm still surprised that you remembered me. You must have seen a great many broadcasts."

"After a while, yes. But I must admit, I went back to *that* one more than once."

Dani was about to say something else when Riker preempted her.

"Your glass," he said. "It's empty. Would you allow me to refill it?"

"Well—yes," answered Dani. "Of course." She relinquished the glass.

His mission established, Riker made his way toward the bar.

Dani watched him go. "A charming man, this first officer of yours."

Picard nodded. "The only man I would ever trust with the *Enterprise* when I retire—though that day is, of course, a long, *long* way off."

Behind Dani, Data passed through the crowd. He hadn't yet had the red dye removed from his hair, Picard noted.

Could it be that the android was *enjoying* this small conceit? What a perfectly human thing to do.

Not surprisingly, Data's appearance brought back thoughts of the marshals. And of Ralak'kai.

"What's the matter?" asked Dani. "Suddenly, you look grimmer than that Vulcan."

Picard chuckled. "I was thinking of my friend—Ralak'kai. And his compatriots. I was wondering if our efforts had brought them very much closer to their goal."

Dani shrugged, thoughtful now herself. "I suppose it depends on how well their Council can function without the Conflicts."

The captain grunted. "Exactly right."

By that time, Riker had returned with Dani's glass.

"Thank you," she said.

"You're welcome," he told her.

Picard lifted his own glass, still full of synthenol. "A toast," he said. "To Ralak'kai. And all those like him."

"To Ralak'kai," said Riker.

They drank.

The sudden termination of the Conflicts—owing first to the reluctance of the memory-restored participants, and then to their departure from A'klah—had had a much more profound effect than anyone might have guessed.

The Conflicts had been the only thing that kept the minds of the "lower-caste" Klah'kimmbri occupied. It had been a vent for their daily anger and frustration. With their videoscreens dark, their lives disrupted, the people were willing to listen when street speakers like Ralak'kai offered an alternative.

The balance, always delicate, had been tipped. The atmosphere was ripe for rebellion.

Only a couple of days after Dan'nor's return from the Conflict zone, entire sectors of each factory town along the river were claimed by the workers and barricaded. What was more, the Civil Service tired quickly of spilling their blood in attempts to break the rebel strongholds.

In the end, the truth was painfully obvious: the Military was nothing more than a huge bag of gas, and the rebels had put the first pinholes in it. It might take some time for the entire bag to collapse—but collapse it would.

In the dim light emanating from the tarnished overhead fixture, Fidel'lic did not seem so haughty and aloof as when Dan'nor had seen him last. The shadows took the edge off his lean countenance, making him appear childlike and even a little fragile—at least to Dan'nor.

The back room where Dan'nor had first stumbled upon Trien'nor and the other rebels was furnished now much as it had been then. It had a table and some chairs and some cobwebs in the corners where the walls met the ceiling.

Of course, the place was a little more crowded tonight, and not only with workers. Fidel'lic's personal bodyguards had to stand behind him; there were only so many seats around the table, and they were all occupied by rebels. The one exception was the chair graced by the councillor.

Ralak'kai smiled at him. "It isn't exactly the Council Chamber—is it?"

"No," said Fidel'lic. "It is not the Council Chamber."

"But then," said Trien'nor, no worse for wear after his short existence as a wagoner, "what you have to say could not be said in that most awe-inspiring of places."

Fidel'lic eyed him with apparent equanimity—though he

knew who Tri'enor was, and he could not have felt anything but disgust for the fallen First Caster. "Quite correct," he said. "Not everyone there is as forward-looking as one might hope."

The councillor took a quick accounting of the other faces confronting him—those of Ma'alor, Zanc'cov, Nurel'lid, Rin'noc. And finally, that of Dan'nor himself.

If he remembered the younger Tir'dainia, he didn't let on. There wasn't even a flicker of recognition.

Just as well, Dan'nor thought. *I'm a different person than I was then.*

"Not everyone," Fidel'lic went on, "takes your movement as seriously as I do."

"That's very interesting," said Ma'alor. "But it doesn't explain why you're here."

Ralak'kai held up a hand. "Let him finish, Brother. The councillor was good enough to come here—the least we can do is hear him out."

Fidel'lic continued as if he had never been interrupted. "It is obvious," he said, "that there will never be anything like the Conflicts again. And without question, that is for the better. The Conflicts were a relic of our former barbarism—a shameful thing that should have been abolished long ago.

"Our true fulfillment as a people—and as individuals—lies not in petty entertainments." His voice took on a different quality—a sort of measured forcefulness. "Our destiny is something much greater—to regain the *stars*. First, Trilik'kon Mahk'ti; then those other systems that we once dominated. And when that is done, we can extend the empire beyond even the dreams of our fathers."

He looked around, snaring his listeners now with his eyes as much as his voice.

"We can *do* that. We are *Klah'kimmbri*. But it will not be easy. To begin with, we must work together, forgetting our squabbles of the moment. We must redesign our factories to make not shoes, but the components of spacegoing vessels. We must redevelop the engines that propelled us from sun to sun, the armaments that made us masters of every race we encountered. And we must improve on these technologies —so when another Destroyer comes through our home system, we will be ready for him.

"The future is remarkably bright," said Fidel'lic, "if we take hold of it together. You, representing the people. And I, representing the government. We can bring everything to a halt by fighting one another—or heap glory on ourselves by simply reaching out for it."

He leaned forward. "A new day for the Klah'kimmbri— and all I need is your word that you are with me. Do I have it?"

The rebels all looked to Ralak'kai. The smile had never quite faded from his face.

"I don't think so," he told the councillor.

Fidel'lic couldn't mask his exasperation. And what was that other thing Dan'nor saw in his eyes? Fear? After all, Fidel'lic had risked much to come here—including his alliances on the Council.

He shook his head reproachfully, as if they had lost more than they knew. Without another word, he rose from the table—and would have exited, if Trien'nor hadn't stopped him.

"Councillor," said Dan'nor's father.

Fidel'lic turned to look at him.

"A'klah *does* have a destiny. But it is not the one you conjure. Nor is there room in it for *you*. If I were a councillor, I would run as far and as fast as I could. For if you try to oppose us, make no mistake—*we will bring you down.*"

Fidel'lic's mouth curled into an expression of disdain. "That remains to be seen," he said. And then he *did* leave, pulling his entourage along with him.

For a moment after the councillor's departure, all was

silent in the room. The enormity of what Trien'nor had said was still sinking in.

Finally, from somewhere—from *everywhere*—a cheer rose up to fill the silence. And it became so loud, so deafening, that it threatened to shake loose the very rafters and the cobwebs that depended from them.

Dan'nor had no doubt that Fidel'lic could hear it as he made his way out of the tavern.

Only now that the labor of settling the refugees was over, and the ship's crew had settled back into a routine, had Worf taken the time to return to the gym.

He found it full of humans—more so than usual. In fact, there were too many of them for him to concentrate properly on his exercises.

However, Worf did not balk at the situation—not as he might have a few weeks ago. For he had learned that humans were very much like *eurakoi*.

Both were burdens that needed to be sustained, with one growing stronger for the sustaining of them. And it had taken a stint on A'klah to discover just how strong his burdens had made him.

Worf thought about the Klingon veteran he had confronted in that mountain pass. The poor bastard had succumbed to the dishonor of killing for the marshals' purposes—even when one of the tenets of Klingon warriorhood was to fight solely for one's *own* causes, and never for anyone else's.

Stripped of his memory, his heritage, the veteran had not had the force of character to resist. Nor had any of the other warriors in the Conflict zones.

But none of *them* had endured the daily challenges that Worf faced. The never-ending temptation to strangle some bureaucrat with his own proverbial red tape. The insults heaped upon him hour after hour by well-meaning ensigns.

In a very important sense, then, living among humans had made Worf a better Klingon.

Of course, he would never give any of them the satisfaction of telling them so.

Raising the *eurakoi* to shoulder height, he darted a glance at the digital display.

No minutes and one second . . . two seconds . . . three seconds . . .

The First Star Trek: The Next Generation
Hardcover Novel!

STAR TREK
THE NEXT GENERATION™

REUNION

Michael Jan Friedman

Captain Pickard's
past and present
collide on board the
U.S.S. *Enterprise*™

POCKET
BOOKS

Available in Hardcover
from Pocket Books

444-01

THE

STAR TREK

PHENOMENON

- ABODE OF LIFE
  70596/$4.99
- BATTLESTATIONS!
  70183/$4.50
- BLACK FIRE
  70548/$4.50
- BLOODTHIRST
  70876/$4.50
- CORONA
  70798/$4.50
- CHAIN OF ATTACK
  66658/$4.95
- THE COVENANT OF
  THE CROWN
  70078/$4.50
- CRISIS ON CENTAURUS
  70799/$4.50
- CRY OF THE ONLIES
  740789/$4.95
- DEEP DOMAIN
  70549/$4.50
- DEMONS
  70877/$4.50
- DOCTOR'S ORDERS
  66189/$4.50
- DOUBLE, DOUBLE
  66130/$3.95
- DREADNOUGHT
  72587/$4.50
- DREAMS OF THE RAVEN
  70281/$4.50
- DWELLERS IN THE
  CRUCIBLE
  74147/$4.95
- ENEMY UNSEEN
  68403/$4.99
- ENTERPRISE
  73032/$4.95
- ENTROPY EFFECT
  72416/$4.50
- FINAL FRONTIER
  69655/$4.95
- THE FINAL NEXUS
  74148/$4.95

- THE FINAL REFLECTION
  70764/$4.50
- A FLAG FULL OF STARS
  64398/$4.95
- GHOST-WALKER
  64398/$4.95
- HOME IS THE HUNTER
  66662/$4.50
- HOW MUCH FOR JUST
  THE PLANET?
  72214/$4.50
- IDIC EPIDEMIC
  70768/$4.50
- ISHMAEL
  73587/$4.50
- KILLING TIME
  70597/$4.50
- KLINGON GAMBIT
  70767/$4.50
- THE KOBAYASHI MARU
  65817/$4.50
- LEGACY
  74468/$4.95
- LOST YEARS
  70795/$4.95
- MEMORY PRIME
  70550/$4.50
- MINDSHADOW
  70420/$4.50
- MUTINY ON
  THE ENTERPRISE
  70800/$4.50
- MY ENEMY, MY ALLY
  70421/$4.50
- THE PANDORA PRINCIPLE
  65815/$4.99
- PAWNS AND SYMBOLS
  66497/$3.95
- PROMETHEUS DESIGN
  72366/$4.50
- RENEGADE
  65814/$4.95
- ROMULAN WAY
  70169/$4.50

more on next page...

THE
STAR TREK
PHENOMENON

___	RULES OF ENGAGEMENT	66129/$4.50
___	SHADOW LORD	73746/$4.95
___	SPOCK'S WORLD	66773/$4.95
___	STRANGERS FROM THE SKY	65913/$4.50
___	THE TEARS OF THE SINGERS	69654/$4.50
___	THE THREE MINUTE UNIVERSE	65816/$3.95
___	TIME FOR YESTERDAY	70094/$4.50
___	TIMETRAP	64870/$4.95
___	THE TRELLISANE CONFRONTATION	70095/$4.50
___	TRIANGLE	66251/$3.95
___	UHURA'S SONG	65227/$4.95
___	VULCAN ACADEMY MURDERS	72367/$4.50
___	VULCAN'S GLORY	74291/$4.95
___	WEB OF THE ROMULANS	70093/$4.50
___	WOUNDED SKY	66735/$3.95
___	YESTERDAY'S SON	72449/$4.50

• •

___	STAR TREK–THE MOTION PICTURE	72300/$4.50
___	STAR TREK II–THE WRATH OF KHAN	74149/$4.95
___	STAR TREK III–THE SEARCH FOR SPOCK	73133/$4.50
___	STAR TREK IV–THE VOYAGE HOME	70283/$4.95
___	STAR TREK V–THE FINAL FRONTIER	68008/$4.50
___	STAR TREK COMPENDIUM REVISED	68440/$10.95
___	MR. SCOTT'S GUIDE TO THE ENTERPRISE	70498/$12.95
___	THE STAR TREK INTERVIEW BOOK 61794/$7.95	
___	THE WORLDS OF THE FEDERATION 66989/$11.95	

Simon & Schuster Mail Order Dept. STP
200 Old Tappan Rd., Old Tappan, N.J. 07675

POCKET BOOKS

Please send me the books I have checked above. I am enclosing $_____ (please add 75¢ to cover postage and handling for each order. Please add appropriate local sales tax). Send check or money order–no cash or C.O.D.'s please. Allow up to six weeks for delivery. For purchases over $10.00 you may use VISA: card number, expiration date and customer signature must be included.

Name _____

Address _____

City _____ State/Zip _____

VISA Card No. _____ Exp. Date _____

Signature _____ 118-40

STAR TREK ®
THE NEXT GENERATION ™
Technical Manual
Mike Okuda and Rick Sternbach

The technical advisors to the smash TV
hit series, STAR TREK: THE NEXT
GENERATION, take readers into the
incredible world they've created for the
show. Filled with blueprints, sketches
and line drawings, this book explains the
principles behind everything from the
transporter to the holodeck—and takes
an unprecedented look at the brand-
new U.S.S. *Enterprise*™ NCC 1701-D.

Available From
Pocket Books

POCKET
B O O K S